Strong Hearts Are Mandatory
Straight to Video

D1002651

Written by

Teelia Pelletier

ISBN: 09988513-1-0
ISBN-13: 978-09988513-1-0

DEDICATION

To my family, friends, and the supporters who helped me in making this story possible! ♥ I couldn't have done it without you!

NOVELS

The Classics:

Book 1: Strong Hearts Are Mandatory: Heart of Glass

Book 2: Strong Hearts Are Mandatory: Straight to Video

Book 3: Strong Hearts Are Mandatory: Stars of the Silver Screen

Book 4: Strong Hearts Are Mandatory: Truth and Phantasm

ACKNOWLEDGMENTS

I would like to thank Dr. Muscavitch my editor, my friend Yvonne for being one of my biggest inspirations to continue this series and to pursue my goals, and my local library and beta readers, who were my biggest support in finalizing the novel. I couldn't have done it without the help my mother, father, brothers and sister, as well as every friend, follower, and beta reader who was a part of my social media that made this story possible to continue with their support!

Thank you!

- PROLOGUE -

Water droplets fell from the trees above, down to where a lone primate lounged beneath a thick canopy of leaves. The primate, a spider monkey, leaned his head back and sighed. He took in his surroundings, gazing at the trees that were as large as any structure within the massive cities of Media. It was raining once more. The water drenched the recently scorched land of the Capital. This was the second wave of storm clouds to have hit Media after the first one had passed the day before, extinguishing any of the chaos that the monkey's colleague had initiated. The rain only seemed to mock him after the fires were extinguished, as though reminding him his former associate was gone. After relaying the experience and his thoughts out loud, he closed his eyes to think about the loss, and then turned his head to face his new cohort in the shadows.

The monkey liked keeping them there. It was nice to not have to look at them but still know someone was there to listen. He let the individual take in his words before saying, "All my life, I lost friends, associates, teammates—everyone close to me. It's really hard, you know?"

The shadow's blue eyes opened, blinking apathetically at the primate.

The spider monkey huffed with slight offense, his gaze going back up at his canopy when another drop of water fell on him. "I had a bad week."

"It was only five days," the other's voice scoffed.

The primate shut his eyes with annoyance. "There were bad days before the incident—that's what led to it happening! How could that not click for you?" He then chuckled, opening his eyes again. "Nothing ever does, though, does it?"

The other voice sighed. The monkey listened to the cohort as they got up and turned away, walking deeper into the shadows and away from him.

He let them go and smiled. He had resolved worse issues by talking to a non-sentient magic block. He whipped his head further back and fell against the vines, lying there in misery. "I think it started when I was a child, you know; unloved by everyone, the outcast, the weird one. It always left me feeling like that," he said, crestfallen.

The form stopped, and the monkey looked over at his cohort, *the fool,* with hooded eyes. Of course they found all of this relatable; they *were* the weird one...the dullest knife in the drawer. The primate snorted and carried on, shaking his head. "I couldn't keep friends after leaving that unwelcoming place. The one person in my family who loved me, my brother, died, and the one friend I made afterwards was sabotaged and killed in a trap meant for me. I went back to the only family who treated me as their own once I was considered an outcast from my own blood, only to find they had been slain by the same monsters that ended my brother and friend."

The blue eyes blinked back at him, wide and round with surprise. The primate blinked slowly at them in return, suddenly realizing they didn't belong to the same being. They were much smaller. He pulled his head up this time, looking into the shadows and watching two pairs of blue eyes regarding him. The monkey hadn't realized the other failure had woken up. He arched his brow and decided to elaborate, anger seeping into his voice as he said, "After that, I took revenge. I chased down the culprits, following them to the very forest we sit in now, and eliminated the population. I claimed it as my own and chased after the ones who had escaped."

The smaller one's eyes scrunched up with sadness. The primate rose up from the vines he was lying on and cocked his head with a grin. "That's when I came across my friend," he growled, the grin falling almost immediately. The urge to yowl over losing his associate was in the back of his throat, but he had to control his temper. He hadn't told the smaller set of eyes that his colleague was dead yet, but he knew he would soon. He would say it at the right time. For now he could concentrate on something else. "And I killed the ones who had wronged me, knowing he was in my midst, ending the collared ones who took away the ones I cared about." His eyes squinted at the smaller pair of eyes, and they quickly looked away.

He then focused on the first pair of eyes, the ones who stared intently and fiercely at him. "Once that was finished, I had already gone further than I had ever thought I could. To have murdered the village, to have ended those who destroyed my life and those who were a part of it…" He lifted up the palms of his hands, and looked back at the two with hooded eyes. "...Well, I let it overtake me at that point. The few times I failed in my quest I was never the only one walking away maimed," he growled and outstretched his hand as he pulled the other toward his chest. "And it won't be the case for this time, either, my new friends." The monkey smiled and straightened his posture so that he looked down at them both. "We're going to take down the person, no, the people, who wronged you both."

He grinned and walked around his open, lit area while the two fumed in the shadows. He took a small bit of enjoyment in having the two just sit and watch from their little patch of darkness, taking in his words slowly. It was his favorite spell to only have the eyes visible as his target. He had to focus on nothing else if he needed to strike.

These two had gone through enough as it was, though. "I will make the next attack, but your use for me will come. We'll take down this Video once and for all."

Once the two agreed, the primate took off into the trees. He climbed up into the canopy and jumped from branch to branch to get out from the jungle as quickly as possible. The vines met his hands on cue and propelled him through the forest. The feeling was wonderful; the magic flowed through his jungle freely as he controlled it. The entire area glowed cyan as he moved through it faster, flowing with his energy and strengthening as he stimulated the jungle with each swing of his arms and hands to reach for the next branch. Cyan threads swam through the bark of the trees, down the vines, and into the roots within the ground below, making the grass glow.

He stopped when he reached the outskirts of the jungle and ventured into the deeper forest, taking his gaze to the sky. The barrier that surrounded Media shimmered the same beautiful cyan as his jungle when he moved through his territory. There was little he loved more than to watch as it slowly turned back to white. The shield's panel had the same rhythm and flow as the shimmering, flowing water in the pool within his jungle, which always brought him comfort. He took in a breath and then jumped into the forest. Twisting around, he allowed the darkness that surrounded him to consume his whole body, evaporating into the dark shadows as he imagined his next destination.

He had to materialize the area around him and land perfectly, a practice he mastered ages ago. The only fault was that the primate always had to remember to start breathing again. He exhaled quickly after dropping against the ground and looked around.

Here he was, back at the castle. It had been one wretched week, and he was not about to run into the king again. He needed to prepare for the moment his new enemy returned.

Revenge before pleasure, he reminded himself, walking down the halls. *Video...*he thought of her name, the one who killed Radio, burned Pictures, and "betrayed" Stereo. Fools of his forest. He grinned, his tail whipping in excitement. What a night it was to resume what he had yet to finish. It didn't matter if things didn't go as he had planned. He could tackle it directly this time, which is what he would do once he finished dealing with the individual he had just bumped into.

"Aah!" The short, dusty tom grumbled. He yelled out when he looked up to see it was, "The Jester!" he hissed.

The monkey growled, lifting up his fist to strike.

Smash!

The tom fell over with a thud and the monkey sighed. Why did it feel like he had already been through this? He really wasn't up for more castle hall roaming. He flicked his hand and pulled it back to himself, but then winced a little at the amount of pain he inflicted upon himself from the severity of the hit. He wasn't sure if it was out of panic or out of anger at being referred to as a jester, but either way, he had to take care of the body.

He came up to the short-legged feline and blinked with disappointment when he realized that he was still alive. He took note of the breathing and looked down at his hand. Was he losing his touch, or was it just because he hadn't thought of using his magic so the blow was weaker? He sighed and scooped up the small kitty, swinging him over his shoulder and carrying on with his prior task. He had to find someone who would know about Video's hearing tomorrow, not just a simple staff member patrolling or here because of having forgotten something at their office.

"Note!?"

The primate lifted his head up and groaned, turning around to see a tall, lean, white feline with a couple of black patches on her fur. He really didn't expect this, but he had stopped trying to hide after wearing the Jester outfit. It had become his nature to make a scene.

"Sorry, I've got none on me."

He dropped the munchkin tom and the other feline yowled.

The monkey followed the feline's gaze and blinked down at the short-legged one.

"Oh, that's Note. Well, on that *note...*" He lifted up the rug to trip the leaner cat and leapt forward. He grabbed the tall feline, swung her into the window, and then waved his hand out to cast a quick sleeping spell over them. They seemed like good pals, at least the second one was. The monkey decided to call her Dot. He hoped Note knew how much Dot was there for him, but that wasn't his biggest concern for the night. The primate sighed and raised his hand to strike the other feline down, with magic this time. His hand slowly lowered as he contemplated keeping his anger directed toward those who caused it in the first place. He had to change and not take life because he could. That had stopped working for him.

The monkey walked down the empty halls again, trying to remember what he was told about the castle. Even with how long he had lived, the castle, even the Capital City itself, had never caught his eye. It was boring. The people were snobbish and all of his enemies were there. He wasn't really someone of action until this point, not to his standards, anyway, but now he had to get used to it.

He needed to find Video! If not Video, he needed someone who could *kill* Video. The castle halls were free of magic. Nevertheless, when he entered the unguarded rooms close to the drawing room, he felt weaker. He couldn't cast his magic. He thought it had been because of the heart of glass and its enchantments, but something else was going on within the walls that was making him sick. It was almost like shadow magic...which was unsettling. He was the only one who would be able to cast the shadows now as far as he knew.

He started reading the door signs and nameplates to see if there was someone's office worth peeking into. He could have probably used the archives to locate everyone in charge of the jurisdiction system, but he had lit them all on fire and didn't save the copies for his own library. He was just about to give up when he looked up and read "Judge Select."

"Ooh!" His tail waved. It was time to get busy.

He opened the door with a wiggle of his fingers, picking the lock and sneaking inside. Looking around, he stuck out his tongue at all the books that greeted him. With a clap of his hands, they all disappeared into shadows. Relieved, he turned his attention to the desk. He searched rapidly for anything: addresses, cards, locations. Something that could give him what he needed. His hand came across a printed photo. He held it up. It was a picture of a tall horned owl with a partner and three owlets in a family portrait. The area was obviously the Meridian Stretch from the detail and quality of the homes behind the group, which wasn't surprising. The primate looked closely until he could recognize one of the homes and grinned when he realized the owl was only two houses down from the Cinema residence.

He could get there and have everything taken care of before dawn.

"Splendid!" He hummed, slapping down the photo. With a clap, darkness took over his form, and his eyes narrowed with glee before he dissipated into the night.

- CHAPTER 1 -
KIDOLOGY

Pounding…chattering. Aching…shouting. Video couldn't decide whether to focus on the noises around her or the burning, pulsing, stabbing pain in her face. As she thought of all the other ways she could describe the pain of her head than the clamor and yelling frequenting the area, she knew the conclusion. The pain was all she could think about. Her heart beat to the sound of the chaos surrounding her, but it pounded in her face, head, and paws. Without realizing she had to regain her footing, Video's lack of focus caused her to stumble.

After being yanked up, Video realized she wasn't walking through her own will. No, she was being forced to walk forward, pressed against and prodded forward anytime she slowed her pace. Video swore the ruckus became even louder after she was pushed forward, and she struggled to keep stepping unswervingly. The noise made the inside of her head feel hollow. Each step on scraped paws made her legs burn, but it still was nothing compared to the pain at the side of her head. It felt like she had been in and out of consciousness. What was she doing here with all these voices around her? She hadn't heard this much noise since she was in the city.

That's when Video realized she had no recollection of what happened or why she was being made to move in this condition, but she knew by the close press of the bodies against her that she was being escorted. This was no city stroll. The idea of being transferred like a criminal made fear rush to her head. Her heart's feeble attempt to pump the blood to her burning wounds accomplished nothing in the way of either healing or soothing them, only making her panic more.

She had lost focus from the amount of pain, the wounds on the side of her head and face feeling like they were surely going to burst. Her legs gave out on her again and she fell to the ground, doing everything in her ability not to struggle as the fenders on either side of her pulled her up to stand on her shredded paws again. How did they get so damaged? Video couldn't remember. It hurt even more to be touched than to move, causing her to wince when one of the two who escorted her growled at her. It wasn't the growl of another cat, either, which made fear press against Video's chest.

In that moment everything sank in. Video wasn't with her old companions anymore. She forced herself to open her eyes and focus on the two beside her and her surroundings. She had to figure out what was happening.

It was a fox who growled at her, one she had never met before, that she assumed, anyway. The fact that it was a fox was something she should have recognized by his scent alone. She sniffed to test her nose and could barely make out his scent through the overwhelming smell of dried blood. To her other side was a large bobcat. The long limbs and wild fur on the giant feline were almost unreal to see up close, towering over even her. That height wasn't something she came across often with her family being one of the strongest bloodlines in Media. Or were, depending if they were alive or not. With round eyes, Video blinked up at the tall figure, alarm starting to flood in, and then looked at both of the escorts' necks to see their collars. The two carried her land's valued insignia, the tear-shaped emblem only the most trusted officials held around their necks. Video made herself relax at the sight of them, knowing there was no reason to fear for her wellbeing. These were workers of Media's government, and she was safe.

However, it was then she realized there were bandages pressed against her head and knew they were only enhancing the pounding pain against her skull. The cloths were likely a factor in her pain because of their quality and binding; they were wrapped around her so tightly it felt as though they were cutting off circulation. The more Video assessed herself as she walked with these two, the more she realized what poor condition she was in, with or without her injuries. Her wounds didn't even feel treated! Her fur was unkempt, and she was sure that she detected the dust under the bandages. How could the land's officials let this happen? Her herbalist mother up in the mountains could do better care! As she moaned from frustration at this knowledge, a new wave of pain radiated from the side of her head at the screech of a hawk. She tried to increase her awareness and understanding of her surroundings as she realized her situation might not be what it seemed.

The factor that didn't help Video's headache was that she was inside a brightly lit building, both with artificial and natural light. She looked at the large windows at both sides of the room, the large metal posts beside them holding the cloth banners of Media's regional symbol that had always brought Video comfort to see. Even now, she felt her racing heart slow down at the sight of the tear-shaped insignia outlined by the light of the day outside. She admired the two tendrils that curved around the symbol and the arches above the main emblem before her vision clouded again with her varying lack of consciousness. She swung her head back and tried to remain calm despite the surrounding chaos and glaring lamps above her head.

The commotion behind her came from other felines, avians, and animals. Sounds she could barely decipher raged around her, and she failed to understand them as much as she failed to see them. Everything felt like a pulsing blur. She barely saw the table in front of her until she pressed her paws against it to keep herself standing. The question repeated itself: What was going on? Every bone in her body ached. Video grimaced at the pain of her paws against the table, but she needed to focus on why she was here, not what her health condition was. What happened? So much occurred before she found herself on either side of the two national staff, but she still wasn't sure where *here* was.

There were so many places in Media that carried banners and flags of the land's symbol, many structures where guards were stationed and escorting others, seemingly endless amounts of areas controlled by the powerful governing body of the Council. It should have been easy to identify her location. However, even with taking all of that into consideration, there was nothing like the commotion happening here. She looked down at the table and recognized it. She had stood in this room many times with her father in training to be a monitor, but never on the side of the accused.

It was Media's judicial court.

Video began to recall the events leading up to where she was now. She and her companions—her former companions—had been inconceivably close to reaching their objective: to collect all the crystal fragments created by the strange mage that had tossed Video and her companions together for simple entertainment. The assignment had been going well. They had collected every shard except the last, but everything had fallen apart in the end. Video killed the noble she was assigned to protect and had slain the monitor whose duty it was to watch over all of them.

Video's two companions had fallen for the temptation of using magic, the forbidden practice which nearly ended all kind unlike its own. The two had needed to be stopped at all costs. There was no working around it—there never was with magic. Video had no choice but to stop them. If only she had kept the mage that started it all away from the noble in the first place…even if there was no saving the monitor for his crimes, she and the noble might have had a chance then. All Video could think of was the monitor's eyes before she took his life. The moment his multi-colored eyes had both become golden, Video had known of the mage's influence upon the monitor. What did they expect her to do when the cat had been working with their enemy from the beginning, even before the mission had started? Why was she at the table of the accused after all she had done to protect the land? It *had* to be a misunderstanding.

She gazed up the judge's stand ahead of her and stared face-to-face with the owl that had the power to decide her fate in the eyes of King Capital's Council. His long, feathered horns rose high above his orange face, and his sharp amber gaze pierced into her fur. His look alone did not comfort her into believing this was going to be a fair trial. No, Video could tell by his eyes: this case was already decided and the judgement was sealed. This bird wanted her dead. Her gaze hardened as she looked up at him, knowing he was not even going to give her a chance to convince him she was in the right. She stared at him for as long as her blurring vision allowed it and held back from growling at him.

"Video of the Mountain Top Region, you are clear to make your opening statement." The owl drawled out his words as he spoke in cat, and Video gave a nod once he gestured out his wing to her.

She had nodded, but she didn't know where to start. What opening statement? They had said nothing to her about preparing *anything*. She was standing here with a pulsing head injury caused directly by a magic artifact, and they expected her to have a clear mind ready for defending herself? Video realized she had to give a whole overview of something she had no prior preparation for. This was far-fetched, even for the court.

"Sir, if I may ask, what am I defending myself against?" Video answered, then with as much effort as she could still manage, she lifted her chin back up enough to glare directly into his cold and merciless eyes.

The crowd yowled and hissed in protest at her words, making Video's ears ring and head pound even more. She made sure not to make a noise, as the fox beside her seemed to be looking for a reason to nudge or push her. Instead, she looked to the bobcat beside her, who appeared to be keen on looking at anything but her at the sound of the uproar.

How peculiar, Video thought, her brow arching. The judge let out a screech and banged his talons against the surface before him to silence the audience. He unfurled his expansive wings, the inner feathers stretching out like white flags. The room quieted at once. The owl looked down at Video and the coldness from his eyes melted away, consumed by a fire of inextinguishable fury.

Video met his gaze, preparing for his answer. The monitor, Pictures, had orchestrated so many things against her. Video had no idea what evidence and forgery Pictures might have conjured up while he travelled with her and the noble, the Radio Star, on their mission. The tomcat had been a part of plans which had worked against them the whole time. She wasn't even taking into account he himself had been a mage, he was already a traitor just by working with the very creature who made the three venture out on their quest in the first place—the Jester.

Nevertheless, Pictures knew the systems far too well as a surveillance leader. He had been a citizen who worked with Media's Council directly, and he was the one who had the know-how to successfully manipulate them. Video couldn't blame the land for not detecting such a well-designed infiltration. She only wished she could have stopped their plotting before it had escalated to all of this...before they lost Radio.

"You, miss, are being accused for the unjust murders of Pictures of Clowder City, the Radio Star of the Meridian Stretch, and Tape and Sensor of the Capital."

Video's brow immediately furrowed, and she stared at the owl. Did he say *unjust*? Video bristled at the very idea of the accusation of her of killing Tape and Sensor, the two monitor assistants who were responsible for saving the last shard of the crystal heart she and Radio were to collect. Rage filled up in her chest, but she forced herself to gain control before she snapped anything at the owl. She knew it could be worse. She could have been framed for more by the two mages, but she was shocked they managed to somehow squeeze in the death of Sensor as her fault, too. It was such a loss the bird had died at all, but Video knew Sensor had been no match for the Jester. He had sought to provoke the enemy so Video could escape from the monkey's clutches, but his efforts had been futile in the end.

Video had no defense against the death of either the Radio Star or Pictures, as they died by her tooth and claw. Still, she ventured to explain: "The first two deaths were under general advisement of the Council. My duty as an observer was to end anyone I came across in the possession of magic. As for the other two: the accusation is false, sir. Tape was killed by my former companion Pictures before I arrived within the castle walls, and Sensor died after I left the eastern hall where I last saw him, presumably killed by the jester that took our King away, sir."

"So you say. I will call the chosen witness to the stand, then." The judge sneered, lifting up his beak.

Video blinked. There had been only one witness besides the Jester, and that was the youngest Council member, the Studio Star, the aunt of Radio. She had escorted Video to the Capital personally once everything went wrong. Video travelled with her side by side the moment after the loss of the Radio Star. The deceased noble was Studio's youngest niece, but was also secretly a distant cousin of Video. Studio saw it all end, right from when Radio died. The city leader could vouch for her, as the dark, striped noble had seen Video fight directly against Pictures' magic and was witness to seeing Tape dead even before they arrived inside the castle. She was even there to witness Sensor keeping back the jester mage that was responsible for Media's calamity in the first place. There was no stronger witness than a noble of Media besides the King, not to mention she was a member of the Council itself, which was something Video had found out on their way back to the Capital. There were endless factors in how much the Studio Star could turn the tables in Video's favor. She would be able to get Video out of this easily.

But it was not Studio who came forward.

It was unbelievably foolish of Video to disregard everything she had trained for as a kitten in the first place, and yet somehow in her hopes to see Studio, she completely discounted one of the most powerful eyes in all of Media, the monitors' surveillance. There was no one worse who could come to the stand than her father, Signal. The giant, long-furred tabby believed anything he saw on the screens of his monitors as fact. The dark tomcat would not otherwise be wrong in believing so, but under the attack of mages, one of them being a monitor, Pictures, who had the power to alter technology and devices, the chance of the recordings being edited was certain.

The Council had hired Video's father to exclusively regard the mission Video and the other two had been sent to accomplish. Video came across his surveillance bots often on the four day venture, as well as on the last day of battle. Everyone in Media knew the outstanding consultant and monitor did not prioritize anything above his service to the Council and didn't offer a single concern when he was hired to survey and watch over the venture Video and her companions were enduring. Video was aware that Signal was loyal to Media above all else. He swore his devotion and life to serve under the Council, so standing against him in a case orchestrated to lead to her demise was shaking. Video swallowed as she made contact with his bright but unfocused silver eyes and knew she wouldn't be angry with him, or feel betrayed by him, no matter what decision he made, to either defend or oppose her, with or against the judge. Immediately, she straightened her posture to show everyone else as such when the judge began to speak.

"Signal of the Rich Top Mountain, you were assigned to assess and observe the mission to assist in ensuring its success. The objective was completed, but not without this traitorous behavior brought to light. After presenting your assessment you will be freed from your current contract with the Council and may return to your freelance, but until then, please present your evidence against the claims of the defendant in front of us." The owl spoke firmly, and a control panel was wheeled out and placed in front of the giant cat as he gave a nod.

"Video of the Mountain Region," her father growled, turning his head up to her as he pushed his paw against the toggles that brought down the courtroom projector. Video struggled to not bring attention to Signal calling her home location the "Mountain Region," knowing it was Signal refusing to admit Video resided in the Rich Top Mountains with him and her mother, Audio, before all this had happened. Video looked at him closely as he continued his statement, "You claim to have not ended the life of the feline Tape, however, the recordings about to be presented suggest otherwise, and infer more closely that your travelling companion Pictures was horrified to witness the scene."

Video's eyes narrowed as she recalled the very moment when Studio had pointed out her father's surveillance bot as they came across Tape's body with Pictures. It had been good timing, but if it had just caught a single moment before Pictures began his act and blamed her, she could use it to defend herself against the manipulative magician.

Conveniently enough, however, the recording started right when Pictures had made his accusation.

"'Video...what have you done?'" The recording started with Pictures' stammering over the dead body, staring up at Video with his bright, multi-colored eyes. *Those should have been enough of an indication for me to know he had been influenced by magic in the first place,* Video thought. She growled as the recording continued, her brow almost as furrowed as it was in the recording as she watched herself hiss at Pictures, stepping over Tape's bloodied body to get closer to the other tom.

Her tail lashed seeing Pictures flinch dramatically in his apparent fear of her in the recording, stepping back and crying out, "'N-no, Video, stop! I'm your friend!'"

Why couldn't Video have seen it was all an act then? She almost winced as she heard herself growl, "'You're only a friend to me, dead.'" Video had to watch the screen closely as she had extended her claws into the castle carpet in the recording, ready to attack Pictures for what he had done. She sighed, knowing what a lunatic she looked like.

Then came the clincher. All Pictures needed was to suggest whose crime it really was, and he did just that, even going so far as to gesture to Tape's dark brown form as he asked, "'How could you do this?'"

Video's tail still lashed the same way it had in the recording, watching Pictures stare up at her in complete and utter horror on screen, now knowing how fake their entire relationship really had been. How fake his love for Radio had been.

All this confirmed for Video was how much she didn't regret ripping her claws into the silver tom's throat when given the chance, but to everyone else, they saw proof of the helpless monitor seeing one of his co-workers slain by a rogue courier.

"Do you have anything to say to defend yourself against the evidence given, Video?" The judge turned to her, one of his horns raised high above the other with the arch of his brow.

Was it worth it to say otherwise? The truth had never failed Video before, but then again, she had never gone against magic or the outright tyranny of her Capital before, either. Even her rogue brother, Stereo, who had abandoned the Capital's laws once his mate was slain for spying for the Kingdom's enemies, held no candle to the maniacal Pictures and his jester lackey.

But it didn't matter. Video couldn't go to her grave knowing she hadn't said all she knew to be true, and quickly lifted her chin to answer the judge. "Sir, I believe Pictures' experience with monitor technology and his knowledge of the devices, which are very often used for surveillance, show there would be no feline more capable of orchestrating a perfectly shot scenario to make something appear to be what it really was not." She ignored the gasps from behind her and continued, "In this case, it being Pictures using me to take the fall for Tape's death, not knowing my own capabilities to be able to bring him to justice for his crime and forgery afterwards."

The crowd cried in outrage behind her, pushing against their benches and yelling at her in anger. Video didn't know what could be said of Pictures' magic. He didn't actually use his abilities during the interaction between the two of them over Tape's death, so she found no point in bringing it up yet. She ignored the cries against her. Another screech from the owl silenced the ruckus, and he looked down at her coldly.

"Do you claim not to have slain the body you stood upon and threatened your travel companion over?"

"I am innocent, yes. You can provide no evidence of the death of Sensor or any recordings of me killing that cat, as I did not do it. I entered the castle and Tape was already dead when I entered the hall."

"And you claim the monitor Pictures instead was the one who murdered the monitor assistant, his own co-worker, in cold blood?"

"Pictures made no direct confession he had done so, and I am only assuming he did with the same information you are using to decide I am guilty of the crime—which I am not. Pictures was standing in front of the body when I entered." *With his blood, fur, and flesh embedded into his paws, but apparently that doesn't mean anything*, she thought to herself. "So I humbly request you rescind that accusation." Video blinked, clearing her bitter thoughts, and looked back up at the owl.

His eyes narrowed as he asked, "You expect us to be so sparing toward you after slandering one of our most respected Monitors?"

Video blinked and raised her chin higher, feeling the blood rush to the back of her head. "Guilty until proven innocent may be your judgement, but I have the Studio Star as witness to these accounts. I request her to be called to the stand to further this investigation and trial before you make any final decision on the verdict."

She held back her emotions when she saw her father raise his chin and already dreaded the owl's response. Something else had happened for Signal to give such a reaction, and Video knew it wasn't likely to be in her favor.

The judge almost seemed proud as he stated, "How fitting that you to find it reasonable to call the individual who was recorded interacting with the mage prior to our King's return. It might not be a stretch to have you tried for being in *cahoots* with the monster yourself after what we've witnessed." The owl snapped his beak as he raised his head, and Video stared in shock as her father pushed another series of toggles that played a different recording.

It was a recording of the Studio Star turning her head up from a writing desk on her balcony to face the Jester. She looked shocked and the camera was angled to show that, but before the Jester began to speak, the screen broke into static, switching to another recording of the two. They seemed to be speaking to each other, Studio very clearly growling and bristled, but the Jester was fearlessly positioning his artifact toward the subjects below the balcony. It looked to be an entirely different night, and Video almost startled when the screen eased into static again before playing the next recording. It was Video and Studio in the castle, Video's paws dripping with Tape's blood, having just left the body. The two were both facing the monkey, who jested and teased cruelly, but before the recording showed the attack, the screen shut off.

"That is unfair and becomes an entirely different story by taking out just a few seconds! Neither she nor I were pleased in any of those shots!" Video snarled, stomping her paws onto the stand and glaring up at the judge. "I am in disbelief! All of these recordings have ended at very convenient moments for your case!"

"Silence, cat!" the owl screeched, holding up his wings warningly. Video growled, flattening her ears and clamping her jaw shut when the guards started drawing closer to her.

Once she fully relaxed, the guards stepped away and the judge continued, "All this brings us to one conclusion. These two were associated with this Jester and must atone for their crimes. While the Studio Star's trial will be held by King Capital's Council privately, the jury and I have reached the verdict for the murderer we face today." The owl stared down at Video and narrowed his golden eyes into slits. "Video of the Mountain Region, you have been found guilty for an uncountable amount of murder and for being an accomplice to the mage that attempted to take away our King. The only sensible decision I can bring myself to give is to sentence you to immediate death, and to have your remains removed through the same technique as you yourself used to dispose of your former traveling companion, Pictures of Clowder City."

The castle furnace. Video gaped, and looked up at the bird with squinted eyes, knowing that was far too personal to not have been an emotionally-made verdict. Something wasn't right. Just as she began to be approached by the two guards, now executors, the owl smiled down at her. She focused her eyes onto the avian closely, and shivered when darkness surrounded the bird for a split second. It wasn't from her headache or panic, either. His eyes glittered the same blue as the foes she had faced on her mission when protecting Radio and Pictures. At that moment, Video knew this wasn't orchestrated by a real official. Her eyes rounded as she came to the realization that the King and Media's subjects were still in danger from infiltration. The Council had one less cat to help take the mage down if the monkey was to succeed in her execution, and she was not about to allow that.

The owl startled upon seeing the new awareness and determination in her expression. "Take her down!" He screeched.

The fox and bobcat leapt for her, and with surprising speed for the condition she was in, Video ducked and scrambled passed them. She staggered, feeling a dizzy sensation in her head at the sudden movements she made. Hearing the gasp of the audience from behind the stand alarmed her even more, but she didn't dare let herself collapse. She whipped her paw across the muzzle of the fox when he approached her again and took a step back. Every inch of her hair stood on end when she hit the back of the judge's stand, but when she looked up at him, he made no movement towards her. He had the same dark, bored stare of the mage jester, his eyes amber again instead of the magical blue. His cheek was resting on the tips of his wings as he looked down at her, the base of his wings having just enough feathers to hold his head in place. His horns were completely arched in his annoyance. It was like he was impatient for her to be taken away to certain death, but too lazy to do it himself. Video looked back down in time to see the two guards coming at her again, and leapt over both their heads.

The crowd screamed, but for anyone who tried to rush out, the guards threw them back and stood with their paws firmly against the doors. Between the two and the meat shield of the crowd, Video knew there was no escape that way. She rounded on the fox and bobcat again, batting her paws against their faces and chests. They flinched and rounded back as her claws scraped against their faces. She snarled at them to keep them back for a moment, just long enough for her to catch her balance.

Video whipped her head back to see the third guard who had been behind her when she was getting escorted to the table. The red tailed hawk was flying at her. Video looked back down to the scene in front of her. Adrenaline rushed in her veins. She felt the fear fill up her chest as she took in her surroundings, bracing herself to jump away from the avian's grasp. Her mind was sharpened, despite still feeling the dull, aching pain of her head injury. She needed to figure out something fast, and she only had her legs propelling her away from the bird. She scanned the room and saw the windows with Media's banners draped across the upper half of them, as well as the flag poles beside the windows hanging the same insignia.

Those might be just what she needed to give herself some leverage. She finished squaring her haunches, and leapt as far as she could without buckling her legs, having to dismiss the pain burning in her limbs from her injuries.

She narrowly dodged the hawk, feeling the air brush through her fur as his talons swiped past her. She landed on all fours gracefully, and bolted for the flag poles. She leapt up from the ground for the vertical posts, ignoring the darkness that threatened to consume her sight from the head wound. Even with the corners of her sight darkening as the sensation in her head worsened, her paws landed perfectly against the pole closest to the window. Video ducked her head to strike it with her skull once the rest of her body followed, giving just the momentum she needed. The pole toppled as the rest of her weight fell against it. Video swung down with it, digging her claws into the fabric as much as she could for the silver post to fall towards the window.

Her ears flattened against the back of her head in anticipation. Her eyes shut tight as the flag pole made contact with the glass. The sudden force of Video's pull was enough for the hard edges of the banner to shatter the window and make a narrow opening, and enough for Video to escape. The hawks and owl screeched and the mammals hissed and yowled. The clamor made Video's head ring with the sounds combined with the intense shatter of the large pane of glass breaking. With the loss of focus, she leapt down from the flag banner and landed unsteadily, toppling over.

It was enough for the guards to catch up to her as she scrambled to her paws. Video gasped, wincing as one of the hawk's talons successfully grabbed her flank. Her tail whipped up and smashed into the avian before his talons could fully grip her. He ducked under the other birds on her way to the window, knocking past the bobcat and fox as she did so.

"Stop her!" the owl cried out, fear evident in his voice. He turned and looked pointedly at Signal, but the tom did not move. Some of the other animals focused on Signal, surprised by his lack of action, giving Video enough time to jump past the collared fox when he stepped over the glass to block her. She landed just carefully enough onto the deep windowsill to not cut her paws on the broken glass fragments, and then leapt out the window.

Video wished she had a fantastic getaway plan or at least some knowledge of what the outside of the courtroom was like before she jumped out of the building, but she hadn't, at least, not enough to remember the immediate rocky incline that awaited her fall. She extended her paws and managed to keep her balance on the first surface she landed on, but the rock crumbled under her weight. She staggered and fell roughly down the incline. The sharp rocks sliced into her, yet followed her fall and hit her, doing damage yet again as she failed to steady herself. She wailed in pain as her paw pads scraped against the edges of the boulders, peeling them raw.

Before she could examine her bloody paw pads, she heard the screech of the raptors behind her. She had to regain her balance before they reached her. With a gust of energy, she slammed her claws down, cracking them as they gripped an uneven group of stone. She growled at the pain, but blinked and became alert once she caught a steady hold. One falcon swooped down and narrowly missed Video as she pulled herself up, leaving her hissing and spitting at the avian. He fluttered and squawked as Video pounced her paws on top of him, but Video had no intention of using him for anything more than a launching pad. She propelled herself further down the incline, fearlessly projecting herself into the air to gain more speed. The soft cushion of the bird's pelt was just the surface Video needed to get her bearings around her and take in the sight of the area, hopefully enough to escape even while other birds circled the area.

Yet there was nowhere to hide from them. Video scanned the boulders, rocks, surfaces and stone, but there was no ledge large enough for her to find shelter under or possibly hide herself from the view of the courthouse. Even if she did, she already heard the drones of the monitors of Capital City hovering above her. She had to figure out something. Her pelt wasn't a close enough match in color or pattern to the rocks for her to blend, and everything beyond the rock terrain was just one forest and then open valleys stretching out for days. They were going to catch her, whether or not it was by following her down, or waiting for her below, unless she thought of something fast.

Her thoughts and plans left her to the conclusion she always ended up with: kill the problem. She would have to end these birds if she wanted to be able to get out of sight, otherwise they would only continue to trail her.

Video leapt forward just as one of the falcons flew down for her. She spun around, waiting for the next attack. A buzzard flew down next. Video was just prepared enough to pounce. She propelled herself forward by kicking her back legs down and flew through the air, landing right on the avian's shoulders. Her claws hooked in deeper than the feathers and well into the skin of the bird, and she swung it down into the rocks. She bounced at the momentum of the collision, then smashed her paws down on the buzzard's head to knock it down into the stone.

It was dazed instantly. Before she could end it for good, she heard another attack approaching. She released the buzzard and leapt back, letting the falcon catch his colleague instead of her. Just in time, she turned onto her paws and landed perfectly onto the stone, and began running farther down the incline. She had to make the killing shots quickly and accurately when the birds came down, or they'd figure out they couldn't attack her and would stay in the skies. She drummed her paws down on the stone with each second, waiting for the birds to catch up to her and begin another team attack.

Was it right to kill these followers of Media, though? Video realized while the judge may have been possessed by the mage, or was the mage shapeshifting, these individuals were just following their orders, obeying policy and protocol to protect their land and leaders. They didn't deserve death because they were trying to kill her; they didn't know better. Video almost lost concentration on the path when the idea came to her, and she barely dodged the falcon's attack.

She flipped the bird around with a pounce and swung herself in the air with the bird still in her grip, knocking him down into the stone. She whipped the falcon's head up and shoved it back down into the rocky terrain until the avian no longer responded, and carried the bird onto the pathway once she knew he was still breathing. That was one down, without death. Video knew if she could survive from the Queen's artifact to her temple, these birds could deal with a bit of stone. Now she knew it was possible to do that with the rest, the buzzard already being taken care of earlier.

How many were there? Video looked to the sky and saw two more shadows, then winced when the headache worsened upon looking into the sun. She groaned, and kept going without any more hesitation. She needed to get somewhere safe quickly, before her injuries were too aggravated, and take care of the other two as swiftly as she could. She kept on, hoping she could find something to rest in and head towards while she waited for the next attack.

As if on cue, Video heard the swish of the bird's wings above her, and she knew the avian was going for a swooping attack. She jumped up to dodge the falcon when it swept down to grab her. Just before the bird could take back to the air, Video came down from her leap and landed directly on the falcon's shoulders. She dug her claws down, and drove her fangs into the bird's delicate throat. She held on as it struggled, holding the bird against the stone earth with her claws pressed down into its wings, and squeezed gently until the falcon was unconscious, all the while keeping an eye on the last hawk flying above.

She dropped the bird down, and yowled up to the flying hawk, recognizing him as the same one who had escorted her into the courtroom, "I am not against Media, fellow follower!" She stomped her right paw, keeping it away from the unconscious falcon. "I spared each and every one of these guards, the protectors of this land, because I am still one of Social Media myself, and I will prove my innocence!" She released her other paw off of the falcon, and flattened her ears as the hawk screeched a rejection of her words.

He flew away even with his outburst, though, leaving her alone with the unconscious birds. Video swallowed nervously. She wasn't sure what he might be calling out for, so she quickly continued onward, travelling down the rocky path away from the court, hoping there would be somewhere she could find and make shelter soon.

35

The red-tailed hawk slammed open the door with his talons burst into the judge's office. "Sir, we need reinforcements! Who can you send out?"

"What? You didn't capture her?" The dark owl turned to the brightly colored raptor, and narrowed his eyes. "You were the one who escorted her to the court. Where are the rest of you?"

"Well," the smaller avian hesitated, fluffing out his amber feathers and murmuring, "It was the cat, sir." He then straightened, speaking as clearly as one could muster to his intimidating superior when the owl turned away. "She is formidable in her attacks, even with her injuries. We weren't prepared. We need a crew sent out to rescue the men and to tackle this tyrant. She claims she's still a follower, but we know better..."

The doubt was evident in the tone of his voice. The hawk startled when the judge rounded on him to screech, "And you think sending reinforcements is going to do anything to help? Those were your best!"

The owl towered over the hawk as he nervously answered, "I-I know, sir...but the more ground she travels, the bigger circumference there is to search. She could be anywhere by the time our team has recovered. We need to find birds from the Monitor's District, maybe from the Western Coast..."

"I'm not wasting my resources on your incompetent lackeys! You fool!" The owl went to shove the hawk, but once the lighter bird flinched, he instead grabbed onto him and pulled him close with his piercing talons. "Don't give me a reason to end you; it won't take much more." The judge's orange eyes turned to ice, and the hawk wasn't sure if they really changed color, or if it was the lighting as the judge continued, "You're going to find those other two that brought her in; that fox and cat-thing, and hunt her down yourselves."

"Sir, they're ground animals–"

The owl silenced the protest with a tightening of his grip, hissing low through his beak, "Find where they are and work with what you have."

"Yes, sir." The hawk nodded, his eyes round. He stepped back as soon as the judge released his grasp on him, and ruffled his feathers before fully composing.

"Good." The owl stared down at the officer, his horns seeming to rise before turning his back. "What's your name, again?"

"Sprocket, sir."

"Well, Sprocket, once you find our runaway, you're to bring her back. May you have your king's blessing on finding her. Someone will die once you return, so you'd better not be empty taloned."

The threat on his own life was enough. Sprocket gaped slightly, his eyes rounding, but at the first sign of movement from the owl's head, he flew off, leaving the judge alone.

"What rubbish." The owl murmured.

- CHAPTER 2 -
IMITATION

Video trekked across the rocky terrain until her shredded paws were blistered. Even with all her travel the rough skin of her pads was no match for the unsteady and rough surfaces of the Capital City's mountains. She looked out in the distance, far beyond the valleys to the Rich Top Mountains, and took in a breath. That was her next objective. There in the mountains she knew the terrain, every dip and every peak. She would be safe there, as long as she could figure out how to avoid the Capital's drones looking for her. Everything was about the timing.

Video found she had chosen the right path by going down the long way of the jagged terrain. Even if her limbs and paws suffered, the officials had the drones searching all of the fast trails and shortcuts, completely skimming the path that only badgers might consider. If she could make it to the abandoned dens she could hide from the sharp eyes of the avians and cats looking for her. She might be able to carry on to the mountains undetected the next day. It almost seemed suspicious the search units hadn't found her yet, but she was going to take advantage of it for as long as she could remain free and pushed forward.

There would only be so much time before they put together she took the jagged path. She would have had even less if she had a tracker on her. Sudden alarm filled her thoughts; Video realized that she had an ear chip that would keep her location marked on the monitor's trackers. It had been placed on her when she began her mission with Pictures and the Radio Star. She froze, horrified while contemplating what to do upon when concluding that fleeing was futile, and sank down onto her belly. She stretched out her back leg, whipped off the pathetically ineffective bandages, and reached it up to her ear where the tracker was placed, hoping to be able to locate it along her ear enough to tear it out, and got a clawful of dried blood instead.

Video startled, and pulled her hind leg back. It took a moment to rekindle the memory of how she got the injury. It had been the magic of the Jester, used by the noble Radio Star, that struck her ear. She had been so furious when it had happened, but after the battle for the heart, she had forgotten all about it. Had the magic really struck the chip? Video let her hind claws slide back and gently probed her ear, trying to feel for any unnatural indentation or swelling from the chip, but it wasn't there.

She was safe! That way, at least. Video swallowed, realizing it was probably going to be the only break she was going to get with the current turn of events. She let her breathing regulate, it having gone irregular at the thought of the magic. Once composed, she quickly whipped back up onto her feet and started down the rocky incline again. She had to keep moving and couldn't dwell on what happened. Radio had tinkered and played with the most forbidden allurement in Media: sorcery, and Video had the wounds to show for it. Her side still felt raw from carrying the bag of shard fragments during the journey, the bag that had been taken by Radio while she had slept. Video had chased the smaller cat down, only to find she had formed some pact with the jester mage that caused the mess which put them on their mission. The beast had given the noble the ability to manipulate the sorcerer's magic to her own wishes, free to use upon her will.

It was an act punishable by death.

However, Video had first assumed the situation concerning the Radio Star was even worse when Video took the young noble's life. The Jester hadn't been beyond possessing the innocent, taking away any form of who they once were, and Video had come to the conclusion that Radio was the beast's final victim of possession. It *seemed* worse, anyway. On further thought, with a first look, the original assumption made the situation more dire, but wasn't it even more diabolical that Radio had been aware of her criminal actions? Video was left dumbfounded by it all. It was worse that her other traveling companion, Pictures from Clowder City, had been assisting the Jester, and above that, had magic of his own, too. It seemed the two mages manipulated the young noble to do their bidding, and Video hadn't been aware enough to stop it. Now she was fleeing for her life.

She wondered about the other's fates, the ones who had assisted the three on their mission, but then comprehended there were none to worry about. Pictures and Radio were dead, Sensor and Tape had been killed by the Jester. Video couldn't imagine any other fate for Sensor after he had bravely attacked the beast. If it wasn't for him, she and the Studio

Star likely would have died that night, too.

That was just the deaths she had witnessed personally. How many did they kill to get into the castle? How many lives did the Jester take when the mage wasn't there with Pictures? Did they kill Recorder? Cassette? Widget? All of the surveillance crew had worked both day and night for the three. There may have been deaths after Video was knocked unconscious, as well as deaths during their mission.

The five day mission; four days of travel, one day of chaos...how could so much go wrong that quickly? A missing king, the administrator over all of Central Media, was just the start. A noble turned against her subjects and took on magic, a consultant had gone rogue with the same influence, the best surveillance team in the region lost over half of its staff from mass murder, a mage's sorcery possessed the consciousness of several individuals, and countless subjects of Media were killed. All of it made Video's head spin, and with her head injury, she was sure she was missing other terrible occurrences. Who knew what else happened?

Video had to focus on getting away before she could dwell on the events any further. She could get to the mountains and reside there until everything cleared itself up and the Jester was found out. She moved on through the terrain until her vision blurred, barely noticing the shadow just out of the corner of her sight. She focused her eyes and blinked when she realized it was an opening to a den, and quickly moved toward the area.

Most of the city officials were diurnal and wouldn't be searching for her at night. If she could just stay there until then and hold out, she might have a chance of making it down the incline alive. During the twilight she could travel through the forest undetected, then make her away across the valley towards the mountains at night when everyone but the owls were back in their homes.

Step by step she could do this.

In the depths of the throne room, a large, golden striped feline prowled. His tail wound up and lashed with each step, making his shoulders rock with his movement. He growled when the door opened to the large hall, his eyes narrowing when he saw a proud owl step into the room. It had the same arrogance as that monkey had when it took its box, the strange, floating cyan cube, to his head, but he knew this judge had served his Council for years, and he didn't owe him any disrespect.

"Did you find her?" he asked.

"No, my Liege, they lost her." The owl sighed, and explained, "We sent ground animals and our top avian scouter after the traitor, but I can't make any promises they'll be successful. She took down at least three guards."

The king cheetah slammed his paw down and snarled, even more upset the bird didn't flinch at his wrath, but instead almost looked like he was going to roll his eyes if he was able to, the flick of his head corresponding with the initial movement. "Send someone who can. We can't have more threats with that chimp wandering around, and I have my own work instead of taking the time to be making up for your incompetence."

After a pause, the judge narrowed his eyes, but then lifted up the tips of his wings and said, "I'll do something about it. Whether or not the three succeed with bringing Miss Video back, as long as they find her, we'll have her location. I can take the situation into my own talons if they fail. One way or another, these three and this traitor will all pay for their incompetence. I will rule over the verdicts, my Liege."

Without waiting for a response, the owl turned away, beginning to walk out of the room.

"I thought you could fly, Prominence."

43

The owl's talons clicked against the smooth stone floor. He turned his head around to look at the King. "What can you do after being struck by a cat, sir?"

The King scowled, and looked away to climb back onto his throne, allowing the dark bird to leave. It was then he realized that it was the judge before this owl who was named Prominence. This was Select, but the arrogant bird had made no correction of his mistake.

The owl took in a breath once the doors closed behind him, his eyes rounding as he let the panic set in. He didn't have his cube on him! If something had gone wrong it would have been a disaster! Who looks to see if a bird flies!? *Owls walk all the time...or I thought so, anyway.*

When he heard paw steps draw towards the door, he knew it was time to make his exit. With a swing of his wings, shadows climbed up from the owl's legs up to the tip of his beak, and vanished in a burst of black shrapnel. He was done here; they could figure it out once they found the remaining feathers of the former judge's body behind the court podium.

Now he had to get another update. The shadows reformed in the dark jungle that the mage called home. The primate came out from the darkness, walking out into the clearing with his tail waving in the air. The king wouldn't think to reorganize the patrols, no, he would just start screeching about finding the mage. The primate chuckled to himself and carried on into his territory.

His nose wrinkled with the smell of cat. His tail lashed and he leapt up into the trees, but continued further more cautiously. With each step he grew quieter until he knew no noise was made over the trees. He kept his eyes peeled for anything unordinary, and then darkened his form to stay hidden.

That moment he saw her. She was unconscious. He then paused, no, she was sleeping. The deep wounds across her neck and on her cheek looked hideous from the paste and salve he put on the already bloody, dirt-covered wounds inflicted upon the small feline.

The Radio Star... The feline killed in cold blood by Video over a simple misunderstanding from both parties. Radio had believed the terrible, fear-mongering Jester had some regret in regard to his actions. *Regret the plan failed.* The spider monkey rolled his eyes. She thought she could bring the shards to him and he would make it all better, something that sounded just as absurd in her words as it should have in his. *Like I could fix a broken heart.* He scoffed.

Then there was the other side. Video had believed Radio had been possessed and beyond convincing that what she was doing was impossible. She thought by killing Radio she would remove the last threat the Jester had to throw at them, and it might have, if it wasn't for Pictures already having plans on ending them both.

If either had instantly jumped into action, they might have figured out Pictures early, and he never would have acquired the shards. Even when he did, it didn't work out; Video still managed to chase him down. Studio restored the heart even before he and Pictures could extract its magic. Video butchered Pictures in cold blood before he had his curses fully lifted. When the primate saw the spells were nearly complete, after seasons of incubating inside the cat, but could not come to fruition, he had attacked Video himself in a frustrated outburst.

The primate groaned, glaring down at the noble his comrade had wasted his time with. Pictures also became too attached and didn't take his opportunities to put Radio down when he could have. Everything they had both worked for was thrown away because of that. The monkey picked up the mangled collar he hung on the vines above the sleeping feline and sighed. It was a strange concept to have a noble in his abode, but it would be good to keep the collar as a reminder when she woke.

He climbed down from the tree to the vine canopy where she lay, her collar now wrapped up in his tail. He rested the back of his hand on the smooth fur of her forehead. Her temperature was regulating, and the wounds were recovering. Either he unintentionally did this or he may have found the next most powerful mage in Media yet. Radio could be a mage that would introduce the next level of regeneration, a mage that could bring back Pictures, if she learned to control it.

Or it was something he completely missed and something else was going on...It was an occurrence he had a hard time believing, but couldn't deny it had happened. Either way, she had been dead and now she was alive, and he was going to figure out the magic behind it to get his accomplice in crime to return.

I was so close!

The primate scoffed, dropping the mangled collar on the cat so that it would lay on her chest, and then leapt back for the trees. So much went wrong, he couldn't think of much worse that could have happened. Even if there were any worse outcomes, he was still stuck cleaning up these past five days. He felt the memories and final thoughts of Pictures were stabilized with his magic; it was one of the last things he did. If he could just figure out how to recover them, and where they were stored outside of his mind, it would be the next step in getting the blasted cat back to him. One step at a time, he just needed to focus on getting Video out of the *picture* first...

The spider monkey shook his head. He needed to stop thinking about Pictures, too. Once he was back into the higher branches he began scanning the grounds and found his target. There were new things to focus on, new targets and new events. He would have to start where he left off, and with those who already knew him.

"Stereo," he called as he leapt down, "I have some news."

The dark, long haired tomcat looked up at the primate in the trees, his icy blue eyes narrowing when the monkey landed in front of him. He knew that no news was good when it came to the strange monkey and answered, "Then state it."

"We're expecting a visitor soon, maybe a few, and I want you prepared. Make sure our Star above is protected and don't hesitate to send an alarm and notify me to come back if we have a threat. I'm going out."

"Very well." The marble striped feline watched the mage move toward the borders of the jungle, and sighed, asking, "Did you succeed in court?"

He smirked when the primate became visibly annoyed, and turned to walk away, continuing with a smile, "She was always your favorite."

Yet here you are, answering to me. Stereo couldn't tell what was a bird and what was a bat if they were both held over his head, and yet he made a point of asking, provoking him. The mage glared at the white paws of the tom and then whipped away.

Video made it to the valleys by nightfall as she had planned, but now she had to find a place to stay out of sight. She was a big, fluffy, brown brute in a sharp, shiny, grass terrain and she would have to find somewhere that would keep her cover so she could actually get some sleep. It didn't really matter, no one was awake searching for her, she could just lay down for a few moments.

She let her body sink down into the grass, and rested her head down, feeling the rest of her energy drain from her. She was so close. Her mother's home was within a day of Calotype's Forest. When she reached that far, she could figure out what to do from there.

Once she woke up, her head would be clear.

Video startled when she found herself back at the castle, back in the drawing room. She swallowed nervously, feeling the heat of the fire outside the room and within the fireplace where the furnace was out of sight. She scanned the room carefully. Where was everyone?

She screamed when she was suddenly shoved down, and found herself face to face with Pictures. "No!" Not again! She kicked the tom off of herself and bolted for the door, but he tripped her with a whip of his orange magic, and leapt for her.

Video ducked down and backed away, but had to defend herself against another blast of magic, jumping right into his path and forced to fight once he attacked. They raked each other's pelts with their claws and fangs, the room becoming a complete blur once she was locked into battle with the tom. She didn't hesitate again to drive her fangs into his neck and bite down, pulling and ripping until she felt his warm blood drip down on her paws, and quickly ripped her claws into his neck to open the rest of his throat up.

She grabbed him again by the neck and pushed back the secret lever herself by knocking him into it. Once the lever was pushed back and the back of the fireplace opened into the giant disposal furnace, Video flung him through the chute again. Once he was gone, she sunk to her paws and cried, horrified at reliving it, remembering the events slowly as they recurred, then looked around in fear of having to face the Jester again, too.

He wasn't there, but it wasn't over. Video jumped away from the fireplace when it exploded into orange magic, and screamed when Pictures leapt out from the flames, glowing orange with his plasma threads expanding like the wings of a bird.

"No! By the Stars, no!" Video backed away, and screamed when the tom leapt, no, flew at her with all the magic he could have had behind him ready to strike her dead for good. *This isn't real!*

Video opened her eyes to see the faint outline of a feline above her, the glittering amber outline of his form, the nicked ear, and orange eyes sending her heart into a frenzy. No, he *wasn't* dead!

Horror filled her chest as she shouted out. She swiftly aimed a clawed paw at the neck of the tom, but instead of feeling flesh between her claws, it was solid surface. The panel made an unnatural metallic noise when her claws made contact, making Video jump with surprise. She didn't hesitate to sink teeth into the throat of the cat before he knocked her back with only a flick of his stone-hard paw. Video's fear was building and she wasn't sure how to respond to the sudden strength of her opponent. Her eyes were shut as she struck out blindly at him, only using her whiskers to guide her and what her paws could feel. When she broke skin, he yelled in response, but it was deeper than she remembered Pictures' voice. She gasped out loud as his paw whipped her down and slammed into her chest, pinning her down effortlessly. The paw pads felt unnatural, like a boulder on her chest which caused even more panic to fill her chest. "Calm down and open your eyes, Video!"

He was unbeatable, he was more terrifying than he ever was before. Video would never be able to escape the mages and had to face her death. Video cried when she opened up her eyes to look into Pictures', expecting to see his grinning face.

But it wasn't Pictures. Video's eyes rounded with horror.

She looked up at the giant tom, a cat even bigger than her, and saw the genuine gold on his form, not magic. He was a smoky black tabby, not a silhouette bathed in moonlight, and his yellow-amber eyes were his own. The nicked ear was actually more torn than nicked, but Video couldn't stop focusing on the chest plate and gold laced fur. There was only one cat in all of Media who had such a strange addition to their appearance, one who found themselves beyond wearing a simple collar to flaunt their status.

Film, the director of the Capital's surveillance, had her pinned with a gold plated paw.

"Oh, oh no," Video barely breathed out, her eyes welled with tears.

Film quickly lifted his paw from her chest, allowing her to gasp for air with the release from the pressure of the plate. He stepped back, and lifted up his chin. "Recover and explain yourself, Video of the Mountain Region."

This cat was the highest ranked monitor in Central Media, and easily the wealthiest feline, who wasn't of noble-blood, in the entire region. He knew every subject of Media in and out, he had access to their records, their recordings, their assignments, and he was respected even beyond the central region to as far as the Monitor's Districts of Western and Eastern Media, and was even called there on occasion, requested to assist them with their events. This was a cat not to trifle with and Video had just attacked him blindly.

He was the one who had directed their mission through the surveillance team.

"I mistook you for someone else, sir. I-I am so sorry." Video bowed her head in shame, awaiting his strike.

"I would have waited until you awakened, but I couldn't risk having to chase you." The Smokey tabby flexed his heavy golden claws and asked, "Do you know who I am?"

Video swallowed and nodded. He likely came to escort her back to the Capital City for her sentence, so she began to cry. "Please, sir, just allow me to explain myself. I didn't betray Media, I–"

"No, you didn't, Video. Walk with me."

She hesitated in shock before she quickly stammered, "Y-yes, sir."

Video felt more worn out than she did before she slept. No rest was accomplished from her nightmare and any energy gained was wasted on a foolish attack. She wouldn't be able to run if she tried, each paw step was barely enough to remain standing. Besides all that, she had to focus on everything she could to remain calm enough not to begin shaking in the fear of being beside this cat.

"The situation we're faced with is hard to fathom, and has been even harder to contain, Video. The recordings proving the reason behind your actions were destroyed and all the witnesses have either been sabotaged or have died. I need you to explain what happened, so we can decide how we're going to handle getting the evidence to show what really occurred."

Video nodded, trying to keep the story in line with what she told the Studio Star. "The Radio Star of The Meridian Stretch had fallen under the influence of the Jester. Pictures of Clowder City had been working with the Jester, from what I assume was the beginning. The Studio Star discovered the last shard of the crystal heart after we were bringing back the other four fragments. The bag that contained the four shards gathered from our mission was taken by Pictures, so Miss Studio and I went to the castle, driven by rickshaw, to pursue him. Tape was dead already upon our entering, with Pictures standing over his body." Video hesitated again before continuing, the image of the dark brown tabby dead before her former traveling companion locked inside her mind. "There was so much blood, sir...we were attacked by the Jester and Pictures. The last shard was taken away and the heart was restored because of the presence of the Studio Star as the Jester's message promised. When Pictures fled with the heart of glass, Sensor attacked the Jester, allowing Miss Studio and me to chase after him."

Film remained silent, making Video nervous, but she took in a breath and continued, "Pictures stood in the throne room and fled when Miss Studio and I split up...I should have stayed with her, but his eyes glowed of magic, both the Jester's blue and his own orange magic... I chased after him. After losing him in the halls, I went to the drawing room where I found both him and the Jester. I had pushed the heart away when attacking Pictures, as it seemed the Jester couldn't be in contact with it." Video began talking quicker as she grew more anxious, stammering, "Studio found us and kept the Jester back while I fought Pictures. I threw him into the furnace with Studio's help, and then the Jester attacked me. Studio activated the heart...I think to release the King, but I couldn't focus from there. The mage...it struck me and left me with this head injury via

52

its own cube. Everything was lost from there. I saw the King, and I fell unconscious." Video stopped, almost breathless as her eyes started to blur with tears again. "I don't know how it went so wrong, sir! I've never failed a mission before."

Film shook his head. "But you did succeed, Video. The King is back."

It wasn't my assignment to end the Jester. Video's eyes rounded when she looked up at Film, realizing he was right. Her heart pounded with the very idea.

"You did everything you had to, Video," he murmured, and looked back to the path ahead. "It was a rough time finding you, Video. The chip in your ear, did you remove it?"

"No...I lost it during...the attack with Ra...the Radio Star." Video blinked, feeling the dizzy sensation return when her suddenly vision unfocused and asked, "I must know, I'm so sorry to ask; why are you walking with me, sir? You're putting yourself at risk for accusations from the Council..."

"Video, I know what danger lies ahead, and accusations are the least of our worries. Right now we need to worry about...Video?"

Darkness. Video saw nothing as she suddenly felt the soft grass against the side of her face.

"Video?"

Video blinked her eyes open slowly once the sun glared into them. It hurt to move, but she felt as though she had slept for weeks. Had that all been a dream? She hadn't remembered travelling any further than past Faith's Village. She looked around to see she was hidden from the outside

53

at the base of a small den, formerly dug by something likely akin to a fisher. She either was near Calotype's Forest, or was past it and in the Crater Valleys.

She went to get up and winced at the pain. All the pain from the wounds given by the avians who chased her had set in and her paw pads looked even worse than they were before. She sighed and went outside, relieved to see she was at Calotype's Forest, but out of danger from the inner Labyrinth.

She sniffed and looked around for any prey or herbal plant life and was relieved to see some plantain. She ripped up some leaves from the plant, and chewed them until they were a poultice she could lick against her pads. Her hind pads felt as though they had broken and cracked, but the softer fore pads were blistered and raw. She had to treat those before anything else.

Once she arrived at Audio's home, she could be treated with her mother's salve and remedies, but for now, this would have to suffice.

She startled when she heard a deep voice saying, "Try to mix it with this."

It was Film.

It hadn't been a dream.

The giant cat placed a honeycomb before her and stepped back to clean the honey off his muzzle. Video bit off more plantain leaves to mix with the honey, licking up the rest after she finished treating her paws.

"I would have brought moss, but I didn't think I'd be able to get you to sit long enough."

"A clever assumption." Video nodded, and looked at the rest of the plantain leaves. She had treated her wounds the whole journey with Pictures and Radio, but only Pictures had noticed while Radio was still sleeping. He hadn't asked her about it until she started treating Transmitter in the Ruined City, but Film even brought her something to help.

"How did you not get stung by the bees?" she finally asked.

"I have my ways." A flash of something crossed his face. Video thought it might have been an arrogant smirk, but his face was one of serious concern when he asked, "Would you mind if I treated your sides? They're scratched badly."

Video blinked with surprise, but wouldn't refuse a request from Film. She let herself relax enough to rest her head down. The tomcat worked carefully to apply the poultice to the wounds from the avians, allowing Video to close her eyes and breathe in the scent of the honey and plantain. Soon she would be with Audio and the smell of remedies would be in the air, impossible not to take in. She missed her mother, not having seen the smaller feline since her early missions. Video wondered what she thought about all the news, if it was getting out, and what Audio might be thinking about if Faith had told her what happened.

Once Film was finished, Video rose and looked up to the mountains where the feline resided, then bristled when Film walked past her on the path.

"You're coming with me?" Video asked, her eyes widening when Film gestured her forward with a wave of his tail and began to lead her up the incline.

"Yes, and we better get a move on before it gets too hot out." He said insistently, not turning to look at her.

Video's eyes rounded, not realizing he ever travelled up the mountains, but she remained calm and smoothed her fur to inquire softly, "And you're doing this, because…"

"You're safest travelling with me, Video." Film stated firmly. "While you don't have your tracker, regular drones still could locate you by monitoring the area. Right now I've got my status set not to be disturbed, which means any surveillance bots travelling on a trail will not monitor within sight of me. You won't be seen and no one will suspect I'm holding you under my supervision."

"Uh." Video clenched her jaw when she nearly corrected the dark feline's arrogance, now wondering how many convicted criminals he might have done this with that weren't innocent like her. Instead of pressing the accusation, she held her breath, seeing his method was probably better not being questioned while he still had the power to call for reinforcements.

After she released the breath quietly, starting to walk with him up to the mountains, she asked, "Why risk it?" She flicked her tail, hoping her voice came out monotonically enough for the tomcat not to realize she was suspicious. She already began to regret letting him treat her sides, forced to consider the idea he could have attached a tracker chip or something.

"Because no one would disobey my command, and because I believe, with enough time, we can find the evidence to prove your innocence."

Video narrowed her eyes. She decided there should be no "we" to prove her innocence, but before she could even formulate any objections, his eyes flickered gold from the contact lens that his rank had to survey the area with additional information, and for immediate reporting. He had technology that was on par with the power of magic.

Pompous, gold laced, arrogant pile of over-shampooed fur! Video had so often heard her father insult this tom: the cosmetic surgeries to embed gold into his fur and flesh, the pampered lifestyle anytime he wasn't out in the field. The cat lived better than the King and had an ego the size of the enormous cheetah, too, with a third of the brain size. Video walked with Film without another word, but his chuckle at her expression let her know that she gave her annoyance at his directives away.

The path quickly lost its softness once the grass eased into earth and stone the further they travelled. It still wasn't nearly as rough as the path down the Capital City. With the treatment of the plantain and beeswax, the only thing that Video had to complain about was her headache. The only thing she had lost being accustomed to was the incline. The entire mission with Pictures and Radio was along hills and valleys, usually the easiest path for the pampered felines. With the constant injuries Video received battling for and against the two, though, the travel had its own wear on her, as well. After climbing the first ledge toward the Rich Top Mountains, Video caught her breath and stated, "I'm going to hunt while we're still somewhere where there's prey."

Film shrugged, and kept walking. "Don't go too far."

Video blinked before her tail lashed. She wanted to continue to insult the tom, daring him to stop her, but in reality, he had. Pampered or not, the cat could hold his own. She woke up and struck him in a frenzy earlier and even if she was half asleep or not, he hadn't even flinched. He apprehended her, had her explain the situation without a moment's hesitance, as though nothing was wrong and he wasn't speaking to the homicidal maniac the Council was making her out to be and what she proved when she went for his throat without thinking. Video swallowed and sighed. Now he treated her wounds and offered the promise the Council wouldn't find her.

Still! The promise was only good under the restriction that he travel with her. He just thought he could demand whatever he wanted. Now she had to bring him back to Audio.

Alarm filled Video's thoughts. What if he pressed her mother for questions? He knew her whereabouts either way, but Video didn't want to lead him to her parents' home, and didn't want to possibly face Signal with him, either. Video quickly relaxed her shoulders before they bristled, knowing it might work out that she had Film to explain the situation was not as it seemed.

If that was really the reason he was with her. Who knew what plans could be in that cat's mind? Every possible solution also had a possible ulterior motive. If Video kept thinking about it, she'd get nothing done. Video stopped when she heard the sound of small prey, and let her ears focus on the tiny noise. She let her eyes follow the sound, and saw a nice, plump vole. She licked her lips, sunk down slowly and began to creep up on the rodent, keeping her tail up just high enough so the long fur didn't make any noise.

She pounced on the vole and swiftly bit it in the neck, not hesitating to begin to eat it. There could be songbirds and maybe some moles up in the mountains, but it would likely be solid day without eating until they were at Audio's, and Video would take any energy she got.

Then she felt the warm breeze of the forest from below again, even after they had climbed as far as they had. There was an endless amount of prey within the borders of Calotype's Forest, but nearly everyone who entered the jungle ceased to return. The idea then came to her mind. Video would never be found if she just went in the depths of it. If Radio was wrong about her theory of it being the Jester's hide out, and the Jester wasn't there, then Video could live the rest of her life hidden in peace.

Even if it was the mage's territory, then Video simply gained another try at finishing what she started. Film would never find her in the enchanted jungle, and there would be no worries about his intentions.

Unless he still went to Audio's and interrogated her. If Video wasn't there to be the focus, the questioning might be directed towards the older feline and her own encounters with magic. Video swallowed, not knowing if her mother's presence in the forest was ever recorded. She was the one cat who could enter the Unending Labyrinth and leave with ease. Video couldn't risk Signal having disposed of all the previous recordings involving Audio roaming within the enchanted jungle for her medicines after he had rid Media of Phantascope.

She had to go back. When it came to her courier work, she answered to this tom, anyway. Everyone did. She needed to respect that if she wanted a chance at getting back into Media's good graces, as well as keep her mother safe.

Video started making her way back to Film, but a moment later she jumped at the sound of an explosion. The sound was unlike anything she ever heard, and made her ears ring to a stunning degree. She whipped back around to Calotype's Forest, and her eyes rounded as she watched a beam of cyan and green light spiral out of the Unending Labyrinth. It shot up to the sky towards the plasma barrier that surrounded Media. Video startled when it connected with the force field. Everything happened instantly. Video screamed in terror when the barrier suddenly broke into sheets of magic, splitting into the sky separated by the threads that flowed over the land.

It didn't stop there, though. Video flattened against the ground as the sheets began exploding into bursts of light, covering the sky in nothing but white for heartbeats at a time and decreasing in amount little by little as they fell from what had once been a complete, enormous dome. The sound alone of the explosions dazed her, but the sight horrified her.

Video's eyes rounded as the threads she had seen her entire life split apart and dissipated: the barrier she was told that protected the land from danger. The barrier had been, supposedly, the only magic that lasted after the former Queen, Satisfaction, had died. It also was supposed to be indestructible.

It was vanishing now. She hissed in surprise at the explosions as they drew closer to the ground. Video fled the clearing, hoping Film was okay and hadn't been struck by any of the magic's shrapnel.

She climbed back onto the ledge where she had left the tom and quickly scrambled in the direction where his paws left a trail, desperate to get to him before something worse happened. She halted when the path led to a grassy open area within the mountain, seeing Film perched on the highest rock in the clearing.

Video stared in shock. The gold on his pelt was glittering in the magic light, the only additional light shining from him being his hovering monitor screen as he seemed to be looking for reports. His slightly curved ears turned towards her as she approached him. Her eyes widened in further disbelief. When she made no movement towards the boulder he rested on, he came to her instead.

Her ears flattened as he jumped down in front of her, the weight of his gold paws making an indentation in the earth once he landed, making Video's claws twitch under her paws. *This cat literally leaves a print wherever he goes.* "Did you see that?! How can you have not?"

"It was hard to miss, Video, but it was not caused by our government, so there are no details yet in the reports."

"That's what you're worried about? Of course it wasn't by the Council, or they would have done it ages ago!" She looked around in case any magic possibly was coming at them, and startled when one of the dissipating panels hit the ground, causing the plant life to burst with sudden growth and flowers.

What would that do if it hit a cat? She whipped around and stared at Film with round eyes. "Why were you in the most open area in all of Central Media, Film!?"

Film ignored her. "All it seems to be is that we're running out of time when it comes to taking out this Jester. We really need your name cleared as quickly as possible."

Video stared at him in dismay over his lack of concern, but nodded subtly, still in shock over the sight. Had he wanted to get hit by the magic? He could take it as an accusation if she asked him, so she would have to keep her mouth shut. She blinked, left to follow Film once he began moving.

She tried not to think about the barrier and to refocus on getting to Audio, but then she realized this was another opportunity. "But wait...Film, if we can't, and there's no additional surveillance at my father's..." Her voice became quiet as she looked up at the taller feline. "This is my chance to leave Media. There's a land bridge past the mountains to a northern land. I've seen it during my missions." Video blinked, and looked up into the tom's eyes. "I could leave."

It was the first time she had seen annoyance from Film. She quickly flattened her ears, dipping her head when he stated firmly, "I wouldn't set for a different path just yet, Video. We haven't even reached our second source yet and I'm not going to agree to give up this easily."

Video stared at him in horror, realizing her own words. "O-Oh. Yes, sir." She nodded.

What had she just done? Video could answer her own question. She just had proved she was as disloyal as the Radio Star, willing to abandon her morals when she was given the opportunity to find an easier way out. The only thing which helped her justify it was the fact that she was so *frightened.* The feeling was new to her. What was going to happen now?

When she didn't speak up again, Film sighed, turning to her once he saw how much she deflated. "Video, you're young, and it was an immediate thought. I wouldn't hold you to it, especially given the circumstances, but the reason why I'm fighting for you is because you fought for your life to defend this land against the Jester. That integrity and loyalty is not something I want to see you throw away because you're scared. We're all afraid of this threat, Video, especially with what just happened." The shakiness in his voice betrayed his composed expression, making Video's eyes widen before he continued. "We don't understand it yet, but that doesn't mean we can abandon it."

"Yes, sir," she whispered.

"It's going to be hard to fight this, but we can do it once we solve how the Jester gets his inside information. I don't know how the mage knew when your hearing was, but since information was leaked of the policies, I believe it still has some connection within the monitor system. At first I thought it was Pictures, but now he's gone and information is still being given out, so it seems I was incorrect. I had nothing I could offer your hearing for evidence; Pictures and the mage infiltrated the surveillance room when they reached the castle. They tarnished my recordings, and I believe it may have been the reason why Tape lost his life; because he tried to stop them. Why, I wouldn't even doubt Pictures was still alive if it wasn't for your account."

Video knew her nightmares weren't real, yet she had to acknowledge, "With the power of magic, any concept of deception is beyond limitation. We can't take for granted he's not still alive when we're in the face of illusion and falsifying reality."

"Exactly, anything is possible under the threat of magic, and anything can just be a trick of the eyes. Did you just throw Pictures into the Capital Furnace, or did you deal him some wounds?"

Video blinked, stared up at the crystal clear sky, and then looked at Film. "I ripped out his throat."

Film gave a slightly rocking nod, his ear flicking uncomfortably. "Right, well, maybe we don't have to worry about him."

"Except that regeneration isn't beyond mages. My father had a lot of trouble with Phantascope when facing the beast because of that fact."

"Yes, it made the Shadow Advisor quite the foe for years."

Video stopped, needing the tom to elaborate. She had grown up hearing about Phantascope being Signal's greatest foe, but never about who else had faced the mage.

It was only when Film turned around to look at her, when she saw the deep scars across his eyes, the same scars her father had been branded with after their final battle.

"The monster got you, too," she whispered.

"I was lucky enough to keep my sight, though." A sly grin slid across his face. "Phantascope always had trouble with the tall ones."

Video scoffed, not wanting to find light in the situation, and kept moving. "You almost refer to it like a person."

"Not at all. Signal and I weren't the only ones who suffered the paw of that beast during its final days. While the papers state the trouble caused in the Unending Labyrinth, that creature had been attacking villages under its Advisor name since I was a kit. It had a fascination with eyes, and told me they were windows to the soul. I believe mages may lose a part of their magic if their eyes are damaged, and I think Phantascope took that advantage when battling a foe. There were many more mages when that cat roamed around."

That was new to Video. "Who else did Phantascope attack?"

"At the first sighting of its aggression there was a young nursing female who died from a throat wound with her eyes gouged out. Her milk had dropped, but no bodies of any kittens were found. They were assumed stolen. The situation was unlike anything we had ever seen. It's not often included in the case of the destruction of Calotype's original sanctuary, but the events occurred only days apart from one another. It was common among the monitors to assume it was Pictures' mother because of the similarities in markings and coloring as well as sightings within the area."

Video's eyes widened. Another mage had killed the tom's mother? What of his littermates? She clamped her jaw shut when Film continued, "Over time there were a few instances, other mages, small villages, and our own monitors." Film paused, as though thinking of an example, and finished with, "Screen from Clowder City was also blinded by a mage attack while he lived in the northern mountains. His entire town was destroyed by only one mage. I wouldn't be surprised if it was Phantascope from the description of the perpetrator."

Video nodded, frowning. She had been concerned by the strange blindfolded tom when she met him, doubting his loyalties, but it sounded like he had been through some sorrow himself. She couldn't believe that even Phantascope would kill a mother to a mage, though. She was left to wonder why Pictures had turned on the subjects of Media if he had a better reason than most to hate mages, if what Film said was true.

It was as though Film knew where Video's mind headed. "Back to the issue of Pictures, Video; I don't think he would recover from a fatal wound dealt from your claws. I was able to watch live when you faced the wolf in the Ruined City. Analog cameras attached to the decaying building above where you faced him were still on. You three worked together well. You all went through a lot, but it was you who faced the brunt of the combat. I know you often delivered to Faith before your mission began, and I'm sorry about what you had to face with her guardians."

Video blinked, dreading the moment he said Faith's name, and tried to keep her paws from shaking while she walked. She had played with the rats when she was young; they had welcomed her into their village on her first assignment and escorted her to Faith like she was some noble. "I knew them before I even had my title…" She had been delivering her mother's remedies, her first courier mission, when she met them.

"It sounded like it was a terrible experience, but a noble one. It's why I know you choose Media over your own desires, Video. Your loyalty is something to commend."

"Thank you, sir," she murmured.

Film seemed content at that and kept on moving. Video knew the path from here by heart, and wasn't worried about falling behind. She looked back at the path behind them, and found her gaze travelling back to the Unending Labyrinth. Video looked into the dark forest, able to see the upper canopy from the elevation. She thought of how readily Radio had wanted to travel into the jungle to confront the Jester. It had only been a few days ago, but knowing Video would never see the young feathery feline again, it felt more like an eternity ago. Video stared past the overgrown brush of the canopy and into the darkness beyond, wondering what the source of the magic was that destroyed the barrier, but then turned her head back to follow after Film.

They could make it to Audio's by tomorrow if they didn't stop, and even with Video's paws in the condition they were in after the Capital Mountain hike. Knowing she was going to get treatment made her endure it. Once they were there, they'd be a step ahead. Video had a place to hide and Film had a secondary source of recordings.

When nightfall came, though, Video's anxiety also returned as she grew more tired. If her father didn't have backups of the recordings, which was likely with how the Jester destroyed his surveillance drone in the castle, Video was back to having to prove her innocence by other means. She wouldn't know what to do at that point. Her mother would probably recommend trying to "talk it out" with the Jester or something and Signal would question why she hadn't gone out already to look for the monster so she could end it once and for all. She sighed and looked toward Film, wondering what he had planned if all else failed.

Film stared back at her with his yellow eyes, the amber rims around his pupils reminding her just enough of Pictures that she turned her gaze away. The idea of being with another mage made her stomach sick. Having met him after the nightmare did neither of them any favors. She sighed, and closed her eyes. "How long do you think this is all going to take, sir?"

He hesitated. "To stop the Jester, or prove your innocence?"

Video blinked, and opened her eyes again, turning her gaze to his gold-lined tail. "Both."

Film's nicked ear slowly tilted as he seemed to ponder a response, as though from the time the ear turned from the front to the back of his head, he had to give an answer. "I believe the moment the other monitors get back to Cassette with their own findings, we might find something that caught a glimpse of Pictures' foul play or Radio's…"

"Magic use," Video finished, her tail giving a lash once she realized Film wasn't going to finish his own sentence.

"Yes. If the Radio Star ever used magic externally like the Jester, any recording of that could be used to prove you were right with your actions, Video."

Video realized the tom hadn't known her reason for killing Radio, only having said that much to allow her to finish the sentence, yet he travelled at her side. Video realized she hadn't told Film that Radio used magic until this point, but that was because she assumed he heard the court hearing, or knew from his recordings before they were tarnished. Even in the court, Video only said Radio was in the possession of magic. That could be as simple as standing next to the cube. She really had assumed Film saw the battle through the surveillance bots if he was going to come all this way to walk her to her mother's home and infiltrate her father's records.

How much of all this *was* for his own agenda? She masked her expression from showing her sudden concern, afraid the larger cat might suddenly change his approach. She was at his beck and call while he wasn't being disturbed by the other monitors. The moment she chose to disobey him, she could be reported and taken back to court. Or just be killed by his own paw, seeing as how she had already been sentenced to death by the mage. She swallowed nervously when she stared down at the tom's paws, thinking of his sharp metal claws and strength, so easily used to defend against her frenzied attack when they met.

Then it clicked for Video; if the monkey already had impersonated someone as high ranking as Enterprise from what Pictures' said, and continued to impersonate the judge, what put it beyond being anyone else with the right information? How did the monster know so much about the high ranking officials and exactly where to infiltrate? Only monitors had that clearance, Film said it himself. This meant the mage had to have had eyes on the inside. Video herself shouldn't know the ranking of all the officials, and even while she did know many of their titles and their placements because of her work and training with her parents, she didn't have clearance to see them. The Jester did, in the right form, and it knew how to take these high class officials' appearance with no suspicion, and when to do it, too.

Video swallowed, wondering if perhaps Film was the one who had been giving the Jester the reports and the know-how to infiltrate. He could be one of the most powerful felines in all of Media, controlled and led by the land's most dangerous criminal. She glanced at the dark feline's gold paw again nervously. She wondered how much was of his appearance was really surgically altered, or if those amber rimmed eyes were the same as the Jester's dark blue to show the mage's magic. Was it was all mystic fabrication? Could he be leading her to a trap?

"Is something wrong, Video—"

The two both startled upon hearing another burst of an explosion from the Unending Labyrinth, and looked over to see a second plasma beam shoot up to the sky. There was no green in this one, and it shot directly up to the clouds until another explosion sounded, and the beam began extending down the sky like the threads of a spider web.

"Oh, that's not good." Film's brow furrowed.

"What did it do!?" Video gasped, her eyes round in horror, and she immediately bristled. The monkey was responsible, the barrier was always spoken of as something that protected the folk of Media, a beautifully woven plasma that kept everything bad away, but this web of magic splitting through the sky was a clear message that it existed to trap the folk with the darkness and evil inside. It made their land nothing more than a prison, and a playground for the Jester's fun. Video took a step closer towards the jungle. She knew the borders of Media were days of travel away, and at the speed of the barrier, there would be no fleeing the land. She whipped her head and looked at Film, hissing, "That was my chance to leave this place for good! Why did you hold me back? You knew this was going to happen!"

"I knew no such thing!" Film gaped up at her, making no movement to stand. "I don't know what's going on, Video. This is magic! I know no more than you do!"

Video narrowed her eyes at the tom. Her lips curled to snarl at the cat, and her claws dug into the earth as she prepared to strike him.

"Now before we get hasty, my dear..." Film's neck fur began to rise.

Video went to snarl at the tom, and then heard more blasts from the jungle below. She startled in fear of a possible ambush, whipping around to see who was coming, but the cat wasn't heading her way. Instead, they were heading for the border of Media now. Video focused her sights on the fluffy feline, who had abnormal, glowing green eyes even for the moonlight's reflection. Video swallowed nervously when realizing it was the same green that was cast before the barrier was eliminated before.

Would she have a better chance if she followed the strange mage? She would have first assumed the mage was Phantascope, but it had too much color on it compared to the photos of the Shadow Advisor. It carried a long staff attached to its belt, the handle glowing the same green as its eyes in a helix spinning up the rod. This tri-colored cat seemed to have the power to weaken the barrier cast by Queen Satisfaction herself, possibly still giving Video a way out of Media for good. One bitter, spiteful glare from the calico upon its realization of being watched answered whether or not to follow it. She had never seen such hate. Video stepped back to Film, her fur bristling at the idea she had even considered following such evil power for her own gain.

"Trouble will catch up with that one, Video. Look how the shadows follow it. We probably should get moving." Film murmured in Video's ear before effortlessly dodging her swipe for his face.

Video slapped her paw back against the ground, not daring to wince when the raw skin pressed against the rough earth. She whipped away from him, going back up towards the path to her old home.

"You wouldn't have made it to the border if you left right away, anyway."

"You think I don't know that?" Video bit down to stop from yelling at the tomcat. She had been upset, but it was clear there was no escape from her troubles, or him, at that.

"I was hoping you'd figure it out. There was a cat by the name of Authentication that was sent to monitor the Jester there two days ago. He was more than happy to accept the job, I only hope it won't lead the young tom to his death after seeing that power."

Video wondered if the cat would be bold enough to actually try and attack the mage, but also knew that she herself would likely do so if given the opportunity. She stared at Film and asked, "If it was just a couple days ago, maybe he's yet to reach it…"

"We can only hope."

- CHAPTER 3-
LATENCY

Video and Film travelled until they reached a ledge where they could rest. They decided to sleep at that point. Video wasn't sure what the next day was going to bring them, so she was going to enjoy what little rest she could get before they experienced the consequences of the new barrier. Film left to hunt and brought back a rabbit for them to share.

It was plump for a mountain rabbit. Video ate her fill, almost in disbelief that Film could catch one so easily. After the meal, both curled up on their respective sides of the ledge. She relaxed herself and settled in slowly, keeping on high alert of their surroundings out from the ledge, as well as within her space when it came to Film. Once she saw that Film's breathing slowed, she let her eyes close.

She gasped when she found herself back in the drawing room. She stepped away from Pictures, who was in front of her this time.

"I just want you to stop!" Video choked out, and glared at the silver tabby.

He looked surprised at her willingness to speak, but then his eyes hooded. "There's no other way, Video. You can't keep fighting like this forever, and you will die in due time." He grinned with malice and struck Video, sending her down to the ground and forcing her to fight until she had to play over the same exact actions to kill him again. This time, from the last strike of his throat, before Video could grab him, she blinked, and found herself staring down at Radio in the valley instead. The cat was crying out the magic through her eyes and looking up at her with horror, pleading silently for her life. Video's eyes rounded as the cat's mouth moved as she tried to speak; however, nothing but gurgling blood came out. The feline began spasming under Video's paws, the blood spilling out of her throat and soaking Video's paws as though she had just spilled a teacup.

"Radio, no!"

"Video, wake up!"

Video gasped desperately for air, not knowing she had been holding her breath, and coughed. She felt her vision blur as tears welled up in her eyes. The burning sensation in her eyes and face from the tears didn't help her feel any better as she lifted her head up.

Guilt washed over her. She could barely speak. "I-I killed her! I killed her and she's gone! She's gone and it's all my fault!" she sobbed, her voice at an unusual high pitch from the distress.

She rose and pushed Film away; thankful the tom allowed it and didn't continue to prove how weak she was from her exhaustion and current state. Her breath was heavy. She was shaking with every sob. Not only was she covered in wounds that weakened her physically, but she felt like guilt was tearing out her throat just like she had done to Radio. She prowled around the ledge where they rested, feeling the blood between her claws and soaking her fur, even though nothing was there. The blood had been washed from her body for days now, but the wounds she received from Radio still burned in her face whenever her heart raced. Her body wracked from another sob. She kept moving up the path, trying to control her breathing and not to get stuck in a coughing fit from her anxiety and guilt.

She did everything she was supposed to, but she did nothing beyond that and it didn't feel like she had looked for any way around her actions, either. Had she *wanted* to kill Radio? Is that why she didn't look for another option? *No.* She thought it was the Jester, she thought it was the beast that killed and warped her childhood guardians and twisted them to be a different life form in their own bodies. She struck Radio with the same anger she would have for the Jester, and now the noble was gone because of it. She couldn't have risked listening to Radio's pleading, not when it could have been more of the Jester's games. Yet now the young cat's life was taken from her, in one of the worst ways possible.

Video didn't realize Film was following her until they reached the rocky terrain of the mountains. His gold paw pads struck against the stone with each step, making an audible noise that was impossible not to hear. At first she was thankful it took her thoughts away from the scene in her nightmare, but after the sixth sequence of the rhythmic paw steps, her appreciation wore thin. Even worse, Video had just spotted prey that immediately fled upon hearing the large tom's movement, making her furious.

He gave you his rabbit, you can't complain. She told herself, and part of her wondered if Film made sure to follow her to the rough terrain just to keep her mind off her nightmare, or he was so full of himself and arrogant that he didn't realize the noise he was making was chasing off prey. He probably ate up the idea that he made a sound with every step, giving everyone and everything an announcement of his presence. Video slowly looked over her shoulder to stare at him, and he gave her an assuring, sympathetic smile. She glared at him, and carried on. Her eyes still burned from the image of Radio, but the sound of his clanking paw pads didn't allow her to think.

"How do you ever catch anything!?" She finally snapped when she saw another small rodent flee from the two of them. "Do you just make a call through your little report log and some servant comes to bring you a meal? Or do your pompous riches allow you to have some technology to generate it from a screen and it appears in front of you? Did someone bring you that rabbit?"

"I hope you know how ridiculous you sound, Video. No one was going to come anywhere near that jungle after seeing that magic coming out of it. I ate yesterday, and we'll be up in the grassy ledges above before tomorrow. You really…"

"I really *what?*" Video's spine began to arch defensively.

"Need to wait for your thoughts to come to you before you ask your questions, dear." He smiled, and his tail brushed against her head as he walked past her and began to lead the way. Video bristled from head to tail tip, and stormed past him, her tail lashing as she climbed up the steep way to get to their destination faster.

Now she was sure she wasn't going to stop for a break. She climbed and prowled for the rest of the morning, ignoring Film's quiet comments of concern over her wellbeing. She could stop for water when she was there, they could get shade when they were there, her pelt was not going to overheat her, and he could just be quiet! She travelled for the past two days effortlessly as far as she was concerned, she was not about to stop it all now just because of some pampered monitor ringleader.

Video looked up at the cliff edge above and knew it would be a fast shortcut if she climbed up it now. She looked to Film, who shook his head. She narrowed her eyes. He could worry all he wanted, it wasn't going to get him anywhere. She squared her haunches and leapt up with force, slowly beginning to climb the rest of the way up once she got a grip on the ledge.

She startled when the ground shifted and started to sink. She gasped, quickly starting to climb up the rest of the way, but her exhaustion got the better of her, and her damaged claws did her no good for a grip, either.

Panic rushed to Video's head. She thought of her mindset moments before and how she thought of the travel being effortless, but the weight of her legs told her otherwise. She wasn't going to make it. Before she could reach the surface above, the ground crumbled underneath her. Her hind legs weren't strong enough to give her the kick she needed to get to where it was safe.

"Video!" Film shouted, but it was too late. Her claws couldn't get a hold of a steady surface in time, and she fell from the ledge. Video's head knocked against the stone below, and the world went black around her.

Within what felt like moments, Video jerked awake. She looked over to see Film going through reports again. She felt as though her skull was cracked open, but when she pressed around the area, it was just a gash, treated with who knows what by Film.

She sighed, fought against the pounding in her head, attempted to stand, only to collapse. She quickly looked to see if Film had turned his head to see her fall, but he hadn't moved. She took in a breath and tried again, a bit more steadily now, and got to her paws. She puffed out her chest once she got her bearings, and then walked past the smoky tabby. She lifted up her chin when he looked over at her with a censuring stare, but kept moving, unbalanced or not. Maybe she could get ahead while he was finishing work, being such a busy kitty.

Video thought of her own process and words and realized it was probably pretty evident she'd gotten her head knocked around a few times by now, but she still wasn't going to waste the opportunity to get some of her own space.

"Video, what's the rush?" Film quickly caught up to the poofy feline, and raised his gold tipped paw to halt her. "You have suffered from more than one head injury. I think you might want to consider a bit of rest."

"I already wasted my day of rest by sleeping the night before and getting knocked out now. I can't stop, Film."

"Video, I *carried* you up the incline to the cliff you so desired to climb. You're where you wanted to be, and now you can take a moment to heal for a bit. We lost no time. You're not heavy. If worst comes to worst I'll just carry you again, but I don't want to wait until you hit your head again for that, Video." Film shook his head. "Eventually you might not wake up."

She couldn't deny that was a possibility if she were to injure her head again. Video frowned, her words barely above a whisper, "But we're so close..." They could reach it if they just kept going.

"I know, Video, but no one's going to find you, and it'll be okay. I'll catch up with my work, and you can stop splitting that noggin of yours." Film smiled, pressing against her shoulder, slowly turning her towards the grassy clearing they were walking away from.

Video sighed, and nodded. She went over to the clearing and curled up, blinking slowly when Film settled next to her, and looked over his shoulder to read his reports. Even her father didn't have the advanced technology Film did. The device was quite out of the ordinary. She could read the text clearly, and illustrations popped up on the subject with the slightest gesture of Film's golden tipped paw. She looked up at him, and asked, "Do you have a report on how the avian capital guards are?"

"No, I wasn't assigned to track or assess your situation this time around because of the surveillance team. Their reports would be forwarded to the monitor who was. I'm not sure if they hired Signal again. I think he was done after the hearing..." Film swiped a few screens away, and then pulled up a document. "Yeah, both he and I were reassigned to watch over Authentication."

Video swallowed nervously in fear for the cat. "What's *his* status?"

Film clicked on his screen with one gold claw, popping up an image of a complexly colored, golden-eyed, dusty brown tabby tom. "He went off the radar when entering the Unending Labyrinth this morning and so far no more news. It's the waiting game from here and out of our control."

Video nodded, resting her head back down. She settled in beside the large dark feline, but then had another question. "With the surveillance room destroyed and the loss of your team and the recordings, how are you still in contact with the Council?"

"Cassette's still there. She's been keeping me updated during the hiring process for the new staff, and has been doing above and beyond for reconstructing the new station. She's my eyes and ears for the Capital, and I'm more than happy to have her after losing my formidable team to those two."

Video remembered how bold the feline was, even to confront and ask Radio about the missing records of her birth within the logs, and was glad Film had someone he could rely on. "I'm sorry for your loss, sir."

Film sighed, his eyes softening, but then rose. "Loss is something we all have to face, but I would give anything for it to be under different circumstances," he exhaled slowly, "And to be able to see their faces again." He shook his head, and stated more firmly, "I'm going to go hunt for us. Stay here."

Video looked up doubtfully at the tom and looked down at his gold paws, making him chuckle. She rolled her eyes, but she was glad she could give him something to smile about, and didn't dare protest when her head began to pound again. "Good luck, sir."

She was half tempted to stalk after him and see if those plates were removable, but her aching limbs and pounding head said otherwise. She stretched out, relieved she could sit out in the sun without worry, and then curled up. Even with how much she wished she could just fall asleep, her mind drifted elsewhere. It was a treat to lay in the sun, left as no more than having a rogue status like her brother.

The difference was she had Film with her. The cat had his own agenda and needed her along for the ride. The idea of being a thread in the webbed plot of such a power in Media shook her. Likely, as soon as the Jester was defeated, *if* Film wasn't on the Jester's side, she would probably be turned in and handled by the proper court. Video looked at the spot where Film had been before he left.

Unless that was him going to get reinforcements now.

She got up as quickly as she could and started back on the path to Audio's abode without him. Hopefully the plates were undetachable and he would be hunting for a while, or he had no signal connection from the mountains to his headquarters if he was calling for help. She would at least get away far enough to a place where she could decide what to do if he spotted her.

As long as her exhaustion didn't get the better of her, that is. The more she walked, the heavier her paws felt from her weight and the more her head pounded. She growled when she realized her eyelids felt like they were going to drop over her eyes from the pain and exhaustion after she had made her first leap to another ledge, but she had no intention of stopping. She wasn't going to rely on this over-ranked furball to get her from place to place if her life depended on it—which it *did,* but she wasn't going to feed his ego. When her eyelids were too heavy to keep open, she walked with her eyes closed, sighing as she did. It only made her paw steps feel like they weighed more with each step.

She could do this, and she could get enough information from Audio about hiding spots to get away from Film then, too. Audio could speak about nearly every resident living in the Rich Top Mountains with her time as an herbalist, treating injuries, sickness, and any other kinds of ailments over the seasons of her and the rest of the residents' lives.

Through them, she learned more about the mountains than any traveler could during a regular life, including the best spots to hide from predators, or in Video's case, the Capital.

She opened her eyes to see how far she travelled, and realized she was at one of the destination points she used to mark before she returned home. Alertness flooded back into her tired gaze, and she rushed the rest of the way forward. If she could gain enough speed so Film would lose her trail, he might panic enough to push things forward with his plans. She could be done with his games then. As a rogue, she didn't have to answer to him right now, no matter how much she wanted her verification back. She needed to concentrate on getting the truth out, not to follow Film on his path of doing so. After that, all she needed was to find something that could put down the monkey for good.

Her paws weakened and she stumbled, startling when she realized how close she was to the mountain's edge. She backed up and looked around cautiously, hoping there was no danger around while she passed the narrow area. The sky and higher cliffs were clear. She took in a breath and hesitantly continued, working her way up the mountain until she could find somewhere safe enough to take a breather and not be caught by Film. Within a few more steps, she saw a den opening and quickly moved towards it.

The space was vacant and was nearly impossible to see to the untrained eye. Video saw an alpine tree with a collapsed branch attached to a lower limb and grabbed it. She tore it off from the tree with a tug of her neck, and then began dusting away the particles that made her trail. Once she was done, she flung the branch down and watched it fall out of sight. After checking to see if any eyes were on her, she went into the den and settled down. All she needed was a moment to catch her breath, and then she could pick up travelling back to her mother's, no Film attached.

The moment went by with a blink, though. Video wasn't sure how long she had slept, but with no nightmares about Radio or Pictures, she woke up more refreshed than she had in days. Her paws felt a little better, and after getting her sides treated, they didn't ache or burn nearly as much, either. This trek was possible; she was going to make sure of it. She groomed herself quickly and set back out.

She really had to give some thought as to what she was going to say to Audio when she arrived. She didn't know how open the Council and King Capital were going to be with everyone about the mission and the Jester still being on the loose, so she would have to decide how she was going to handle that as Audio's questions came out, especially whether or not she told the truth about Radio being conscious during her final moments. Video swallowed, and kept moving. Maybe instead she could just tell Audio about how Studio said they were distant relatives, but then again, it sounded like the Jester butchered the majority of them off, anyway.

She'd probably settle on asking Audio about her latest remedies and inventions. Video gave herself a nod as she tried to hold back tears when it came to thinking about all that occurred. Remedies would probably be the best thing to talk about, anyway. Audio probably knew that as well. She leapt up to a higher ledge, and looked below. The higher she went, the more flowers and plants she saw with which she was familiar. She thought of all the times she would gather the remedies' ingredients with her brother Stereo and their mother. Everything was simpler back then. She spotted more plantain and treated her wounds before continuing.

When Video came across the stream she would fish as a kitten, she knew her home was just up the hill. Her tail began to wave in excitement. She looked out over the cliff side to see Calotype's Forest below. She let her shoulders relax. At any other time, it would have only taken a day to climb up from the enchanted growth, but she made it, and that's what was important. She turned back towards the stream and began to follow it uphill. It was late afternoon when she reached her childhood home.

The surrounding area of the structure was beautiful. Flowering herbs and flowers grew like a meadow behind the home. The open areas not taken by the flowers were instead covered by vines and moss. In the front yard, there were several small gardens and paths along with a beautiful small stream which cut across the yard and then traveled down to the Unending Labyrinth. All the stone structures that made rooms and shelter for the guests were built along a hollowed out tree also decorated with plant life. The tree reached high above it all, shading the plants which needed protection from both the sunlight and the harsh mountain winds. Balcony windows lined the trunk, and the vines weaved all the way to the top. This was her home. Video bounded up the stone path to the entrance, her tail waving like a kitten's would. She had to take in a breath before she could enter. She made it!

On alert now, she looked around some more, this time to spot any possible danger, but nothing was in sight or in the air. She was safe to enter. Her mother was in the foyer, as though she had been waiting for her, but once Video finished pushing open the door, she saw Film.

That gold-laced, puffed out furball beat her to it.

"Oh, blast the Stars and sky above our heads, get out of my house!" Video snarled, and launched herself toward the tom.

Film shoved Video back with a flick of his gold tipped paw. Video barely scratched his chin. Video stumbled back and growled, starting for the tall feline again. Audio rushed forward, practically half the height of her younger daughter but still able to hold her still when it came to defending a guest. "Video, this is Film from the Capital City. The one we've talked about with the shiny gold and high tech. He's here to help, sweetie." She started purring as if in attempt to soothe her kitten, but only received a glare instead.

"How did you get here so quickly?" Video looked past the ear tips of her mother to turn her glare to Film.

The large tomcat blinked, and answered, "I came back with our food and you weren't there. It wasn't hard to track you as far as the cliff side and use my log for the rest of the way. I saw you sleeping and figured I'd wait here for you. I explained the situation to Audio in the meantime."

"It would have been more appropriate for you to have been calling the Capital on me! What are your plans? Are you using my parents as leverage to make me cave? What do you want?"

"...*Video!*" Audio gasped, her eyes rounding in shock.

Film arched his brow. "Video, I could pop you on my back and carry you to the Capital City right now if I wanted. I could have done it days ago, but I didn't. You might want to think it's all about you, but once again, it's not." His last sentences were curt, silencing both Audio and Video, but then he continued more calmly, "I'm here to find the truth about the massacre of my surveillance team. If I can clear your name for Radio and Pictures' deaths as well, all the better. You either can take my help, and in return do your best to help me, or stay on your own while I finish my business." He leaned back, his eyes hooding. "It's your choice."

Video's eyes narrowed into slits, and she hissed with fury, "What help can I get from you? You didn't even know Radio used magic until I told you myself! I already told you who killed your team. How do you think I got these marks on my face? No regular scratch would be this deep! Every wound on my face is from a mage, Film!"

"Video, it has been rumored the noble bloodline had magic for ages. I couldn't be sure that was what you meant when you addressed it during your trial, or if you had truly witnessed the use of magic. My surveillance team didn't catch a moment of Radio using magic until you took her life, but it's not an impossibility the other monitors from the Western or Eastern District hadn't, or of it being recorded in Signal's personal archive. We're going to find out what we can to get this solved the right way."

"Oh, Video…" Audio's soft voice echoed through the narrow room, and Video's eyes watered at hearing the dismay and fear in her mother's voice.

She wasn't going to show Film any weakness, though. "The sooner, the better. We won't get anything done by lying about here. This can be our safe point where we can meet and discuss what we've learned."

"No need. While we're figuring out how to talk to Signal about his recordings, we might as well travel together, Miss Video." Film lifted up his chin and smiled down at Video, and then led her out of the home.

Video blinked, the rush of panic flooding to her head again at realizing she was still going to be stuck under Film's direction, and glanced at her mother before looking back at the tom to answer, "We'll be coming back each night to rest here now though, Film." At least that way she knew she was always within a day's journey from Audio.

Film hesitated, as though considering a negative response. He blinked, and continued forward. "Fair enough."

Video let out a sigh, and then kept up with the dark tomcat. Now that he knew her only safe-house, she had to rely on believing he was here to help. There would be no talking to Audio about other shelters now; Film had probably already bugged the home with gadgets.

The two walked out to a long-edged cliff, and looked down at the valley below. Video followed Film's gaze down to the Unending Labyrinth, and listened as Film stated, "Directly from your home, the Labyrinth is only a day of travel."

Video's eyes narrowed. "Are you saying you want to–"

"No, but the distance is an interesting thing to see in person from here."

Video realized the tom was referring to the days of Phantascope's reign against Media, and how Signal was in charge of the department sent to eliminate the mysterious dark mage. The proximity to Signal's office was why the Council commissioned him to direct the other monitors on finding the calico mage's hideout, the hike only being a day to get to from his home because of the direct cut down the mountain edge.

Film looked at her. "Have you ever gone down to the Labyrinth by yourself, Miss Video?"

"No, not by myself." Video kept her voice firm. "I travelled past it with my companions for the mission of the glass heart, but otherwise I only ventured down with my father once to learn how to manipulate the changing ground to my advantage. Audio brought the plant life from there to me for our lessons without ever having me accompany her."

She gave Film a few heartbeats to respond, and when he only nodded, she continued on the path downhill, relieved he ended the subject.

She was always jealous that her brother, Stereo, seemed to know more about the Labyrinth than she did, especially when the tomcat had never paid as much attention to their studies as she did. He would rather learn from experience, apparently.

She startled when Film was suddenly beside her. She glared up at him before managing to mask her expression again.

He saw the initial glare, and tilted his head.

"There's a lot to think about being back here, especially so quickly after the mission," Video said quietly. It was too early to share details about herself. She still didn't trust him. She thought of how Stereo had attacked her twice within the five days of her mission. She knew it was likely some connection he had with a monitor who could track the location of the three chosen with their chips, but it made her wonder when she would see the tom again, and if their next meeting would end with one of them being dead.

Both of them had thrown away their lives and didn't have anything to lose at this point. It seemed almost strange that it had been Film who had found her in the valley and not Stereo, but perhaps the tom was also the reason why she hadn't run into her brother since. Besides their father, Film was the only domestic cat who was able to tower above the two, likely making him as intimidating to Stereo as he was to Video. His gold claws didn't look any more inviting than his solid form for battle, either.

She almost didn't realize that Film was guiding her back to her home, but she nearly tripped when they were suddenly turning.

"Not used to being led, Video?" Film teased.

Video blinked in surprise at the thought, and her brow furrowed as she looked up at him. She might as well answer honestly, "Not at all."

Film chuckled, and carried on with his long striped tail swinging into the air.

"Why are we going back?" she asked.

"Because you still need to rest your head, dear, and you never appropriately greeted Audio, either."

Video couldn't argue the point, especially with the scene she made. She remained quiet the rest of the night, as Film had already explained everything she told him. She could just make small chat about the herbal remedies as she planned. Audio fed them both. Film didn't eat much since he had eaten Video's share from his hunt earlier, but that allowed Video to feast now. The evening went by quickly after she was treated for her injuries. Audio had inspected and cared for all and any wounds, from Video's paw pads to the top of her long ears, admiring Film's makeshift bandaging with the plantain, honey, and lamb's ear leaves for bandages.

Video tried not to sigh when Audio brought them dessert. She watched as her mother went to sit at the other side of the table, the smaller cat's tabby-striped tail waving. "So, you two have been travelling together for *how* many days...?" Her chirp was almost a trill of curiosity.

"I'm going to bed." Video's nose wrinkled, and she pushed away her plate. She was not about to be match-maked with the pompous furball. She could already tell from the volume of Audio's purr that she was hopeful to hear about a possible relationship.

"Good night, Video," Audio and Film called to her in unison, making Audio giggle. Video rolled her eyes and prowled into her bedroom.

Video felt like the rooms had been bigger growing up, but realized that feeling was just par for the course when she was half the size from what she was now. She looked around the rooms, seeing Stereo's room and then her father's office just a hallway down. She lifted up her paw in the slightest when seeing the door to Signal's office. Was he home?

She looked back toward the dining room, but Film and Audio were still talking. She sighed and went to her room without looking at the door again. He was probably still at the castle being questioned. She'd get a night of peace now that she was home. Hopefully, the monitors tracking Film would think he was here interrogating the two about their daughter and not *with* her the whole time. It was something she could hope for, anyway.

One thing for sure, Video was glad her mother had anticipated her growing size, as her plush oval bed she slept in as a kitten still fit her wonderfully. She curled up in a ball and let the quietest rumbles of her purr escape from her throat before she closed her eyes.

She opened them to find herself face to face with Pictures and slammed him into the floor.

"Why won't you just die!?" Video grabbed him with her claws, and began repeatedly smashing him against the burning floor. "Leave me alone!"

Pictures could barely get out the words from Video's force, but then finally gasped out, "...Not until you're dead!" The silver tabby's amber wings extended out and whipped her off of him.

Video quickly recovered, but startled when the tomcat got up. Half of his body rotted away into a dark black skeleton traced with a faint amber outline making a silhouette of the cat he used to be. Orange crystal hearts lined his chest, and his eyes were black with amber slits for pupils. *What was he?* Video screamed out as he screeched at her, pouncing at her with burning nails and driving her into the ground.

Video shook her head, the attack taking the air out of her for a second. She recovered and clawed against his arms, but to no avail. How could she kill a corpse? She yelled for help when she felt her throat begin to close, his claws shoved under her chin, and began struggling when she no longer could breathe from the pressure of his burning paw. She looked up at him, the dark skull's openings dripping burning orange magic onto her face. She kicked him off and jerked against the floor once he came at her again, this time now as a snowy white owl.

"No!" she yelled out, able to breathe again.

She rose up in her room, positive she only slept for a few seconds. Her paws were still shaking from the vivid images, the clear picture of the burning skeleton and the owl...an owl she had seen before in *pictures.*

No, no more Pictures. She shook her head, desperate to get the name and word out of her mind, and walked toward the door of her room. All the lamps were extinguished. Her eyes were hardly able to find enough light to be able to reflect her surroundings. She took in a breath and tried to focus anyway, so she might at least be able to see a shadow in case someone was coming.

Once she was positive she checked each side of the hall without being seen and that no one was waiting out in the hallway expecting her, she slunk out, heading back for the foyer to go outside. Anything indoors was uncomfortable right now, especially the dark wooden walls that reminded her of the warm colors of the drawing room: the last thing she wanted to think about right now.

The familiar hallways did bring her a small amount of ease as she made progress down the hallway. Being home was the best thing for her right now. It was almost enough to lull her to go back and sleep in her warm bed, the tiredness threatening to overcome her as she regained her composure and came out of the initial shock she had waking up, but she needed to get out. She was determined to get some fresh air.

She walked across the living room and startled when she heard the click noise of Film's golden pads against the wooden doorway. She didn't want to see any gold right now, or any amber rims that were wrapped around his pupils. No nicks, no arrogant smiles. She didn't want anything that reminded her of Pictures. When she quickened her pace, she heard him ask, "Video, is everything alright?"

The tom was in the room right in front of her path.

She should have just taken the back way out. There was no way she was going to explain her nightmare or the correlation to him and Pictures, either. Why couldn't he be in one of the rooms near the office? Audio probably did that for Signal's sake. "Go away," she growled, too tired for pleasantries.

She ignored his ears flattening and looked away instead. She didn't slow her pace once he turned to head back to his bed, but she was relieved. She could apologize in the morning, but for right now, she just needed to get out. The door was open and she slid out silently, letting herself be led by her blind steps without giving it a thought.

Her paws took her to the cliff. She perched down at the edge. She felt in even less control than she did when she had been leading the mission with Radio and Pictures. She was a rogue that answered to the highest ranked monitor to Media and had to travel with him in secret. Even going this far away from his immediate area could put her at risk of being caught, but she needed to be by herself for just a moment. Just a night of being alone could give her the time she needed to be able to face what was ahead.

Her paws smoothed the ground and she licked the rough surface of her torn pads until the curled dead skin was gone and the pads were smooth. She cleaned the dirt in her chipped and torn claws and worked until they were as neat as possible again, thankful that Audio had treated them as thoroughly as she had. Once she got the last fleck out, she blinked slowly, and then rested her chin on her paws.

Just one night without worry was all she asked. She looked up at the moon high in the sky and knew she had slept for a few hours already, but she couldn't start her day yet, not without rest that didn't involve having any nightmares. What was she going to do if they never went away? How long did things like this last? Her lids fell over her eyes when exhaustion took over, and she fell into a deep slumber of nothing but darkness, just the way she liked it.

Video didn't wake up until the sun's light was in her eyes. She blinked them open slowly, trying to keep her breathing steady. She was at the cliff, with no burning cat skeletons or weird owl things, and she was safe. She looked down, and saw the lithe brown form of her mother picking herbs just below the cliff. She gave her a chirp. When Audio looked up and chirped back, Video rose. She was about to offer to join, but when she saw movement out of the corner of her sight, she looked to see Film leave the house. She quickly looked down after seeing his gold paw, scanning the ground for any marks, but there were no indentations in the earth suggesting that he disturbed her, nor anything of his scent along the grass blades. Wanting to keep it that way, she quickly headed towards him.

Film blinked with surprise when she walked up to him, and his tail curved upwards in interest. Video narrowed her eyes, and lifted her chin.

"What do we do next?" she asked, forgetting all about the apology she had planned the night before.

Film's tail tip flicked, and then his whole tail sunk. He answered, "Cassette still seems to be working on getting the reports from the other monitors, and my assistant, Settings, is finding what she can from my office, so for now, it's still the waiting game while I wait for my own correspondence to go through. I thought I'd try talking to Signal today, but that's about it, so you can go out on your own."

Video stared at him, trying her best not to give any reaction to his suggestion of approaching Signal. All she could feel was relief it would be Film who did the correspondence and not her. She thought of how Signal did nothing to stop her from escaping in court, but also how readily he provided the evidence that had her sentenced to death by the judge as well. He had always trained her and the rest of her siblings to be loyal to Media's government above anything else, yet somehow both she and Stereo went down the path of rogues. She shrugged and gave a nod before she carried on. "Alright, thanks."

"Where are you headed?" Film called out once she didn't say anything more.

At first Video considered ignoring him, but decided to stop, and turned her head to answer, "Just down to the riverbank, sir."

Film nodded and made no movement to go after her, once again to her relief. She turned her head back to the path and started on her way down, her tail waving as she got to move down the familiar trail. She didn't have any direct memories or knowing as to why, but she always seemed to get bubbly whenever she went down by the water; as bubbly as Video could be, anyway. It was just too nice not to enjoy. She quickly and silently moved past where she had been sleeping and where her mother was picking plants, and quickened her pace down to the stream.

After knocking her paws against a few fish and playing, Video's ears pricked to the sound of a hovering bot. She immediately bristled and looked around, her heart racing in fear of a Capital drone, but it was different. Her eyes rounded at the sight of the familiar gold and nearly exclaimed out loud, "Studio!"

The golden drone had a glowing light to it similar to her Father's, but bright yellow. It printed out a small sheet, and Video quickly took it in her paws and spread it across a boulder to read, desperately trying not to damage it with her wet paws.

Dear Video,

I hope this letter finds you at a good moment. The situation we have ahead of us is dire, and we're all under limited resources while the Council is being cast aside by the Jester's machinations. Our government is against us and we have to do what we can before it's too late.

I was just given the opportunity to write this to you now, hopefully it'll be in time.

The Jester is beyond being the spider monkey mage we've seen this past week. It has been here for ages, and it will strike again. Its magic extends beyond the scope of the physical world, enough to go as far as to read any thought directed towards it. Be careful with what you have on your mind! It's reading this now, for all we know.

During my childhood, there was a mentor of mine that watched over me, advised me on what to avoid with magic and what happened if the magic was tampered with. He was knowledgeable of life beyond the degree of anyone else. This primate mage has the very same magic.

This is dangerous, Video, and it isn't what it appears to be, either. As soon as you're finished reading this, find safety. The monster has a true form, one you might be familiar with–

"What's that you got there?"

Video gasped, expecting the Jester, but was even more surprised to see the guards who had escorted her to the court. She pulled the letter back when the fox tried to reach for it, and growled when he came up toward her face.

"Don't waste time with questions, Wrench!" the hawk screeched at the fox from above.

Video lifted up her chin, her eyes lit with determination, beginning to ask, "Here to try and…?"

"Not *try,* Vid." Wrench wrapped his jaws around her neck at the same moment the bobcat grabbed her paws in his teeth, and the two pulled her down, knocking her chin against the boulder. She yowled and rolled out from the fox's grip, but the feline still had her. Video kicked off the bobcat to run for the trail, but the talons of the hawk clamped shut on her tail. He pulled her back onto her rump just long enough for the fox and bobcat to leap for her.

"No! You have team up to fight the Jest–!" She tried to explain.

She screamed when they got a hold on her sides, her shout cut off when the bobcat shoved her muzzle into the ground. "Say goodbye, rogue!"

Video was going to die if she didn't think of something. She was desperate. What was it she read about, not thinking about *the Jester?* Video tried to struggle to pull out of their grip. It was critical to get back to the letter concerning the *strange monkey,* and she had to find out everything she could about the *beast.*

Just as if on cue, Video quickly scrambled away when the guards were knocked off of her. She stumbled to find her balance and to turn around, her eyes rounded when she found herself face to face with the mage. She hadn't seen the Jester since they fought in the drawing room, and with her nightmares, the reminder wasn't needed. She took a step back. "Did...did you hear–"

"Would Studio ever lie to you? Little gossip." The monkey walked away from her toward the letter. Video stiffened and jumped to stop the primate, but was knocked down with an effortless whip of its hand, the aura from its cyan magic blasting through Video's fur as she was pushed away. She quickly looked up, ready to defend herself, but the Jester busied itself by attacking the recovering guards.

The bobcat nimbly tried to fight, dodging the blasts of magic and driving his fangs into the primate's arm while clawing at its shoulder. Video startled at the crunch of bone from the severe bite, but after a yowl, the monkey's tail wrapped around the cat's neck and began to strangle him. Both Video and the Wrench went to stop the mage, but smashed into a plasma barrier the Jester formed with its free hand. The Jester then gripped the hawk's talon when he dove down, immobilizing him just for the moment the monkey needed. The mage twisted the avian until his wings were muddied in the earth, and pulled him against the ground. Video and the fox both gasped when the mage wasn't satisfied, and the two yowled in unison as the primate flung the hawk into the stream.

"Sprocket, no!" Wrench yipped rapidly, "Sprocket, you have to fly!"

Video and the fox only spared a heartbeat to watch the avian sink under the current, and then clawed against the barrier desperately to save the bobcat as he only tightened his grip on the Jester. "No! You can't! Let him be, Jester!" Video screeched.

The Jester looked over at her, and gestured with its free hand at its mauled arm, the bobcat still attached, as though it was offended at her plea for mercy. The large feline slowly began to release the mage's arm once the Jester gave another shake, leaving the two to watch as the bobcat's grip only continued to weaken. Video shook her head to bring herself into focus and tried running around the barrier. She needed to find a way to stop the monster. What she didn't expect was a different type of barrier, though. Video screeched when the primate put her in a plasma dome to keep her still. She quickly began to look for a weak spot within the force field.

The bobcat released the mage's arm, all the air finally cut off from the pressure of the tail around his neck. Without hesitating, the primate flung the cat's limp form into the stream, causing more shouts from Video and the fox. "Socket, no!" the fox called out to the bobcat as the large feline bobbed up and down with the flow of the water as he was carried downstream.

Video spent a moment mulling the idea their names were so similar before realizing she had to stop the monkey from his course. *He'll die! He's unconscious! You can't do this!*

"The thoughts don't really work like that if you were trying to talk to me, Miss Video." The monkey chuckled.

Video went to press her paws against the dome, and flinched when her paws began to burn upon contact. She almost believed the mage, only for a heartbeat, and then she realized its play. *Yes, they do, or you wouldn't have answered me, you buffoon! Fool! Chimp! Come fight me! Leave them alone!* Video growled and hissed at the primate, running at it once it released her.

The Jester shook its head and sighed, smacking back Wrench with a swing of its tail before it leapt at Video. The two rolled in a frenzy of combat before the fox came to strike again, teeth bared and ready to strike. Video yelped when the Jester grabbed her arms and knocked her into the last guard, whipping him into the stream now, too.

"No! No, no!" Video yowled, kicking the Jester in the face. She hurried to the water and tried to reach for the fox, but he was already out of reach. She had to jump, she had to get him! She squared her haunches and leapt for the deep water, but the monkey yanked her down, swinging her against the rocky bottom of the riverbank and scraping her face and paws.

She was pulled out from the water coughing and spluttering, and then tied down by vines and earth.

"Consider them spared. I'm making efforts to better myself." The mage's eyebrows arched as it looked down at her, throwing its hand up as though their lives were a passing thought. She had no idea what was lie and what wasn't after the lies the creature had already told, but it quickly changed the subject. "She almost got me, just spilling her life story like it was nothing. I swear I wouldn't have been here on time if you hadn't pulled that nifty little trick there. I heard your thoughts earlier–I imagine when reading the letter, but who doesn't talk about me nowadays? I wasn't paying attention." The mage scooped up the letter and finished reading it with wide eyes, then flung it into the river.

"No!" Video called out one more time, and began pulling at the vines and rocks around her paws frantically.

"You always make everything a hassle–"

The Jester had been walking up to Video, but was struck across the face by her claws once she broke free. She reached for the beast's mangled arm and drove her fangs in, making the primate shout in anger and pain. She wasn't going to stop. She held on even when she began to be pulled off, rolling onto her back and kicking at the arm vigorously.

Just when she thought she had reached bone, the Jester's tail smashed against her throat and knocked her back, completely dazing her. Not stopping, the mage grabbed her neck with its tail and slammed her onto the ground, snarling, as its tail began to choke her. "Listen to me! Studio's not the only one with a message, you stupid girl! Radio's *alive!*"

Video had to refocus to hear what the mage said, and then screamed at the lies before it closed her windpipe. She began to kick the monkey again, but then her vision went white.

She blinked her eyes open, and realized she was standing on a tree limb, but nimbly, holding onto it with a tight grip. She startled when she saw the monkey hands and realized she was watching through the eyes of the Jester. Its vision was so *crisp*, like it could see for miles with its magic, but instead it was looking down at a delicate figure. Video was left to watch in shock when she recognized it was Radio. She saw her with a cyan hue as what she imagined was the Jester looking at the young noble, using some detection of magic.

She was *breathing*. Her scars were healing and being treated. Her collar was mangled and beside her, and she was safely secured. Video couldn't believe it. It was so real, Video could feel, see, taste and smell everything within the vision like she was there right now, more fully than any of her dreams, but it was impossible.

When she woke up, her throat still felt as though it was still closed, making her quickly open her eyes. The monkey loomed above her, pulled her up onto her paws, brushed off the grass on her head with a couple sweeps, and then released its tail around her neck. Video gasped desperately for air, trembling from being without it. She growled and shoved the mage's hand away, glaring at it as she did so. Her paws were shaking with fear and her chest felt like it was going to burst from her heart's pounding beat, but she wasn't going to back down. If only she could focus enough for another attack.

"While I've got your attention," the monkey laughed, bringing her chin up for eye contact and giving her a wink. "I think it's about time we really get to talk, *heart to heart,* that sort of thing."

Video's vision was so blurred compared to what she had just experienced, she had trouble seeing what was in front of her, but she refocused on the Jester's arm, and backed away when she saw it was all healed, the only proof of any fight being the torn fabric from its costume on the ground, and then even that washed away into shadows.

"Not so hard to believe now, is it?" the Jester asked as it cocked its head, and then loomed closer to Video. "Radio's alive, and it was as though she never died. Except for the wounds still healing, of course, but it proves to be a nice reminder for her." The monkey chuckled.

Video shook her head weakly and whispered, "No, with your trickery, anything can be said and appear to be real."

"Your father's monitors only show what's true, even if he doesn't always read it right. I promise you, one look at those and you'll see the little damsel in my Labyrinth. You've nothing to fret about. I want you to come to the forest once you see her alive in the monitors for yourself, and we'll work out getting her back to you then."

Before Video could even begin to ask why she'd want that, the Jester answered her, "It'd be an easy way to clear your name for killing the noble, right? Then you just have some assault and battery charges to worry about. Then there's the concept of a cat surviving after receiving those wounds. I doubt the whole magic thing won't be hard to explain to sell her down the river, either." The Jester chuckled again, glancing over to see if the guards were still in sight.

Video looked at the Jester with a dull horror in her eyes. Everything was just a game. Even Radio somehow being alive was just amusement to the mage, nothing out of the ordinary. Why did the Jester want her out, though? Her mouth went dry when she thought of the nightmare she just had a day ago, seeing the decaying monster as he struck her. Was Pictures alive, too? Video looked up to see that the monkey was walking away, and asked, "Is...is he?"

The Jester looked surprised at the question, or more that it came out of her mouth at all, and turned to her, pointing to its temple. *The mind.* "He is only here, sweetie; for now."

Video at first was upset over the endearment only her mother used for her, but the "for now" sent shivers down her spine. She stepped back, frozen to the ground as the Jester turned back down the hill, and slowly looked towards the stream where the Capital guards and her letter washed away. Everything was gone, the fabric pieces, the blood, the roots and earth, even the smell. Was it even real? She looked back to the incline leading to the Labyrinth, but the Jester wasn't there anymore, either.

It could have all been in her head. Video looked down at her shaking paws and started back to the path toward her home, trying to play with the idea that she imagined the whole event.

Every moment she drew closer to the door, the more she found herself further pondering and thinking about the Jester and facing it in the castle. She remembered being knocked down and close to death before the mage's artifact smashed directly in her skull.

With that thought, she was only left with the images of looking down at Radio's body and pleading eyes, wanting nothing more than for Video to stop but not having anything to convince Video she could. Video's thoughts went next to Pictures, the one who travelled with her as another verified follower, still readily betraying them both to assist, or possibly even lead, the Jester in the infiltration of the castle.

Video closed her eyes and thought of the darkness of her rest to keep herself from thinking about them, not wanting the nightmares again nor the monkey to hear her thoughts. Video blinked when she realized the Jester didn't even hesitate to confirm it, but she had been too unfocused to realize it at first. What else was it going to put her through now that it knew her location? What if it hurt her family?

Video looked up at the doorway, having pushed it open with her paw, and looked ahead to see Film waiting in the foyer. Her eyes watered, and her paws and shoulders visibly shivered.

"Video, what's wrong?"

It was all too much, Video came up to Film and cried against his shoulder, telling him about the guards finding her. "They ambushed me, the guards from my trial, they found me...but..." She was going to start to tell him about the Jester, but with the fear of the primate listening, and the fear of Film's response, assumptions, judgement, she just said, "Just when I thought everything was lost, they lost their footing at the stream, and it was what I needed to...to defend myself. They were taken downstream, but I don't know if they made it. I just wanted them to stop, Film, not harmed...not..." She cried, dropping her head and flattening her ears. She was hopeless. "I just want to go to my room for now...I'm sorry."

"I want the full story tomorrow, Video. This could have a drastic impact on our mission, but rest for now. We'll tackle it all tomorrow."

"Yes, sir." She replied weakly before moving past him toward her room.

"I...do have something worth mentioning before you leave."

Video blinked and looked back at Film.

Film sighed, making Video only worry more, but he explained, "Cassette has failed to message me back personally on the back up files, but hasn't failed to take action on spreading rumors about me with my 'do not disturb' status. I'm afraid if we don't work fast to clear your name, the Council may start revoking my rights as a monitor before we know it."

Video knew the tomcat had only put his availability to not be disturbed because of her. Her ears flattened as he continued, "She, out of everyone in Media, knows how seldom I use it. She has started accusing me of associating with the mages. I think some of the castle staff believe her."

Video blinked at the smoky tabby's gold laced fur, amber-rimmed eyes, and thought of his smug, cunning smile that was on par with the Jester's grin. "I mean, is she really wrong to assume?" She cocked her head.

Film looked as though he was going to answer curtly, but instead scowled at Video and turned away. The immediate reaction and then dismissal surprised Video, so she quickly assured him, "N-nonetheless, all of Social Media have the utmost respect for you, sir...I just don't feel you should be surprised by it. What have you done to counter her accusation?" The Jester would have already killed the headstrong calico tabby, which already separated it and its viciousness from Film.

"Nothing yet, I just received two messages last night and another one now." He murmured back.

Video couldn't help but be surprised the tom was willing to share his concerns with her. She imagined he had a better time controlling his tone and inflection to sound more genuine than she ever could if relaying the same situation, though. What he said was likely just an update. When Audio came in, Video was determined to close the conversation before her mother could interject anything. "That's unfortunate, but still good that there are eyes there looking out for you. I'm sure you can resolve it."

"I heard the whole thing," Audio said as she walked up to the two, ignoring Video's warning glance toward her. "If you need anything from here, in light of the fact they could restrict your resources, we all know our way around Signal's equipment and would be happy to help–"

"But otherwise I'm positive you can figure it out yourself, too." Video quickly interrupted. Signal wouldn't be pleased to know his equipment was going to another possible associate of sorcery. Whether or not it was true, which was something Video wasn't sure of herself, the elder feline didn't deserve the additional stress. Audio only smiled at her daughter before looking at Film and giving a small sigh.

Film nodded to Video, but then looked expectantly at the giant marbled tabby, as though waiting for her to speak up more.

Video wasn't willing to go back into the detail about what happened down at the riverbank, but wasn't sure if that's even why Film was staring at her. She just nodded back and quickly turned back around to go into her room. "Have a good night."

"You, too," Film answered softly.

Video sighed and padded down the rest of the hallway as Audio started speaking to the tomcat again. If the chipper feline was determined to give out her partner's resources, Video's judgmental stares weren't going to keep it from happening. She would have to tell Signal directly what Audio was considering, but she wasn't ready to face him about anything yet.

She would just go to bed.

Video waited until the house was quiet before she made her next move. She looked toward the doorway of her room and saw the flicker of cyan light just outside the doorway, around the corner of it. She quickly got up and looked down the hallway. Her head tilted when the cyan light disappeared. She looked toward her father's office where it reappeared, and followed it.

Once it disappeared again and lit up the room underneath the doorway, Video swallowed. Going into Signal's office was not a welcome task, but if Radio was alive, she had to know, and she had to rid the magic from the room before anyone else saw it. She hesitated again when her paw brushed against the door. Knowing the cameras could make things appear not as they seemed, Signal might still think Video and Studio were affiliated with the mage.

Maybe he'd just think it was a screen left on. Video shook her head and pushed open the door anyway. If the Jester's magic was already inside, then there was nothing she could do to keep the mage from entering. It already had the access.

One screen was still on in the room, and Video's eyes rounded when she saw the living form of Radio. She was alive, breathing, bitter, and moving. The Jester was shoving her toward the middle of the screen, seeming to be politely apologizing and shrugging at her questioning, but still making a solid case that she was well awake as she began to more animatedly protest against the posing it was putting her through. Video bristled when the mage looked up at the screen directly into her eyes, and she backed out of the room quickly.

It was so much to process at first, Video could barely keep herself steady, but it boiled down to one thing. She saw her! She saw Radio *alive*. It was through her father's monitors, and there was nothing abnormal about it. It was all the Jester said. The reactions were too spot on and accurate with Radio's natural demeanor to be the Jester's work. The mage itself pointed out Signal could read things inaccurately. She couldn't doubt it when the Jester could have killed her at the stream. It needed her to take Radio out from the jungle. Without another thought, Video grabbed a piece of parchment and scratched, "She's alive." No more words were needed. Video walked out of the house, comforted by knowing everyone was still asleep, and started down the trail.

She stopped. What if it was that angry calico mage shapeshifting *as* Radio? The vision could have been fake, too. Video saw the bitter, unnaturally green-eyed cat leave, though, and couldn't assume it was the case. Her father's monitors would have picked up the shapeshifting magic, right? She had to take the risk.

The path to the cliff edge seemed longer than it had earlier, and Video stopped when she reached it. She took in the sights, the settlements of Media's subjects littered all around the rich top mountains all the way to Faith's Village, and then to Calotype's Forest, where the Jester was awaiting her entrance into the Unending Labyrinth. If she traveled through the night, she might make it by dawn. She had nothing to hold her back and only danger ahead of her.

With a final glance toward her home, Video relaxed her shoulders and started her way down the path to the Labyrinth. A new mission was beginning and the Jester expecting her. It was time to save Radio.

- CHAPTER 4 -
LATITUDE

Video approached the brush past Calotype's Forest, her mouth becoming dry as she felt the heat of the jungle blow against her fur. Here she was, alone. There was so much Video might face within the depths of the jungle, but it was worth it to bring Radio back. She took in a deep breath and paced forward. The forest was always harmless enough, dangerous to enter, but the bountiful vegetation made it attractive to many different animals, both for the prey that looked for food to eat for the winter, and the predators looking for a bite of prey to eat.

The forest was nothing compared to the dangerous Unending Labyrinth, though. Video could feel its magic before it was even in clear sight. When she approached it, the feeling was almost overwhelming. Thankfully she was taught that no matter how tempting and uplifting the magic felt through her breath, the magic was to be resisted. Video shook the thought from her head before she clawed her way up one of the trees at the outskirts of the Labyrinth, careful to look inside before entering completely.

She perched up on one of the high branches to scan the area ahead. She couldn't see anything beyond a few trees, the vines and leaves of the canopy above. It all covered the forest in complete darkness. Without sight, she would have to trust the terrain and that she'd be able to grab onto something once it came to her. At this point, the only conclusion that she could come to was that the darkness was magic, remembering how clear it was for the Jester's vision. She swallowed and entered the Labyrinth, whipping her back legs down to propel herself into the air within the unwelcoming shadows of the Jester's territory, and felt the darkness close around her. She tried not to panic, feeling the heated magic against her limbs and fur. It felt as though she was being pulled forward and moved without knowing where she was going.

With a gust of air, the shadows moved away from her, and she landed on the soft ground of the jungle, easily an hour of travel within the Labyrinth from how deep it was, judging by the canopy. Video caught her breath before further observing the terrain. It wasn't completely dark like before; small pockets of sky beamed down into the clearing, allowing her to see some of the area now. She gasped, looking behind her to see if she could get any idea where she was with the light, but outside the clearing, it was nothing but the darkness again. She had no clue where she was this far into the enchanted jungle, but she felt from the barrier's location above she wasn't going to be making it out of the Labyrinth anytime soon.

She heard a clearing of a throat, and looked ahead to see the Jester sitting with a familiar silhouette. It wasn't one of Radio, though. Instead, it was her brother, Stereo.

Why was she surprised that her brother would go as far as working with a mage to end her? Video's eyes rounded in hurt and shock at seeing her twin. She knew he was capable of killing her, but she never imagined the lengths he would go to ensure it. The monkey turned its head to face her first, and she swallowed nervously. Its expression was blank and emotionless, not giving her anything to gauge a reaction. Something about the lack of emotion made her realize how easily it had moved her into its grasp with nowhere to escape, besides the cat who probably wanted her dead more than any official of Media. Stereo's head tilted closer toward her, but she still couldn't catch his gaze as the Jester began to approach her.

What was she supposed to say to it?

"Calling me *sir* will do, for starters," the primate whispered, suddenly a whisker's length away from her face.

She startled and backed up, her muzzle tickling from being so close to the mage. Had the Jester been listening to her thoughts this entire time? How much thought had she given it? She blinked when hearing the mage's words, then furrowed her brow when she realized it wanted her to refer to it as a person, and flattened her ears. "I don't think so."

The primate's smile fell, and it lifted up its chin with its eyes hooding. "Fair enough, I'll just keep Radio and throw Stereo at you instead since you're so suddenly–"

"Please, sir!" Video stated, her throat constricting as she realized she just went against everything she had ever been taught. Signal would be ashamed.

The monkey smiled again, and turned away from her. Video looked down, humiliated, and listened silently as the primate spoke. "That's better. Trust me; acknowledging individuals as people who are different from you isn't so bad. The concept of mages being beyond the regular living being is flattering, but we're more down-to-earth than you think."

Video glanced at Stereo, then back at the Jester. "You're not suggesting Stereo's also a–"

"No, no, dear girl, there's no worries with him. He's not *there* enough." The monkey giggled, pointing to its head, making Video wonder for an instant if magic was based off of intelligence, but the monkey grabbed Video and pulled her close, ignoring her startle and building panic as its eyes hooded. "But there are more of us than you think, and I think you may have seen a bit of what we're capable, too." The primate pointed up, and the canopy's gaps parted fully to show the barrier, which looked like a spider web that glimmered from a fresh rain storm.

Video shivered at the sight, and then looked into the Jester's eyes. She saw the look before, and screamed when she felt a weight swing down against her head, crumpling her to the ground, unconscious.

Radio stretched out her paws, her gaze dull with the exception of the cyan rim around her pupils. She stared at the small bowl of water in front of her, the thick overgrowth having caught some from the last downpour in Media. She considered drinking it, and then pushed it off her vine-woven hammock. She flexed her claws back and forth, in and out, up and down, but rolled over on her back when that grew boring as well. She stretched again, this time each and every one of her limbs and sighed. She closed her eyes and thought of Pictures, hoping to dream of him again tonight.

She wondered what he was doing now and if he was alright. She was so tired of the Jester's constant games and refusal to take anything seriously. She was kept here just like she was cooped up in her own home, doing nothing except waiting to be checked up on and given an update on things, although at least here, she had Stereo.

The tom was surprisingly sweet, taking into consideration how she met him in Clowder City. His behavior was easily explained. Who wouldn't want to knock their evil twin sister into a wall a couple times? Radio's tail lashed. She had to intake a breath to calm herself down once thoughts of Video flooded her mind. By the time she exhaled the third time, she was calm again. She decided she should think about the situation she was in now. Her paws brushed gently against her healing wound. She licked her paw to rub it against the bald spot on her cheek where she had been struck, trying to keep the moment of how she received it out of her head.

Everything was easier said than done. Radio's paw trembled as she pulled it away from her face. She blinked and had to hold back the tears that threatened to fall. The contact with the wound thrust the night back at her, the instant when the light was gone from her sight. All she could think about was that moment, no matter how many times she convinced herself there was more to her day than dwelling on the past. It was too recent. Radio had difficulty with keeping track of time in the jungle, but she knew all of it was still only days since it happened. The tears fell, blurring her vision and dampening her fur. Radio covered her face with her paws, wiping the tears from her eyes.

She felt breathless for a moment, and inhaling and exhaling deliberately and slowly to relax. The back of her throat burned, but her breathing practices settled her down again and she was able to focus back on her thoughts.

She missed Pictures. She wished the tom had been there to stop it all. No matter how angry he had been at her, he would have never let Video have done what she did, right? Love or not, no decent subject could allow another to do that. Radio still had to figure out if his love for her was ever really there, but it seemed to be. When she dreamed of him it was. She was so afraid to see him again and see it might not be the case.

Radio rolled onto her belly and looked out from the hammock down to the earth below. The darkness made her think of her dreams. The soft outline she would see of Pictures always right before she woke up reminded her she could overcome anything with the hope she would see him again. They could be together happily and accomplish everything he needed after she had held him back so much. She let her eyelids fall again and heard the gentle voice of the tom in her head. She could breathe in his scent, imagine him next to her, feel his presence beside her, but when she opened her eyes, the silver tabby wasn't there.

She sighed and dangled her paws off of the hammock, contemplating just tipping it over and letting the Jester decide her fate as she fell. All this time in the Labyrinth only showed Radio how emotional and brooding the monkey really was and how believable it was that he actually shattered an artifact just because he wasn't satisfied with the results. It seemed like he was more than capable of doing that to all of Social Media, too. This thought made Radio wonder if he had allowed her to die at Video's paws just because he wasn't impressed with how she handled his power. He was *immature,* that's what it was.

Then again, she wasn't much better. Radio had to ask herself about when she was going to do something right. It didn't matter what side she was on, she always brought the party down. Perhaps that was why it was best she stayed with the Jester and his big bulky, but handsome, lackey of a tom. She could hold them back from the evil they wanted to commit just merely by existing and being a weight they had to carry around; a burden upon their shoulders. At least she had use that way.

Radio stood up and looked down into the darkness. She wanted to see what was really there, and why she always felt Pictures guiding her. Cyan mist flooded from her eyes. Radio brought her head up to bring the mist to the sides of her face, thickening and flickering like fire as she thought of how to use the magic she had in order to find her answers.

She focused her eyes on the canopy above to sharpen her sight, and the shadows began to slowly dissipate from the clearing, allowing her to see every leaf, vine, branch and twig past the magic the Jester used to cover the Labyrinth. With the shadow enchantment, the regular vision could only see about two trees ahead, but with magic, Radio saw the entire jungle not sealed off by overgrown traps. The only downfall was that Radio only saw Pictures if she was directly in the shadows of her dreams or magic. Maybe if she could remake the shadows to appear beside her where she felt the tom, she could see him again.

These were good questions to ask the Jester. She couldn't wait, either. If she could solve this and keep him by her side in the waking world, then maybe it was one step to teleporting him to her somehow so they could get out of here together. That part she wouldn't tell the Jester.

Radio squared her haunches and leapt down from the hammock into a knot of vines below. She landed solidly, but when the vines began to strain under her weight, she leapt down onto a solid branch, and then began making her way through the Labyrinth to find the monkey.

Video woke up and groaned at the pain in the side of her head. For one day, she finally hadn't experienced pain at the wound where the Jester had struck her when in the drawing room of the castle. Now it was reopened and throbbing. Of course it had to hit her in the same exact spot. At least the second strike wasn't nearly as hard. She thought of Film's concerns and realized she was lucky she wasn't dead. She lightly touched the outside of the wound with the dark side of her paw, and felt the stickiness of her drying blood around it. *The blasted monkey.* She stood up, trying to get her bearings, and looked around to see her new surroundings.

Video only saw darkness. There were small glimmers of light showing through the outline of the canopy, but it wasn't enough to see what direction the sun was, and knew she probably couldn't until evening. Video sighed, and started forward, knowing she would probably have limited time before the forest started changing around her, trapping her in the Labyrinth forever.

She had to figure out a direction to go, and how to follow it while the jungle started changing. Usually the trees themselves didn't change, just the growth around them. The Jester would have to be determined to thwart her to go as far as moving the earth to such a degree, but with a forest already enchanted, it might be easier than she would otherwise assume.

That would be a problem she could face when it happened. Video left claw marks in her tracks as she walked, hoping it might do her some good if she came across them later, and carried on carefully. All she needed was to find a pattern in the movements and how to track where she'd been previously. She would be able to handle it as long as her headache didn't send her over the edge.

116

She startled when she heard the brush shake above her head and looked face to face with the clothed monkey. She watched as the primate gave a couple tilts of the head, shaking the bells on the jester hat the animal wore. *Animal.*

The Jester's eyes narrowed, and Video clenched her jaw, knowing it realized she had just stopped referring to *it* as anything at all. It didn't last long, but it had still been worth a shot.

That's what you get for being so invasive, beast.

"I came all this way to help you when, as you might have figured out, I have better, bigger things to take care of..." The Jester's hands extended forward and showed a small string of threads making a spider web in almost perfect replication to the dome now covering Media. "But no, even then, you have to be unappreciative and rude."

Video blinked at the replica with surprise, then looked back up at the mage. With a flick of the monkey's wrists it turned into a cage, trapping an image of a dusty tabby inside. Video recognized Authentication from Film's reports. She swallowed nervously when the cage shattered with a clasp of the mage's hands, and looked up at the monkey with round eyes, staring into the half-lidded, blue rimmed eyes staring back.

"Now, I don't have the time I need to be able to watch you roam around here endlessly, so I'm going to make this as easy for you as I can, all the while still entertaining and beneficial to me."

"How sweet." Video clamped her jaw shut after realizing she had sassed the mage that took away her king and led her to murder her two companions. Should she apologize? She realized the primate probably was reading her thoughts, anyway, and looked up for an answer.

The monkey just gave a small head shake, and continued, "I'm also thinking of giving you some hints to be able to find our darling undead friend, too. See, it relates to what you three were already looking for, a shape of sorts, like–"

Video didn't need anything more. It already made sense that the Jester put her in the center where it was best defended. "She's in the *heart* of the jungle, isn't she?"

The monkey's face fell, and Video took that as a "yes." She started back for the core of the forest, understanding that all this monkey seemed to be looking for was a good joke. While Video would never try to tell one, it seemed the Jester also had no problem making someone out to be a joke. She determined she would face that as it presented itself. It was *too bad* the Jester couldn't even have a clever sense of humor, if she could figure out the punchline before the delivery was even completed.

Video ignored the monkey's screeches of offense at her sarcastic thoughts of it as she walked into the jungle, looking around at the sights and trying to find which direction would lead her to the thicker growth of the terrain. The primate had indeed been reading her thoughts and was so insulted there was no pretending otherwise. She was going to keep it up if it didn't stop, too.

She walked past the vines that stretched toward her, trying not to be bothered by the jungle already moving around her person in attempts to fool her. It was disorienting, feeling the ground stir and twist under her. It was to the point there was no path she walked which hadn't been altered. She growled, and whipped around, glaring right into the monkey's eyes, the primate hanging upside down to be at her eye-level.

"Stop," she commanded.

"No," the Jester responded curtly. The expressionless face had turned bitter. It pulled back into the trees to sulk.

Video's eyes narrowed with her loathing of this childish primate. She moved forward, ignoring the trees and vines turning and moving in attempts to catch her. How was she going to do this? Didn't the mage just say there were better things to do? She jumped over a vine that came up from the ground, and ducked as a tree branch came uncomfortably close to her ears.

Finally, a root got her, tripping her by wrapping around her paw. She fell and slid against the ground. The mud stained and dampened the white fur on her chest all the way up to her chin, making her growl in anger before she untied herself from the root. She raked it with one swipe to turn it into a pile of threads and continued forward with her tail lashing.

The Jester seemed to figure out her irritation point as soon as she growled, and her retaliation towards the root only confirmed it. The ground under her became more and more unstable within heartbeats, softer and wetter until she was practically dragging herself through a marsh. She raised her paws up higher with each step as the watery ground continued to give away, but her pace slowed as the terrain became harder to move through as more and more of her body became soaked with filth.

Video remained persistent, storming through what seemed to be a giant mud puddle until it was nearly impossible for her to move. The mud had now soaked her white fur all the way up to her chin. She dug her claws out into the dirt in attempts not to shout out in her anger, and then whipped up her head to glare at the monkey. The mage had been following her through the trees the entire time.

"You're lucky you even have fur there," he murmured, stroking his naked chin.

Was she just going to travel endlessly suffering under the mage's torment? How long was she really going to be looking for Radio? She sighed, looking into the ever-moving Labyrinth around her. Why had she not expected this? Should she have expected the Jester was going to follow her every step of the way to find the former noble? Video shrank back and pulled away when a stick looked like it was about to impale her as it fell from one of the high branches. She brought her gaze up to look at the monkey with round, furious eyes after the debris hit the side of her face.

"If you ask nicely, I'll make the Labyrinth work in your favor."

Video narrowed her eyes.

"How long has it been since you've actually been sweet about something? Like, asked politely for anything? Have you ever even smiled since your kittenhood? Please don't say never, it'd break my heart. I'd be sad for weeks, you know."

Video's ears flattened to her skull, not remembering much about her kittenhood at all. She opened her mouth to yell at the monkey, but was silenced by two fingers being pressed against her muzzle, the primate having lowered the branches to be at her eye level.

"No, no," the Jester cooed, giving a small headshake. "You should just...not."

Video growled when the monkey pulled away. Once the earth began solidifying again, allowing her to climb out, she continued walking back the way she had started. It was bad enough she came here at all and now the mage wanted her groveling and begging for the knowledge to find her way through the strange enchanted forest. She couldn't stop to clean her fur either, knowing it would give the Jester some sick satisfaction that the filth bothered her.

It wasn't until her nostrils flared from exhaustion she realized the monkey wasn't there. She looked around, no shape or form in sight, and let out a breath before she again moved forward. She traveled through the entire day, but the canopy began to close up as night approached, trapping her in complete darkness.

She settled down against the largest tree she could find, cleaned the dirt and mud off her pelt, and closed her eyes. She had a long mission ahead of her, one of direct danger, but she was where she was supposed to be. Her father would be proud of her tackling the mission, not caving to the Jester's demands. She could sleep with ease.

Until she was in the drawing room.

Video gasped and panic flooded through her. This was the most vivid dream yet. Everything was in crisp color, and she saw every detail in Pictures' face as though he was really in front of her. The two locked into battle. Every hair on Video's pelt was standing on end from her fear. What was she going to do when he started to decay? She couldn't handle it this time, not with how real it was. She bolted away from Pictures, pressing her paws against the burning door and ignoring the scorching pain as she shoved with all her might.

Fire burst out from the exit. It thrust Video back at Pictures, who caught her in an embrace to hiss, "I'm going to kill you."

Video sliced his face, stripping the skin right off, and kicked him back. She had to keep herself from screaming when the skin started to decay, slowly easing into the dark skeleton she saw last time. Bright, orange, solid wings sprouted and expanded out from his shoulders. He snarled at Video in pure fury as his eyes lit with amber fires. He charged toward her again, flying at her as the skin came off his claws and turned into black bones.

Video ducked to dodge him and scrambled over toward the fireplace. She looked deep into it past the regular structure and into the furnace, seeing if there was anything that could keep him there. She barely escaped his next attack, letting him skid to a halt and slide right into the fireplace. She closed it behind him and held her paws over the burning metal, crying over the pain it caused her paws.

She yelled out when the walls burst open, and a bright, pure white owl flew out, only darkening to show his black spots when he wasn't charging for his next attack.

Video was left out of ideas, she gasped for breath and then a thought clicked.

What would the Jester think to do? What would the Jester think of this strange snowy owl with amber magic? Or her recurring nightmares? Did its magic extend beyond the waking world and into her dreams? Was that the cause of it?

Video screamed when the owl flew at her and went to slice for its face before its talons could strike her.

She yelled out once a hand caught her paw as she swung it out and held it tight. She blinked her eyes wide open, immediately adjusting them to the darkness. Video looked at the melancholy expression of the mage as it made no attempt to let her go. She pulled her paw away and took a step back, her tail quivering when thinking of that night, and how angrily the primate had attacked her after she killed the tom.

She was surprised to receive only a whisper from the monkey, though. "It *is* every night for you, too."

Too? Video lifted up her chin. "Who else…?"

"Everyone else present at his death, it seems." the Jester answered, and began walking back into the brush. "I actually didn't know for sure when I referred to him the time you asked, but everything's pointing to it.

Nightmares of that awful night would be natural, but this is something beyond that. That owl was *Wisdom,* Video. It's who I'm looking for…"

Video was surprised at the Jester's honesty. Her memory placed the image of the owl, now. She had seen a drawing of it in Signal's documents. It was the mage before Phantascope, the Shadow Advisor. Had it really been Wisdom? The mage's existence ended ages ago, before Video's grandparents, likely. What was the mage's connection to Pictures?

She started to follow after the Jester, desperate for an elaboration, but then put her paw down and sank back down onto the soft moss. It knew the owl just by her vague question. Now what worried her was that the primate mage was searching for the old mage. That and its words would mean the Jester, Radio, and Studio were all having dreams of Pictures, perchance the King as well, if he really was the crystal artifact Video and her two companions had been commissioned to find.

She curled up and wrapped her tail around her muzzle, trying not to be shaken by the Jester's grip on her paw, or the strange sympathy she was shown, either. Was it the same for everyone?

The next day, Video tackled the jungle with a new attitude. Evading the traps, dodging them when they were set off and learning the pattern of how they were set once she moved slowly enough. The pace wasn't hard with her pounding headache, but the pain made it harder to focus. She was surprised to see the Jester again, this time not in the same Jester outfit, but…a darker, armored version. Video gazed at the metal plates trailing along the mage's jester collar and hat with surprise. Horns with the same metal plates rose up from the top of the hat, which was strange. The monkey had jumped down without a word, so Video looked at the mage quizzically while trying to mask the initial startle and glare. Her eyes rounded when she picked up the scent of blood from the outfit, too.

"Go on, you can pretend I'm not even here."

Video's brow furrowed, and she kept moving slowly and hesitantly. This was the mage that attacked her in the drawing room? Was the mage showing truer colors after the night before? Video could tell somehow that this magic was more natural for the monkey, more personal magic. The formed outfit almost seemed like a direct part of the primate magician's form.

She passed a few trees and asked, "I'm just supposed to look for Radio?"

"Mmhmm!" The monkey brightened immediately. "Let me know if you need anything."

Video's pelt and eye both twitched in unison. She kept walking slowly and skeptically, trying to find what areas were warmer than the others and using that to draw closer to what she imagined was the magic in the jungle's core. She tried to focus as much of her thoughts on the ground and just simply the idea of its magic instead of anything else. She wondered if she could just think of monkeys and it wouldn't have an effect on certain mind reading spell abilities. She knew she'd never get an answer from a mage that did have that ability if it did, because it'd give itself away, right? Her gaze caught the flash of the Jester's outfit as the primate walked and she had to remind herself not to think about the mage directly.

"Why? What are you thinking about?" A curious, excited smile eased onto the monkey's face.

"Nothing." She quickly growled, the immediate response betraying the shakiness in her voice. She had to try harder.

The mage frowned, and lifted its chin up defensively as they walked together. When Video glanced at it over her shoulder, she saw its eyes were very directly focused on her. She bristled immediately, and snapped, "Why do you watch me like a hawk?"

"I mean, if you'd prefer me to look the part," the mage squawked and brushed her cheeks with the wingtips of what used to be its arm.

"How dare you!" Video hissed and went to swipe at the monster, but it jumped into the trees. She growled under her breath, and stormed into the forest, her tail lashing.

"I know, daring to use magic in the inspiring presence of Video of the Mountain Region," Video's shoulders tensed when the mage used Signal's wording for her title, getting the reminder that this was the owl that sentenced her to death in front of her father. Film had used it, too. She had almost forgotten that the Jester took the form of the judge, but didn't give any more reaction as the beast furthered, "Just awful, I'm surprised I got through the mission without being severely dealt with."

The mage's words hit her hard. She had tried so hard to end the monster back in the drawing room, back in Faith's Village, the moment Radio died, but she always failed. Her shoulders slumped slowly as she kept walking.

"Aww, poor Video. The attempt is what counts, right? I mean you'd think that would have proved your loyalty. Too bad no one who mattered caught it." The monkey giggled. "I'm used to it. It's just playing."

"But it's not." Video breathed out, stopping to look down at her paws. "Lives matter to us, because unlike you mages, once we die, we don't see the next day." *We never see our loved ones again once we, or they, are gone.* Video tried to keep her tears from falling out from her eyes and continue walking, but they fell when the Jester startled her by jumping in front of her.

"Better than to lose them over and over again." The monkey growled, its eyes glowing threateningly.

Video glared right back at it. "Go on and keep pitying yourself. You've become jaded. You've lost any appreciation of the life you once had. It's an expectation for you and you have no problem speeding up the process for your personal gain. Those rats were my *friends!*"

"Yes, yes. You tore them all apart. Quite literally, I might add. I saw all I needed to through Pictures' eyes, no need to rehash me on it," the monkey snorted.

"You were there!" Video yowled in pain, but then she blinked and looked at the mage with surprise. "Pictures' *eye!* That's how you knew where we were…" She always figured that the monkey just watched them through some weird magic screen or something, but figured it'd always be something from a distance, not within one of their own senses. Pictures' blue eye made more sense. Had the Jester always had that ability? Was it during the whole mission? She watched the monkey grow bored watching her thought process and glared at it more as it climbed back into its trees.

Video thought of Pictures' relationship with Radio and whipped her head up to look at the mage. "How *close* of an eye did you keep on us…? When they were alone, too!?" she screeched.

The mage gasped, taken aback and looking ultimately horrified as it turned its head to explain, "By the skies, Video! He knew when to keep his eyes closed! It's not like you can hear or feel anything through sight, Miss Video! I saw only what was needed for the mission!"

The monkey looked flustered and embarrassed. Video was left speechless for a moment, wondering if its face suggested otherwise, and then exclaimed, "Oh, by our Stars and King!" She hissed, blushing, too, before she dug her claws into the ground as she turned away from the blasted primate.

"I'm eager to change the topic of conversation, I'll take anything. Speaking of the King, it's my question time now."

Video rolled her eyes and kept walking. She thought at first the outfit made the mage more frightening, but it was still the same skewed monster. "I'm here to see Radio, not chit chat with a murderer." She didn't see Sensor die, but she knew the avian had faced the primate mage. The nobles were dead and every animal the Jester possessed as a puppet was just as bad as dead, if not worse off, after being a pawn for its games.

"Nonsense, I gave them something to do." The Jester interrupted her thoughts with its disagreement, but all it did was make Video's tail lash.

The monkey scoffed, and then continued, "When it all began, where were you? Ever since you started working alone I could never track you like I did when you and Stereo were together. You two left a trail where ever you went."

"Don't speak about us like you knew us, like you knew what we went through. It's none of your business."

"You'd be surprised, Miss Video," the Jester shook its head, furthering the question, "I must know, though! How *did* you get there so quickly? I figured we were going to have to wait nearly a complete day, but there you were, sitting in the windowsill."

Video scowled. "What are you talking about, you absolutely strange…" *Creepy, more like it,* "…creature?"

The monkey hesitated, squinting before bounding forward and shaking its head.

Video stopped in her tracks, and gave the monkey a suspicious, quizzical stare. The mage returned the look, slowly mimicking her expression before she moved past the mage and finally asked, "The day I met Radio and Pictures? You expected me to take that long when I knew the King was in danger? You *are* a fool then."

The mage chuckled deeply from behind her before answering, "Danger? I put the King under *cardiac arrest*." Video scowled at the poor joke. "For getting there so quickly, all so passionate, you sure slowed down once you started the mission."

Video whipped her head around to glare at the primate furiously, her eyes narrowed into slivers of amber. It had been dragging on the question just to say that. She knew it. "Because I had two worthless weights to drag around that ended up betraying me, anyway! Is that why you brought up Stereo!? To further rub in that everyone I work with betrays Media?"

The monkey's expression kept the mischievous smile it wore when speaking, but the longer she glared, the more the corners of its smile turned up into a grin, and the primate burst out laughing as she prowled away.

The mage had laughed, but Video knew it had something on its mind, because it never came back down from the trees. By the time the day was at its highest peak, Video didn't sense its presence at all and was left to handle the traps and dangers alone.

They weren't as dangerous as they had been in the beginning, though. Instead of dropping down branches to impale or having pitfalls that dropped one down to their death, they eased into set branches that snapped in Video's face if she hit the vine incorrectly. What she was most amazed by when exploring the Labyrinth, not that she ever would commend the spider monkey for its work, was that a lot of the vines were designed into patterns similar to webs. The further she walked, the more she realized the entire Labyrinth had long woven vines through the canopy that were tied together as an enormous plant-made spider web. It likely worked well in case the Jester needed to make a quick get away, but Video realized how similar it also looked to the new barrier.

She walked cautiously once she realized the area was consistently changing around her after her thoughts. It was a lot more open and had space to move around in. The ground was smooth, without *any* vines or roots visible. The further she walked, the fewer trees there were, until finally she heard voices in the distance.

Her blood ran cold when she swore the second voice was Radio. It was her *shouting.* Video hurried forward, desperate to see the commotion and to see if Radio was alright. She saw the two in the trees, high above in the tallest branches. She quickened her pace, hurrying to them as quickly as she could, as the Jester's tone sounded no less pleased than Radio's.

At the moment the Jester looked at Video, she could decipher their words. It was like there had been an artificial muffler over their voices before the mage allowed her to listen. Radio still didn't look around so as to become aware of Video's presence, however.

"I just want to see him again."

The monkey laughed, and shook its head. "You want to see him, I want his memories and his magic. With further thought, I'll explain. I just found out how to harvest the spell he cast on us, the one that makes us dream of him. I learned it trying to be rid of it from my own, so now I can for you." The mage's hand started reaching for Radio's face, making her bristle and step back.

"No! Don't take him away! It's the only way I get to see him before he comes and rescues me from the likes of you!"

Video's heart stopped. Radio didn't know Pictures was dead.

The small noble looked at the monkey in anguish when it chuckled, "Oh, aren't you up for a disappointment."

"He'll come. He has to." Radio hissed as her tail swiped around her belly.

The amusement faded to rage at the quickest heartbeat. The Jester snarled at Radio, making her shrink down to her paws. It progressed on her quickly, forcing her to back to the very edge of the branch where her collar hung. "Well, good luck with that! He's dead, Radio! Sliced across the throat and thrown into the furnace to burn like old memories! He suffered slowly, and lost everything at once, all at the same moment he gained it! You'll never see him ever again, because even when I bring him back, you'll be *dead!"*

Radio's face fell into tears immediately. "You're lying!"

"Nope! And the killer's right here for you to thank!"

You bag of dirt! Video bristled from ear to tail-tip as the monkey gestured its hand out toward her, the grin wide on its face.

Radio whipped her head around to look at Video. Her cyan eyes widened with horror, fear, then complete betrayal and fury.

Until the primate took another step. She looked back at the mage, flattening herself again when its hand lifted threateningly. "No! Don't! You couldn't bring me back just to kill me!"

"If only I could take the credit, but if you're so powerful, or really not allowed dead, you'll just come back again, and I'm going to figure it out then."

"What!?" Radio screamed out in fear when she lost her balance on the branch, scrambling on for life. Video's eyes rounded, and she bolted forward, seeing the monkey's hand raise.

"You shouldn't be alive, anyway!"

Both Radio and Video yelled out when the Jester grabbed Radio by the neck. It gripped tight to cut off her shout, and then flung her off the branch with her collar.

Radio spiraled in the air in desperation, scrambling around for any grip on the surrounding tree limbs she could grip into, but with a swipe of the monkey's hand, all of the branches parted from her path.

Video yowled, and hurried to catch the cat before she landed. She already could tell Radio didn't know how to catch her balance. If she landed before figuring it out, she'd be a goner. Video ran as fast as she could, tightening her muscles and bolting across the clearing, but she wasn't going to make it.

No! Video couldn't see Radio alive just to have her die again, not right now. This was her only chance!

All three startled when a burst of amber light erupted from the clearing out from Radio's chest. Video didn't cease her pace, but was shocked when the ball of light opened up into glowing plasma wings, and the faint outline of a cat wrapped around Radio and gripped her tight.

Video's spine felt a chill when she recognized Pictures with the same magic from her dreams. Video awaited a final kick from the winged and outlined feline mage to send Radio to her grave. Unlike what she expected, though, it wasn't shoving Radio to her death. Video's eyes widened when she realized he was balancing the small feline and breaking her fall.

It was just enough for Video to make it under her. She leapt up and grabbed the small feline, startling when the faint image of Pictures burst into pure light and was pulled into the cube above their heads. She glanced up at the Jester and saw the monkey's malicious glare before she landed, but there was no movement implying an incoming strike.

She landed roughly, holding the smaller cat tight by the scruff to keep her from touching the ground and quickly jumped back from the reach of the Jester, or a drop from it, before she tried anything else. Once her paws were steady, she quickly let Radio go.

Instead of any thanks, startle reflex or panic, however, Radio whipped around and snarled at Video.

"Hey! I just saved your life–"

Video was cut short when a blast of magic sent her across the clearing. She landed on her paws and growled at Radio, but the smaller cat didn't back down, instead facing her paws set and tail lashing.

Video would probably be able to admire her for it if she wasn't so upset, but instead she snorted as Radio yelled, "Pictures saved me and you just took the credit because you snatched me in the air!? You killed him! You killed *me!*" Her voice cracked on the last statement as her eyes welled with tears. She charged at Video with her eyes bursting with magic and took a flying leap for the enormous tabby cat.

Video ducked down and dodged swiftly, glaring at Radio coldly over her shoulder. "Magic users have no other purpose than to die in this time and age. You both had it coming."

Radio whipped around and looked at her in horror, but before she could attempt to attack again, a cyan blast shot down between them, shooting a crater into the clearing.

Video stared at the crater with wide eyes, and then quickly looked up to see the Jester stare down at them with utter irritation and annoyance. Without hesitating, it screeched out in anguish before the cube aimed and shot another blast out like a cannon. Video leapt out of the way and bolted for the woods after Radio, who had already taken off after the first attack with her collar in her jaws.

Before she could catch up, Radio wound up a spiral of magic with her tail and whipped it at Video. Video jumped over it and quickened her pace, unfazed by the attack. After everything that had come at her in the Labyrinth, a few poorly aimed attacks from the noble were nothing. Radio tried to shoot for her feet, for her head, even a low blow to the tail, but Video nimbly evaded all of them as they ran from the monkey following them in the trees. The two kept it up for a while, Video amazed at the fact that Radio wasn't running out of energy until she realized that the delicate feline was using magic to cycle out her energy the way the Jester did.

All seemed well, until the ground began dropping, and soon there was nothing but a giant pit in their path. The drop down was more than what Radio could manage and Video wasn't sure if she'd be able to hang onto her if she struggled. Trees were lined across the edges, the branches making a bridge across the chasm. Video whipped around to see the Jester was approaching slowly, and looked to Radio. "It'll take too long to get around, we need to take to the trees."

"Why would I listen to the likes of–" Radio cut off into a screech when a blast of cyan magic once again struck at them. She quickly bolted up the tree and started across the terrifying pit, with Video close behind.

The two leapt branch to branch in sync. Video kept closer to the trunk for her additional weight and in case Radio decided to try and take advantage of the less sturdy surface to strike her, but Video was more worried Radio would unbalance herself instead of actually striking Video successfully. Once she couldn't see the Jester behind them anymore, Video started to relax, but when she turned her head back to in front of her, she had to skid to a halt when she found herself face to face with her brother.

Stereo smashed his paw against her chest and knocked her right out of the tree. Video scrambled to grab the earth along the sides as she suddenly slid down, panic rising up in her chest after being thrown off so abruptly. Her claws caught contact with the roots embedded into the walls of the pit, and after a bit of skidding down, they held her weight. She let out a breath of relief, and then climbed the rest of the way up with new found adrenaline.

Stereo waited for her and went to attack her again, but Video leapt past him and quickly shouted to Radio when she saw her staring down from the trees, "Go, hurry!"

Radio bolted away. Video kicked back Stereo when he attacked her again, then took off after her. She looked around, desperate for any signs of how to find where they were that she might have missed before.

And she *did.* She looked at the vine webs and traps lined in the Labyrinth, and then paused the rest of her thoughts to study them. She realized that they all faced the same direction. Was it a coincidence? The more Video thought about it, the more she could ponder learning about something involving the directions of webs that the spiders made in her mother's, Audio's, garden. The memory struck her as she and Radio jumped through one. She remembered her mother telling her the myth that mentioned spiders always making their webs facing north. Video wondered if it applied to a spider monkey with a love for references. Knowing the Jester's current habits, it was likely not. She continued forward, watching Radio move nimbly past and through the shadow covered jungle like it was nothing.

She followed Radio's pace and pattern of each step, staying a fair distance away so she could monitor each movement before she copied it. She kept an eye on the vines as she did so, steering Radio in the direction she needed her to go by going on the opposite side of her and watching her automatically move in the other direction. They'd be out of here before they knew it. The noble's eyes were sharp, and so far had taken them around every trap and gadget that Video failed to see from the enchanted darkness of the forest.

The jungle seemed large and impossible to navigate alone, but with knowing the direction and knowing what the surroundings were, the two made incredible speed. Video hadn't travelled so smoothly with a companion since her brother Stereo took on missions alongside her.

Her chest tightened with thrill when seeing the outskirts of the jungle. She gave a leap with all her might through the brush. She and Radio leapt with full force into the rest of Calotype's Forest, and quickened their pace once the shadows were gone from Video's eyes.

She took the lead then, guiding Radio through the forest with ease. She realized the forest didn't look quite the same, but when she looked over her shoulder to see the Jester staring at them from the jungle's canopies, there was no snide expression or cockiness, just underlying irritation and bitterness in its gaze.

She swallowed nervously. The mage stopped following them as soon as they reached the forest, but the anger promised retribution. She quickly caught up to Radio after the small noble had rushed ahead after Video's hesitation and kept pace, then started looking around again. Stereo wasn't anywhere in sight, either, nor was the forest moving like the jungle had. They might actually have a chance to get out and still be intact.

Within a few more bursts of sprinting through the forest, Video saw the open area of the valley, and quickened her pace with newfound energy. Radio was holding up so well with her magic that the two shoved past the brush and into the clearing together.

She looked to Radio, but the small feline didn't focus on anything else but the view in front of her. Even with all the magic that boosted her energy, the noble was still unused to the speedy travel, and kept glancing down at her paws to make sure she wouldn't trip. Her jaw was clenched, making Video hope the cat wouldn't end up breaking her collar more from the strength of her grip. Video shook her head, then brought her line of sight back to the path ahead. They were almost there. Video kicked down her feet again, and flew through the air past the woodland brush.

Almost immediately upon hitting the safe ground of the territory outside of Calotype's Forest, exhaustion washed over Video. Her heart felt like it was going to burst from her chest and wouldn't stop pounding. Her vision was blurred, but she couldn't lose focus in case Radio decided to attack again. The two both turned to glare at each other immediately. Cyan magic sparked from Radio's eyes as if on cue from Video's thoughts, but Video could tell that the small unkempt noble was just exhausted as herself, barely holding her own collar between her teeth. The two wouldn't be finishing any battles today.

"Come with me," Video breathed out, her brow furrowing.

"...What?" Radio asked through her collar, her eyes rounding with surprise.

Video paused to intake another breath and then said, "I didn't fight my way through that jungle being harassed by a crazy magic spider monkey and battling with my own brother just to part ways with you and not get you somewhere safe." Video took the time to exhale, and then softened her gaze as her breathing regulated. "There's a home up the mountain, just a day's journey away from here, probably two, seeing as how we seemed to have emerged from the wrong side of the jungle..." Video looked around their surroundings, realizing she could see the Ruined City in the distance.

Radio followed her gaze, her eyes widening, but looked back to Video as the larger tabby did the same.

"I'm going to take you where you'll be safe and away from these two," Video whispered.

Video started to turn around, but barely caught herself when her paw fell from under her and made her stagger. She winced at the pain and realized she sprained it during their run out of the Labyrinth. The giant tabby lifted up her paw and looked down at it, feeling the inflammation and seeing the swelling. She couldn't believe the amount of injuries she managed to give herself just within a few days. She'd likely carry some of these wounds to her last breath. The feline looked back at Radio who had a flash of sympathy before her gaze hardened, and then continued to turn around.

She limped towards the hill to take her and Radio to Rich Top Mountain. She only looked behind her when she realized Radio still hadn't moved from where she stood.

"What's taking you?" Video asked abruptly.

The small cat looked up at her with shock in her eyes, hurt, and bitterness, with the collar at her paws. Video looked back at her, realizing why the noble was hesitant, but had nothing really that she could say to the cat. Radio had toyed with magic, whether or not she was still herself. Video had to put an end to a threat, no matter how much Radio thought she was doing it for good, and Video couldn't apologize for that. There were probably a few things she could say that could come across as such, but Video wasn't sure how to word it right either.

She swallowed and lifted up her chin. "I just don't want to leave you here, Radio, and I know everything will be fine if you just come with me now."

"Why did it have to be you? Why couldn't Pictures come and get me?" Radio choked out, tears falling down the sides of her cheeks.

Video frowned. All Video could think of was the tomcat who threw fire and plasma at her in the castle halls, the tom who killed the monitor who had helped them on their entire path, and had no hesitation to attack one of the most distinguished nobles in all of Media, the Studio Star, nor had any problem telling the Jester to kill Studio, and Video, for that matter, either. With that in mind, Video realized Radio didn't know that dark side of Pictures, nor knew her entire family was dead as well.

"Because we don't get to choose who is good and bad, Radio."

"I want to go home," Radio started to cry.

Video closed her eyes, holding in a breath, and then sighed, "Radio, there's no home for you to go back to, but I know you'll be safe in mine. I need you to follow me."

Radio stared at Video with concern, not yet realizing what Video meant about her home. Video wasn't about to explain it to her, either. She whipped up her tail to gesture the small cat forward. "Come on."

Video started for the incline. When a burst of cyan light came from inside the Unending Labyrinth, Radio didn't hesitate to pick up her collar again and run after Video.

The two traveled for as long as possible. Video noticed with Radio's magic, the smaller cat had a much easier time keeping up with her enormous companion. Video wished the sprain hadn't been holding her back; otherwise the two could be making even more progress. They stopped at a small dip in the mountain, where a cliff hung overhead, protecting them from the elements. Video instructed Radio to stay at their resting point and clean herself up while she found them both food. It was hard to ignore the bitterness of Radio's attitude, but it seemed the feline knew she wouldn't be able to survive alone when she listened to Video. After catching a rabbit, Video made her way back, ignoring the monitor device floating by when she did so. If the monitor wanted to make an issue by saying they saw Video with the Radio Star travelling up Rich Top Mountain, that was on them to try to explain it to the Council.

They ate in silence together, and Video enjoyed the peaceful moment of rest to eat her fill and be able to rest her leg. When Radio fell asleep, Video found plantain leaves to rub into her wounds and paw pads, preparing her for continuing the journey. The sprain to her paw wasn't as bad as she was afraid of, and she'd be able to walk regularly again in no time. She came over and curled up beside Radio for a while, keeping the mangled collar wrapped in the smaller cat's paws out of her sight. Video couldn't quite bring herself to look at it, and tried to avert her eyes to the scar on Radio's cheek, too.

It made her wonder of what Radio thought of the deep wounds Video still had on her face. The noble was probably proud of them, if anything.

She rested her eyes for as long as she could, and drifted off into a light sleep. After a long moment, she sensed Radio starting to awaken, and quickly rose up to move over to the trail before the feline noticed her closeness.

Radio's head lifted up from where she was sleeping, and Video gave a nod before she started back on the path, relieved when she heard the small snowshoe cat following behind. One thing she noticed was that Radio still hadn't groomed herself since leaving the jungle, but she wanted to refrain from scolding the small noble for as long as she could.

Once they were on the move, the guilt and worry cleared from Video's mind. Travelling at night was much easier than in the day, especially after leaving the Labyrinth. The summer night breeze felt like wonders on Video's fur compared to the humid grounds of the jungle of the spider monkey, and the night sky was much more welcoming to the eyes, with the exception of the glittering web that now enclosed Media. Video hoped that the Jester hadn't taken away the barrier that Video knew forever, but she had a feeling that any last devotion the Queen had to her people was gone after the events of the crystal heart. Video almost frowned, but kept a still expression when she felt Radio's gaze on her, seeming to be seeking some way to confront the marbled tabby about her actions.

Video was hoping to speak first about the situation, but still couldn't find the words to explain herself and what happened after the small feline had passed. Not only that, but she wasn't sure how much Radio already knew and also how much power the cat may actually have from the Jester, easily making her capable of reading Video's thoughts if that was the case. She would just have to take it as it came, and hope that Film and Audio would be able to comfort the former noble once the tale of her family came out. Even Studio was accused of magic foul play, and could suffer the same fate as her sister's family under the hand of the Jester playing as the judge.

The two travelled until dawn, and reached the home of Audio shortly after the sun finished rising above the summit of the mountains. Alertness flooded into Video's gaze as she saw the welcoming structure. Video led Radio to the home excitedly, her tail beginning to rise with anticipation of seeing her mother and the distinguished monitor, Film, to further prove her innocence. With Radio being proven alive with magic, the Council had to take into consideration the possibility of Pictures also having the magic influence, and that Video and Studio only being in the wrong place at the wrong time. All of it seemed possible once she walked through that door with Radio. What she hadn't expected, though, was her sight beginning to blur in front of her.

Video gasped with alarm and staggered. What had happened? She had gotten sleep! Her vision didn't clear, though. Video tried to slow her pace to refocus, but her sight only continued to darken, and her paws fell under her, making her fall against the earth only a few paces from the door. She tried to get up, but her paws were shaking and couldn't grip the earth steadily enough for Video to be able to pull herself up. Out of the corners of her sight, she saw Radio begin to turn away, backing out of Video's sight at that moment. Panic shot against Video's chest that her work would be for nothing, but the flash of black and gold comforted Video by knowing Film was taking care of that.

Her paws refused to move, but upon hearing Audio's voice calling to her and her mother's gentle white paws brushing through her mane, the giant feline let her head fall, letting the darkness surround her.

It was going to be okay.

- CHAPTER 5 -
ENDURANCE

Video woke up to her leg getting bandaged, and opened her eyes to see her mother Audio and a familiar dark pelt. It wasn't the charcoal stripes of Film, though. Video blinked in surprise when she found herself staring into the teal, hazel, and sea-colored eyes of her sister, Jukebox.

"Hey, Video," her older sister said, the reassuring smile and mild concern making Video immediately relax her shoulders after they had begun to bristle with surprise.

"J-Jukebox." Video dipped her head. She looked around. "Where's Film?"

"Jukebox came with Console once they heard the news of the court's verdict of your case, Video. After you arrived and we all knew you were safe, Film left with Console to try and tackle getting the backup surveillance and Cassette's accusations within the Capital City, while Jukebox decided to stay here and help you and Miss Radio settle down while we figure out what happened." Audio answered it all without hesitation as she finished bandaging Video's front leg, as though having rehearsed it all before Video woke up. "You haven't been asleep for too long, so don't think you missed anything."

Video nodded, but she begged to differ after hearing Console had been here too. She hadn't seen her other oldest brother since Stereo and she had their verification ceremony. She looked to them both now. "Thank you. Both of you." She then swallowed. "How's Radio doing?"

"She's pretty good, considering." Jukebox frowned, and held down Video's head as Audio began checking the wounds on the lighter tabby's face and neck. "She's asleep now, but she's been listening to us pretty well."

Video was surprised, but before she could answer her darker-furred sister, Audio added, "Film directed her to stay here and to listen to what we say, so I think that's why she hasn't been doing too much. The poor dear." Audio began cleaning Video's wounds, and grabbed her bandages.

Video wanted to refuse the bandages, but thought she might as well keep quiet in case she could learn more of what the situation was. "So everything's going well?" she asked. She quickly lifted up her head to let Audio begin wrapping her injuries, fighting against a brief wave of dizziness.

Both ladies hesitated to answer, making Video frown as Audio silently started wrapping her head, but then Jukebox chuckled, "Yeah, pretty much."

"Besides Signal coming out of his office when he decided to speak to Radio..." Audio muttered.

"Is she okay!?" Video burst upwards, nearly knocking the bandage wrap out of Audio's paws as she looked over in horror at the two, as no one detested magic use more than Signal. "What happened?"

Blood rushed to her head, causing her immediately to settle back down, but Jukebox answered before any more panic could build up in Video's mind. "He just refused to acknowledge her as a noble without her collar. It wasn't much of a deal, but since Radio came with the mangled thing in her jaws, she didn't..." Jukebox's words eased into a laugh.

"She threw the collar at your father, Video." Audio murmured quietly, not half as amused as her older daughter.

Video winced, unsure if it was from the pain as Audio began reapplying the bandages to her head, or from the idea the Radio Star had actually flung a metal object at the giant tom. "And everyone's okay?"

"Radio's been sleeping since, so that's pretty good." Jukebox offered, and then continued, "The collar kind of...broke apart more after she threw it, though, so she was a little upset when Signal pushed it back at her in mangled pieces and left."

Video nodded. She thought of asking more questions, but stayed quiet and kept her head still when Audio sighed and tightened the bandages. "Jukebox, would you mind giving me a moment with Video? I want to catch her up a bit."

"Sure, I'll start getting everything ready for the meal later." Jukebox nodded to them both, smiled at Video, and then headed off.

Audio purred as she left, but it lowered to a quiet rumble once her older daughter was out of earshot. "Video, Radio has been doing well as of now, but we received the report that her family and head servant were victims of the attack...and she's not aware of this yet."

Video swallowed, and looked at her mother nervously.

"She's still mourning the loss...of...well...Pictures, dear," Audio murmured quietly, her white paws kneading against the bandages apprehensively as she continued, "I wanted to ask if the Studio Star, may the King honor her heart, caught you up on our history together."

"S-Studio said we were related." Video blinked, hoping that was all Audio possibly had to share.

Audio nodded, and sighed. "Okay, good. Radio was aware but I wanted to be sure. Radio doesn't know we're now the only family she has anymore besides Studio." Audio swallowed, and the kneading sped up as she continued, "Video...I need us to be there for her. I know it's going to be hard, likely for you most of all, after what happened, but you're going to need to be very patient with her...especially when she hears the news. I don't know when, or how, but we need to be ready."

The lithe, tan feline finished bandaging her daughter and sat back down. "I just don't know what else to tell you, Video, but I'm glad you know, too. Family is important."

Once Audio's paws were off of her, Video immediately hopped down from the bench, and stretched out her functional limbs. "I know, and I understand."

"Good." Video saw her mother visibly relax at her response, and then her mother rallied and offered cheerfully, "Why not get some more rest, Video? We'll care for Radio if she wakes, and that way everything I treated you with can set in and start working. You'll have a chance to heal before you deal with the rest." Audio began chirping through her purr, which Video suspected was a way to further encourage her compliance with her mother's request.

Video didn't really know where she could go from here, anyway, besides getting Radio back to the Capital. "So be it, but I'll leave at dawn tomorrow. We can't afford to waste any more time after how quickly the Jester showed its plans are moving forward."

"Good enough, dear. Get some sleep, Video."

Video nodded, and left the room.

She prowled down the halls as silently as she could, moving in a much more relaxed way, calm now that she didn't have to worry about Film lurking about and possibly watching her. The tomcat seemed to have good intentions, but that knowledge still brought Video no comfort when she felt she had to travel with him under obligation and command. He was still the highest ranked monitor in Central Media below the Council. Tomorrow marked the day of her starting to clear her name, having a magic filled undead noble to prove there was more going on that met the common eye. She just had to figure out what to do from there, and what other evidence she might be able to find against Pictures while Film and Console located the other monitors with Cassette.

Video entered her room and closed her eyes nearly upon the moment of curling up in her bed, ready to drift off to sleep for only a moment to figure out what she was going to do next. She, for now at least, had to be grateful that Radio was really alive...or really brought back by means of the power of something the rest of Social Media was told to hate.

Video blinked her eyes open to stare at the glowing ones of Pictures. He snarled at Video and she quickly jumped back. However, there was no fear in Video's eyes, only exhaustion and anger. She was tired of the control Pictures had over her sleep and healing, fuming that she could feel her head pounding even in her sleep. The tom cat's eyes burned with fire and his wings rose above his head as he readied for a strike. She watched him ignite into a blazing fire form and felt the heat blast against her face, but didn't flinch. Video was so infuriated at not being able to obtain a simple night of rest, she hissed in her dream at Pictures, but then leaned back when her eyes constricted slit pupils as his light shone against her. No matter how threatening he looked tonight, she was determined to feel and express no fear. She knew now Radio had dreamt of the feline mage as well every night, but the young noble didn't have to relive the drawing room battle like she did. It was from Video's own memories the nightmares came, according to what the Jester had been saying before it tossed Radio out of the canopy. Radio probably got to run around in the Sanctified Meadows with the tomcat, never suffering the consequence of her agreement with the Jester.

Video remembered she couldn't be thinking of the mage even in her dreams without it knowing she was, so she stomped her paw and vanquished the thoughts as the silver tom leapt at her. Video sliced him across the face and smacked him back. He looked at her with anger and leapt for her again, but she was ready. She grabbed him by the neck after weaving around his claws, and then pulled to the side. He stumbled down, so she grabbed him by the throat with her claws and started tearing into him. She had to deal with this night after night, but she never got tired of this part. It was the one thing she was happy to do over again. After he failed to gasp for air from the damage she did, Video grabbed him again with her jaws. She whipped him around and threw him into the fire, as usual, but this time she shouted at him that he was not real. Immediately after Pictures had been whipped into the flames, he was truly gone as far as she was concerned, and she was in no mood for facing him again. Video didn't want to deal with Pictures returning with his plasma wings or the decaying, black, skeletal form. As soon as she realized that, growling as the fires began to flare out from the furnace, she woke up.

Video figured she had vented out some frustration in her dream. She felt refreshed as she rose up to her paws and looked around in her old room, gently shaking off the bandages. She let out a yawn, lashing her tail when she realized she was still exhausted from the energy exerted during her sleep due to the fighting. She looked at her claws, but there was no blood or fur caught between them, and they didn't feel as sore as they did in the dream. Video stretched out, picked up the bandages and tossed them into her wastebasket, and then joined her family in the common areas of her childhood home. She brightened as she realized she could partake in the breakfast with Audio and Jukebox and came to the well-laid out spread with a lift of her tail. Audio and Jukebox both murmured their greetings and comments of her apparently improved health, and Video thanked them again for their help and treatment for the recovery. After her dealings with Stereo, and the suspicion which crossed her mind with Console, it was a comfort to be with family members who showed her real concern and gave real comfort.

In her relaxed state, she felt she could ask Jukebox a question. "How can you possibly make time for the situation up here in the mountain region with your current schedule?"

Jukebox huffed in indignation, as though offended at Video's question might imply she had prioritized her schedule wrong. Audio quickly placed her paw gently on Jukebox's, and Video's elder sister smoothed her fur for a moment and answered instead, explaining, "I came from Clowder City after receiving permission from Speaker, Screen's assistant. Screen is kept very busy right now working as the temporary mayor of Clowder City, as it is without the Studio Star's guidance." Jukebox's expression changed a bit. Video thought she might have seen the beginnings of a timid smile, but then her sister's eyes turned warm, "The tom has been left with the kit for a change, which is good since he's growing up too quickly!" Then she truly did grin. She looked at Video as she tilted her head just a bit, and went on, "I wanted to make sure my baby siblings were okay, though. I couldn't stand to wait for reports and hear it all from someone else, so here I am!"

Video thought of what she'd seen of Stereo, and felt awkward on having to elaborate any of it when both Jukebox and Audio looked at her so expectantly. After a moment of awkward hesitation while Video tried to figure out what to tell the two, Audio brightened and spoke instead, "All my children, and now grandchild–" she beamed at Jukebox and looked back at Video, who watched Jukebox roll her eyes as soon as Audio turned away, but also brightening just as effervescently as Audio as their mother gushed, "–are doing so well! Console is thriving throughout Media, and yet is off traveling with the *glamorous* Film on a very important assignment, Jukebox has to get permission to leave her assignments from the Clowder City's mayor's assistant himself and her family is positively thriving there! 8-track is off playing in the Monitor's District..." Audio monopolized the rest of the breakfast conversation, finishing with, "And my little...well, my very big, Stereo and Video, overcoming the severest of obstacles I don't want to imagine either of them having to face..."

"Being hunted as rogue couriers," Video interrupted coldly.

Audio flinched at the curt words, slunk down, frowned, and then sighed. Her face then turned optimistic and she finished with, "Well, time will tell the truth about what both of you have endured. Goodness and truth will heal both your wounds even more than my remedies, and you will be vindicated. I have to believe that." She lowered her head for a moment, but then looked up and smiled again, and only her eyes reflected a melancholy briefly before her eyes smiled again, too.

Video did not have the energy to placate or encourage her mother in her optimistic beliefs, as that was not anything at all like Video's experiences as of late. She excused herself and took her plate to the sink. Before she could leave the dining area though, Signal entered.

Video was seeing Signal for the first time since their time in the courtroom, and was unsure of what to expect. She did not envision this. Her father and accuser seemed pleasant toward her, despite her nervousness, something he usually picked up on and chastised his offspring and his partner for revealing to others.

Video's head had been in pain all morning, but it had been bearable. Now it was pounding. She was sure it was just as much her confusion toward her father and his current treatment of her, or because of wondering when it was going to change, which was only increased by her mother's optimistic and clearly delusional words. At least Audio could relieve some of the tension by leaving the kitchen to go see how Radio was doing, claiming it was to make sure she was eating enough. "I'll be back!"

Signal not only took a plate for himself, but gave Video another plate. Video sighed, serving herself up more food. Video was happy to realize her father was not going to make conversation, but also wondered why he wanted her to stay if he hadn't planned on it. She decided to talk with Jukebox for the rest of the meal about her travel and the mission to clear her name. Signal listened silently to the point that Video wasn't sure if he was listening, but the sisters knew better.

Once everyone was finished with the rest of the meal, Video and Jukebox worked together afterward and made short work of cleaning up the kitchen. Video waited for her sister to get involved with some reports, and then made her way out of the room. Even now Jukebox was still working remotely after getting permission to be off work. Video decided it was time to face her mother again and found Audio leaving Radio's room. Audio didn't bring up any of the breakfast conversation, but invited Video out with her to harvest some herbs. "I just need to collect the usual...the recent events really left me with a small supply, I'm afraid, and I'm worried we might need more soon. Would you help me, dear?"

"Sure!" Video was happy to oblige. The skills her mother taught her as a child had been what saved her, and others, out in the field. She always enjoyed the opportunity to learn more. The herbal remedies were what excited Video the most about coming back, and Audio probably wasn't wrong in her assumption, either.

She followed her mother out of the house and down the incline to the plants. Video looked around and started pulling up dandelion and then burdock roots, hoping she wouldn't get too entangled within the hooked seeds the stems grew. The dandelion was always easy enough, but the burdock always gave her trouble because of her long fur. She thought she had done well enough, but looked at her side and saw her flank was lined with the seeds. Video let out a sigh of relief when her mother came over to help pick out the burrs from the enormous plant, and settled down with her pile of roots.

Video closed her eyes and sighed, then leaned down and tried picking a few burrs off herself, too. She jumped when the pile shifted, one of the roots falling down and brushing against Video's flank, but then realized it was just because her tail had brushed against it. She felt her heart pounding, and apparently so did Audio, because she looked up at her daughter with concern that moment.

"I-I'm fine," Video quickly stammered.

Audio frowned, but nodded and resumed picking off the burrs.

Video sighed, and then took another burr off her paw. She was much too jumpy, but the idea made her think about Audio going to the Labyrinth when she, Stereo and the older litter were kits. Video figured maybe she could ask Audio about her experience within the jungle and if it moved around for her mother, too. "Audio, may I ask if...the plant..." Video took a breath and started again, "If the plant life ever seemed to change around for you within the Unending Labyrinth? Or even Calotype's Forest? It was non-stop for Radio and me."

Audio swallowed, but answered, "Well, not so much in the forest, dear, but the jungle, yes. The traps and shifting stopped when Phantascope was there, generally, but otherwise it was always throwing me off course. Most of my visits there to harvest were when he was with me," her neck fur raised a little, but settled back down before she continued, "Of course, only if we were getting along while we were there since he could be so moody and brooding at times. He hated me using his title; I'd always have to come back later so he could get a chance to calm down when I'd slip up. I think I only did that twice, though." Video, surprised at the information, was curious as to how Audio somehow had befriended a mage, but her mother switched the subject to plants quickly.

"Oh, Video. I can't leave you alone with these burdocks. What was I thinking? I'll have you pick plantain again, as we can never seem to have enough of that."

Video started to open her mouth to ask her to continue about Phantascope, but Audio glanced to her left and exclaimed to her younger daughter, "Look at the container of valerian! Shoots have already spread below the container and we *cannot* have that spread further. Well, sweetie, happy days for me while I dig up the root systems. I'll put them into jars quickly, as I save them for the other animals. Can you believe it calms them? We can all have tea from the young leaves for lunch; those won't affect us, at least."

Video turned her back on her mother so she could roll her eyes without detection like her sister had before, but flicked her ears when her mother continued, "And do avoid the lovage and borage as you find it. Do you remember how to identify them? Of course, a bit of lovage might do your father some good so he has to leave his office to relieve himself, I suppose..." Video fought not to call out with a yowled, "Mother!" in protest, but Audio saw her face and followed up with, "Don't look at me like that, dear one, I have only his good health in mind. Beware the borage, too, sweetie." Audio blinked when Video glared and quickly assured her younger daughter, "Well, I'm sure you're too old to want to eat the pretty little blue star flowers as you used to want to do when you were little..."

Video scowled even more. She did nothing of the sort. Audio's musical voice, which seemed to singsong whenever she spoke of her kits, would trail off as she concentrated on harvesting the invasive valerians that she claimed had freed themselves of their container living. "I'll just store these in the greenhouse, sweetie. Your father refuses to have the roots anywhere in the house itself..." This time her voice trailed off into the greenhouse, Audio almost bouncing as she stored her morning harvest.

She completely avoided the subject after that, which only frustrated Video further. Video was enjoying the quiet when Audio came back, minus the jarred and bottled roots and leaves for tea, looking at Video with wide eyes, "Ooh, you've likely harvested the hillside while I...mmm, we'll make a green sauce of the plantain to top the meat brought home today. Do leave the muskrat family alone downstream, though, please, when you hunt. I just cured their son of a nasty cough and promised to bring them some seeds I have stored. That would be such a waste if they became a meal for us so soon after I helped their family become healthy again."

Video couldn't believe how she dismissed the topic. "I'd really like to talk more about–"

"They were so grateful," Audio interrupted quietly.

"Ugh, never mind." Video groaned and went inside, weaving through the house to drop the pile of broad plantain leaves onto the kitchen counter. Hunting sounded like just the thing to do, so Video quickly ran out from the kitchen before Audio could follow her and found Jukebox. Her sister was just rummaging through her old things. Video asked her if she wanted to hunt together for lunch, adding the part about avoiding the muskrat family, and Jukebox readily agreed.

The eagerness excited Video. The two sisters hunted well together, with Video relieved this was an activity which required silence and there would have to be no talking. It sounded like something she would enjoy doing with her mother, but Audio rarely hunted—if ever. When Video was a young kit, there had been speculation amongst the older siblings that if their mother had her way she would feed them beans and peas and completely cut meat out of their diet. To this day Video wanted to believe the very idea was impossible, but they knew better.

Video pounced upon the young turkey who thought it had successfully hid on her. She fought efficiently, breaking the bird's neck so minimal muscle meat was damaged. What a feast to bring home! Even with her frustration earlier, she couldn't help but beam with pride now. Video headed off the field of the little plateaued area about half way down to the next summit, and back up the hillside to see if she could find her sibling and hunting partner.

Jukebox proudly bounded toward her sister with a squirrel and a chipmunk held by their tails in her mouth. Her step hesitated when she saw the drake, but Video was happy to see Jukebox's tail didn't droop. They could both be proud of their hunting prowess. The sisters grinned at each other, still holding their kills in their mouths as they headed up the incline together.

Audio came out to greet them, her eyes growing big at the kills. "Just drop them there so you can both wash up in the stream, girls. I'll start on lunch immediately. The green sauce has been made, arrowroot biscuits will be baking soon, but I'll get this drake into the hot oven first so his skin is wonderfully crispy. Back up before I start plucking!"

They did as they were told, listening to their mother growl and snarl while she plucked the feathers from Video's prey. Audio was like no other when it came to plucking. She saved the down for their bedding, too. They couldn't hear her anymore when they reached the stream, but now Video had to listen to Jukebox.

"You should talk with Radio," Jukebox stated, raising her voice over the stream's current. For the second time that day, Video had to keep from growling. "You know I'm right." Jukebox splashed her dirty paws into the water, and then continued with her chin raised authoritatively, "You're going to need to bring her to the Capital to clear your name. You told me so yourself at breakfast with our father. You might as well try to get on the best terms you can with her."

Video was hesitant. Radio never listened to a word she said. She had failed to take the mission seriously. The young noble seldom listened to Video's advice. She was jealous, bitter, and after Video had killed her, she would be beyond finding logic in the situation. Video still didn't know how the two managed to make it out of the Unending Labyrinth and to Video's old home, but she imagined that would be the last time she would get Radio to take her advice.

With a stern look from Jukebox, though, Video knew there would be no disagreeing with her. She lashed her tail and flattened her ears, but agreed to do so. "Alright, but I'm not counting on anything coming from it." She thanked Jukebox in a whisper, then quickly began washing up in the stream so she didn't have to discuss the issue any more. Jukebox did the same, and seemed to be okay with dropping the subject. They walked back to the house without any more conversation, but it was a companionable silence.

Video and Jukebox entered their family home and Jukebox motioned with her head that she was going to the kitchen to help their mother, who was singing. Video grimaced when she hit a high note, the pitch going right through her ears. Video motioned to Jukebox she was going to head to Radio's room. They gave each other a determined nod and Video quickly slipped away.

Once in the doorway, if one could call it that since the only door inside the house was in the doorway of Signal's office, Video found Radio caring for herself. She started to back away, content with knowing Radio was grooming herself again, but knew she needed to speak to her and couldn't back down. She silently padded into the room.

Radio looked up when sensing the movement, saw Video and flinched.

Video stopped mid-step and put her paw down where she stood. "I am sorry to disturb you, but we need to speak." When Radio said nothing in reply, Video continued, "I'll cut to the chase. I need my name cleared for killing you during our mission. You'll need to go to the Capital City with me, and reclaim your title, too."

Radio's feathery fur stood on end. She spoke quietly, but with a determination that was plain to discern in her voice, "I will do no such thing and will go nowhere with you. You *did* kill me!" Her voice grew louder and shriller with every sentence. She continued, now yelling, "How dare you come in here and tell me that! You murdered me in cold blood saying the word, 'Die!' Video! You have no respect, no understanding, and no goodness about you! All you think about is clearing your name and getting everything swept under the rug, but I'm sorry to say it won't be that easy."

Radio continued to rant, no longer looking at Video, but turning away to yell at the wall. "I didn't dream about Pictures last night! The only thing I looked forward to at the end of the day! Of course, that was when I thought he would come for me, but now I know he's dead, and the dreams are now forever dead with him!" Radio stopped her ranting to catch her breath, almost as though hesitating to say her next words, but then added, "...I wouldn't mind helping the Jester to bring him back!"

Video had been irritated with the rant, but had figured it was good to get all of Radio's issues with her aired right away. The last comment, however, set Video off in a fit of anger. "I cannot believe how stupid you can be, Radio! If you knew what was good for you, you would know that using your magic makes you as good as dead to the Council! If you don't help me clear my name, you'll be just as hunted as I am, if not locked up and put away like your Aunt Studio!"

Radio whipped around and looked up at the larger feline, surprised.

Video's anger was lost at the look of shock. Somberly, she explained how Studio couldn't even come to her hearing. "I had to face the Jester alone because he impersonated the judge. There is no help out there for either of us except for what we get from each other." Video's voice had grown soft. As much as she didn't want to go on, she furthered the account, "Pictures was an absolute monster that used both of us to get what he wanted."

"You're lying!" Radio hissed.

Video bristled, and she towered over Radio defensively. "He stole the shard fragments within heartbeats of seeing your dead body and then proceeded to kill innocent people! Our teammates, Radio! I witnessed him standing over the dead body of Tape, and not caring for a second that Sensor was next. Not even the Stars know the status of Widget and Recorder. The only reason why I know Cassette's alive is because Film told me himself!"

Radio's eyes rounded. "They're all dead?" Her voice immediately hardened. "No! You're *wrong!* I have no reason to believe you...you could have been the one who killed them for all I know!"

"If I had done it myself I wouldn't be here, Radio! I wouldn't have been hunted by that mage and my brother; I'd be working alongside them like Pictures had been! He was a mage, Radio! I know you must have realized that blue eye wasn't natural. It had been the Jester's influence the whole time." Video saw Radio's eyes spark with realization, and continued quickly, "It doesn't matter what you shared with him, Radio. Film and everyone else here is aware of the truth. I wouldn't have faced that jungle to save you if the situation was any different. I couldn't lie about losing that team, Radio. None of them deserved the cruelty and torture they were exposed to."

Video caught her breath, her chest tight from relating only a few of the losses. Yet she knew she had to continue, because this was the first and likely the only time Radio would listen to her. "What you did was wrong and by law you deserve whatever punishment the Council has for you for using your magic just as Pictures had, but if you help me, I..." Video swallowed, as this was the hardest part for her to say, "I could look aside for you and we will never have to deal with the likes of each other again."

Radio hesitated. She turned away to compose herself from the tears she shed during Video's outburst and shook her head.

"I just don't want to believe he would be capable..." The small noble whispered.

Video blinked, and then softened her voice. "I can't justify his actions, but I fought for my life that night to make sure you didn't die in vain." She then straightened her posture, rising up her head to look down at the feline. "I did everything I could to make sure the King was brought back. After Pictures took the shards, I saw no other way." Video took a step closer. "I need your help to make this right, Radio."

Radio shook her head and cried. Video let her cry, relaxing her posture and softening her gaze. The noble had a lot to take in, especially about the one she cared most about, but Video had been as considerate she could with it. There was nothing more to say about it.

It seemed Radio realized that, too. She looked up after a moment and after taking in a breath and hesitating, she agreed. It seemed to Video that Radio made the agreement with a malicious gleam in her eye, but the lighting in the room wasn't the greatest, so Video told herself it was just her tendency toward paranoia that would make her think so. The look was gone before she could focus on it, but Video wasn't worried. Video figured Radio would likely pull the strings needed to try and get rid of her, anyway, but also knew her own sources were just as powerful if Film picked his side right.

Video tried to make her voice brighter, saying, "For what it's worth, I'm glad you have another chance to atone for what you did and I hope we both can make up for the consequences of our mission."

Radio said nothing in reply, making Video wince at her own poor choice of wording. It was best just to leave at this point. Video was out of breath and shook up as she left the room, but knew Radio was likely worse off than her. It was a lot of information to process. She walked away from the room and decided to go to her own after getting a breath of fresh air.

She started going to her ledge automatically, but then remembered the battle she had with the guards and the–

Video realized she had to stop her thoughts immediately to keep from them getting read. She succeeded for a second, but instant dread came from the idea they were going to be trailed from the Labyrinth, hunted in retribution because of her brother's temper and the other threats. What would happen if Video stayed here for too long with her family? Could Signal handle another battle with *a mage*, not any particular one, of course, even with the rest of the family's help? What Radio and Video fled from wasn't like anything Video ever read about in her literature before, it was something out of this world.

She wished Film would have some kind of advice for her, but realized she could probably ask Jukebox, too.

She headed back into the house to talk to Jukebox, not noticing the pair of glowing cyan eyes watching her from the rocks above. Before she could get to her older sister, though, Audio met her in the hallway and asked for help with making dinner instead. She looked at her younger daughter with concern as they reached the bright kitchen with its windows. "You, my sweet girl, are not to worry about whatever it is you're worrying about because it'll only stress your head more. Maybe I should add a sprinkle of dried tutsan to the salad." Video was okay with that, she had no intention of touching the salad.

"Mm, no, the gravy." Audio realized.

Video groaned.

Video was helpful while Audio explained what they were going to make and how. Once both of them had a task to keep busy with, Video knew it was her chance to ask more about the Shadow Advisor. "Audio, you mentioned that Phantascope would get...moody." Like every other mage Video knew, but didn't say that out loud as she furthered, "Did the Shadow Advisor have any other quirks? Anything that seemed exclusive to mages?"

Audio looked thoughtful for a moment, but then said she was unsure, adding, "I grew the impression that nothing could hurt Phantascope and that seemed to be the case until the end. He had come to me singed, battered, and weak before he attacked the kittens." Video was shocked her mother could still refer to the monster as a "he" again, especially after knowing it attacked her own children, but Audio quickly assured her, "He was overly emotional at the time, just having lost seasons, if not ages, of work in the Labyrinth." Audio shut her eyes, looking as though she was in pain at remembering the day, but then Audio looked at Video introspectively, "I had never seen that kind of wear on him until that day and didn't...don't understand why the loss of the forest could damage him so much physically."

Video didn't have words to respond, unable to understand her mother's endearment to the savage mage, so she gave a nod and finished setting the table.

"The beast was weak to fire."

Video whipped around to see Signal dropping a giant hare onto an open spot on the counter. Jukebox came in behind him and followed suit with a pheasant. Video couldn't help but have a twinge of envy that the two went out hunting while she dealt with the brooding noble, but instead decided to focus on what Signal said instead. "What do you mean?"

"A mage in Calotype's Forest, back when it was her sanctuary, cursed the creature you speak of during its final attack. Reports state the cursed mage itself was a fire mage before the incident, but after the last battle, no reports claimed to see the same spells used by it again. Fire was the best way to chase the beast out when I was assigned to eliminate it." It was the most expensive Video had seen Signal yet. He almost looked satisfied when he said, "The thing couldn't tolerate it. Fire was the only weapon used against it which wouldn't allow it to regenerate itself afterwards." The satisfaction dissipated instantly as he growled, "Otherwise, it was impossible to kill."

"Astonishing," Video whispered. Video was amazed by Signal's knowledge, but she noticed Audio was listening with a bit of melancholy, which made Signal's tail lash in sync with Video's own.

Jukebox came over and complimented the food spread out on the table, which Video finished setting while Audio quickly started setting out the roasts of squirrel and chipmunk Jukebox had caught earlier with root vegetables and their mother's ever present greens. A mixed fruit sauce was for dessert, topped with a honey drizzle.

"I'll elaborate when the time is right," Signal quickly stated, "But for now, we should enjoy the fragrant meal." The compliment to the food was enough to perk Audio up and she began to purr.

Radio joined them for their evening family meal. Both she and Video were quiet; mostly Jukebox and Audio talked. Jukebox shared the highlights of her hunts, Audio summarized the gardening she did, although Video noticed she didn't mention the valerian harvest, and then Audio asked far too many questions about Jukebox's kitten. Jukebox was more than happy to answer all of them, beaming with pride. It was a quiet dinner outside of the topic, all things considered, as the ladies kept their voices low for Signal's benefit. His acute hearing and his lack of fondness for chatter made all conversation at the table more relaxed, much to Video's contentment.

After dinner, Audio and Jukebox both went to respond to an alarm. Video told Radio they would wait to hear back from Console and Film before moving, but the time for them to go to the Council was impending. "You should be ready when that happens."

Radio retorted, "Oh, yes, because I have so much to pack!" She huffed and lashed her tail, "But yes, I'll be ready." She turned away from Video and stepped out of the kitchen area while Signal had returned back to his office, leaving Video alone.

Video gave up trying to make sense with Radio. She left the room as well to see Audio and Jukebox trying to connect to Film and Console. Video heard the call go through on the monitor and felt the excitement rush through her to hear the news. Audio got out her mic within moments, so Video went over.

"Tell them! Tell them what you did!"

Video was surprised to hear the voice of another she didn't recognize. She flicked her ears as she looked over Audio's shoulder.

"Settings! With due time! Look you–three." Film paused in acknowledging the two felines when seeing Video poke her head up behind Audio and Jukebox. "Hello, Video."

"Have you been caught up with the information on Radio, Film?" Video asked.

"And all that magic and mayhem?"

Video didn't like the light chatter. "She's alive."

"Oh, that, too. You said that in your note. Yeah, we've been working with elder Cinema from the Council ever since Audio sent us the memo."

Video's eyes rounded. Cinema? Alive? She would have to be the oldest member of the Council if Studio's story was true back in Clowder City. The elder was Radio *and Audio's* great-grandmother. "What did she answer with?"

"It was kind of weird, Vid," Console dropped down into the shot of the camera and leaned over the counter. He was still the spitting image of Audio, with a broader build and the darker tint of his brown fur from Signal. He blinked his forest green eyes at his sister when seeing her look of pride, then elaborated, "She kind of inferred she'd been through this before with the Jester personally. I guess this thing's been around as long as her. She told us that if the Jester had timeless magic, ceasing age growth, it wasn't too far out to think a noble like Radio could do the same, and believes she's alive. Either she's condoning the magic or knows the Jester's involved with it, so watch out."

"You couldn't *infer* she just never died!?" Alarm filled Video's mind. Everything could be for nothing if they established that both were involved with the magic. A corrupt influencer could suggest that the two were experimenting.

"Well..." Console grimaced. "Turns out they did have recordings of what happened...the drone must have been a high-distance one you didn't see, but they're looking into the context now."

"Cinema's dealt with cases like this before, which is why she was the best to contact," Film said, ignoring a scoff in the background. "She's going above and beyond her duties to make this work out, looking into what will be best for both you and Radio."

"The judge who held your trial's been missing since having an audience with King Capital, so they're considering giving you another hearing since..."

"The King deemed him a traitor," Film stated.

Video's heart fluttered with hope. The King knew that the judge was an imposter! Things might be on her side yet. She nodded quickly.

Console purred when he saw his little sister's excitement and added, "Your name should be cleared in no time, Vid, you'll just have to get through it."

"Oh, this is so exciting." Audio whispered.

"Yes, but it doesn't change the fact that Film expended nearly all his resources on procuring an audience with her!"

"Settings...!" Film snapped quietly. He continued softly, "We did what was necessary. No Council member was better for the job."

"We can't afford to spend more when we still have to ensure they'll actually make it all the way to the Capital, though! They'll need separate carriages, security, surveillance, comfort..."

The concern in her tone worried Video. How many strings did Film pull to speak with elder Cinema? Had he really gone through that much?

"Yes, yes, and it will all happen, Settings." Film assured softly.

Audio, Video, and Jukebox all jumped in unison when a pair of yellow eyes popped up right on the bottom of the camera. A tiny tortoiseshell tabby walked around and came up by Film, having to leap up onto the counter to be at the two toms' height. Video had expected a tall, authoritative queen to come over with the tone and snappiness thrown at Film, but it was more like a badgering little sister now that she thought of it. The small feline had a large, gold collar lined with silver rings and a dropdown pendant in the center with Media's insignia. This feline was as widely respected as Film for her speed and knowledge of Media's interface and database, but Video never imagined her as the small little cat she's seeing now.

"Nice to meet you, Settings," Audio said.

"Truly! Mutual greetings. Film's only said the best about your family," Settings chirped.

Audio gave a soft chuckle and started purring in happiness. Video and Jukebox's eyes both narrowed, but also gave nods to the small dark colored feline.

"We're doing all we can to help you three, the third being Studio, of course, to get your names cleared. I've never seen these two work day and night like this and you ought to show them your gratitude once you're all shining with your titles again." Settings looked pointedly at Video.

"Yes, ma'am," Video arched her brow as she answered.

"Good," Settings smiled back.

Video then looked to Film. "And what of clearing your name, sir? Were you able to rectify everything you were being accused of in the Capital City?"

Console grinned with mischief immediately, which worried Video, but Film answered smoothly, "Yes, Cassette's accusations went beyond protocol and professionalism, and slandering isn't permitted in my surveillance crew." Film's tone quickly dropped into bitterness. "While I understand the situation involving the team had a strong effect on all of us and emotions are at their highest peaks, it only stresses this should be a unit to rely on each other more than ever. Cassette didn't share those feelings, so she was removed as Assistant Manager of the team."

The three felines went speechless, and Console and Settings both gave them sheepish stares. Video swallowed. Cassette was the last member on the team after the castle's crisis. "Who will make up the team?"

Film chuckled. "Well, that's just the thing. Once she was certain she was getting my position and I was going to be fired from the accusations she made," he scoffed as Audio and Video gasped, "She took the initiative to hire a team from the Monitor's District to transfer here. We have a formidable team of three working for us now. I hope you'll be able to meet them once your name is cleared."

Video nodded, giving the smallest of smirks at the tomcat. "Sounds like a plan, sir."

He returned the smirk, which made Video's face become serious immediately. He laughed at her instant reaction, and then exclaimed, "Wonderful! Have a good night and take the time to savor the news!"

Video waited until the screen went dark to enjoy the idea she could be free and seen as a user of Media again. She purred as she brushed her cheeks against her sister and mother, and then headed to her room. She wasted no time going right to her bed to curl up and go to sleep. The sooner morning came, the sooner she was one day closer to getting to the end of this.

She curled up in a twist and laid on her back with her paws curled in the air. She was ready to sleep well and tackle the new day and the next report from Film and her eldest brother. It was just too exciting! Things were going as it should. She purred herself to sleep with the idea they had worked so hard for the justice of Media and to clear her name, and she knew that no mage could take that away from them. Video drifted off into sleep slowly with that in mind.

She blinked her eyes open to feel the heat of the drawing room.

The warm colored walls and the waves in the air from the radiating heat made her pant. She slowly got up and looked over at Pictures as he approached her. He seemed a bit more cautious and frustrated tonight, but that didn't affect Video. She clamped her jaw shut. This time, she was determined to kill him nonchalantly and leapt for him first. He trembled with surprise and the two were both knocked against the ground as Video came in contact with him. He kicked her off of himself and whipped back onto his paws, but Video just tilted her head and approached him again, blinking boredly at him as they fought. She ripped open his throat slowly once she finally had him pinned, and then took her sweet time throwing him into the fire, too. When he flew back out, he looked outright offended as he landed at her paws. "You think this is a joke!?" He scowled.

Video blinked slowly at him, considering mocking him and his combat abilities, but instead growled, her attempts at controlling her temper wasted. She couldn't believe how stupid he and Radio were, and that he thought he had the right to ask her that. "You have no idea how much work you've made for me! How much trouble and how many consequences there have been because of everything you did!" She stepped forward, advancing on him even when he began glowing orange with his anger. "Not that you care, since you're a foolish mage that can't consider the idea that something, or someone unlike himself, can have feelings!" She said the last words with a hiss.

Pictures blinked, looked at Video and answered, "But that's what you're doing."

Video was shocked by his answer.

Video woke up and quickly looked outside to see it was dawn, but that's not what startled her awake. She woke suddenly to screams of felines outside her room. She immediately rushed out to see Radio, Jukebox, and Audio all watching a report on the living room monitor. Video's eyes rounded in horror at the sight.

It was Clowder City burning, blue and white fire was completely engulfing half the city. Hundreds of cats were running out from the city, while the Jester and Stereo ran down the burning threads. The monkey was chasing them out and shooting blasts of magic at them while Stereo was shoving any brave felines down who decided to try to attack the two. The tabby tom was masked, which made both Jukebox and Video's head slightly tilt, and when it came up on the screen, the headline said it was the work of the Jester and a mysterious unknown partner.

Video wanted to mention how ridiculous it was they didn't know it was obviously Stereo from the Rich Top Mountain region, but the situation before them was too dire to speak out loud any faults of the newscast. Radio was witnessing her aunt's city being destroyed. Jukebox was watching the city burn where her partner and kit lived, not knowing their status as far as Video knew.

Video looked away as the reporter began speaking about the casualties concerning the Resolution Star, the Flash Star, and the Frequency Star from the events of the Jester's attacks on the Capital. Audio went from running her head into Jukebox's neck to putting her paw on top of Radio's.

Radio looked like she was in disbelief at first, but when the reporter mentioned the loss of the family servant, Stella, the feathery feline broke down into sobbing and cried in horror at the news.

Video looked down at the small cat with sorrow, knowing there was no comfort or empathy she could reasonably offer while she stood beside her sister, but when she walked forward, the reporter began addressing the condition of the Studio Star. All four ladies looked up to hear the news, and saw the dark brown tabby on screen, but just as it showed the brassy noble approaching the Jester and beginning to speak, the monitor screen cut off to static. The camera went back to the reporter, who stated they lost contact with the surveillance of Clowder City.

Radio shook her head and continued to cry. Video rested her muzzle gently on the small cat before she rose up and started for the outside of her home.

"Where are you going, Video?" Jukebox choked out, her voice shaking from watching the events on the monitor of the city where her kit was and from Radio's reaction to all the news.

"To find out what I can do to end this." Video responded, and continued forward. She had to bring these two to justice, no matter how much she put herself at risk by doing so. If she had just succeeded in killing the Jester in the castle, this would have never happened.

Audio ran out after her. "Video, dear, wait!" Video whipped her head around, ready to chastise her mother for trying to stop her, but Audio was already right behind her and quickly murmured, "Radio's expecting." When Video stopped and looked at her with surprise, Audio added in a rush, "It could have happened either before, or after her death by how far she is along, and she can't, or won't, tell for sure."

Video fully turned and asked, "Who could be the father after if the father before would've been Pictures?"

Audio looked at her feet and the creeping thyme under them for a moment before answering softly, "Stereo could be a possibility from what Radio's been saying."

"She knew Studio said we were family and *still..!* The cursed noble!" Video scoffed in disgust at the revelation, and stormed off, ignoring Audio's warning, which sounded decidedly more like a plea.

"For the nobles it's different, Video! And Stereo didn't know!" Audio continued to carry on that if she came across Stereo, she should remember that he might be a father.

He might be dead, by the time Video was through with him.

- CHAPTER 6-
DARING

Video trekked endlessly, cutting through the mountain path to make it to Clowder City in one day. She knew her father would be proud of her resilience and knew that no monitor or surveillance drone would check the trail. The path was deemed impossible by their standards. With that and the fact that Console and Film went above and far beyond what anyone could do to clear her name despite the odds made Video more positive that she had her father's approval. With the Cinema Star's blessing, it was likely Video didn't have anything to fear even if the drones did locate her.

The trail was long, but it was nothing Video couldn't endure. This is what she had been trained to endure her entire life. She defined the position as a courier. The only thing that held her back was her apprehension. Her former confidence about her protection turned to dust as she saw the decaying, rusted skyscrapers in the distance. Console and Film may have started to enlighten the Council about the real situation, but it didn't necessarily mean all of Social Media followed. She had to move around the Ruined City, knowing their analog cameras went straight to the Monitor's District from Film's words. If there was just one insider for the mage, or an ally of Pictures, knowing the tom from his seasons of consulting, Video could be hunted within seconds again.

She took the longer route to move around the city, but couldn't bring herself to travel through the Sanctified Meadows, either. The flowers stretched across as far as she could see. From what she remembered, it was barely a night's journey with two weights on her back. She didn't want to see how the meadow had bloomed since she travelled through it with Pictures and Radio, not after what the two had shared. She turned her trail to cut through the rough terrain and traveled directly along the mountain instead. She wouldn't allow any ledge, trench, or incline keep her from making her way to the Clowder City.

When Video encountered a long drop she walked around it until she found a fallen tree that would work as a bridge to get across. She sniffed and inspected for any other residents in the area, but it didn't look like there were any sign of inhabitants near the tree. Not a sound in the air and nothing but the squeaking of bats down below; it seemed safe. She made herself a burrow under the tree with a short bit of digging and curled up under the giant trunk.

Sleep came quick to the giant tabby. She wasn't haunted by Pictures, either, and realized it was because she rested in the day. Her dreams started containing the flickers of his magic right before she snapped herself awake and carried on during the night.

It was refreshing to have a moment to herself. The jungle's current inhabitant had removed all her immediate threats and Console and Film were taking care of the rest. Video was amazed at how different it was traveling alone again. She didn't have to slow her steps, she didn't have to listen and remain patient for others' conversation and she didn't have to stop to rest at every incline of a hill.

The travel was peaceful, until she saw Clowder City.

Video smoldered as she approached the ruins of the black, glittering city. Her tail lashed with anger. The ghost of Pictures could leap out and attack her now and she would rip it apart effortlessly. She wouldn't mind an excuse to take out a few things after seeing the sight.

She was furious. Her brother did this! Her twin! He was in union with the Jester and had no guilt.

Video was ashamed. Her paws traced where others had stepped and she came across a print of the same exact size as hers. Humiliation and disgust washed over her because of how similar they were. That they both had done so much damage to the Studio Star. If Video had just taken the shard from Studio, the city leader never would have been imprisoned and treated like some criminal mage. What if the Jester held a trial for her as well, before it was caught as impersonating the judge? She should have asked Film and Console! She was so selfish and self-absorbed! Video's chest tightened when she realized she hadn't even thought to ask, and yet she wouldn't be alive if it wasn't for Studio. The noble even went out of her way to send her a message when they were both in peril, and it was torn away by the Jester. Video had given no gratitude for everything the Studio Star had done for her.

It was hard to breathe at the realization. She entered where the gates had been and looked at the empty streets that once had been a third of the city. The two traitors had taken out a quarter of the walls and then expanded the fire to burn a third of the buildings on the western side. Video looked in shock at the destruction. The concern was washed out of her mind as she had to pull herself together to become fully alert. She was careful where she walked, as some places were still hot to the touch. Video looked around for the possibility of anyone still being there. Her eyes darted to some shadows moving down an alley. They were large and moving as though they didn't belong there.

She couldn't tell what types of animals they were, the scent of anything and everything being covered by the smoke and burned debris. However, that wasn't going to stop her from any confrontation. Anger built into her paws with every step she took closer to them. Her tail lashed with anticipation when she almost caught up to them. Once they saw her shadow, they took off and she instantly made chase.

Video followed the trail rapidly. The shadows moved quickly, but they were no match for her fury. She raced to the other side of one of the alleys they were heading down and caught the two, leaping at one's neck and smashing them down into the burnt earth.

She found herself staring down at a fox and snarled. How dare such an animal enter after the attack. *No respect!* She hissed warningly at it, allowing it a chance to apologize, but only a heartbeat went by before her anger took over. "Foxes aren't welcome here!"

Her claws raked down its neck, making it yip and bark in fear. Video released it, and then looked over at the older one, which looked at her with more understanding. She knew it spoke cat just from its gaze alone. She tossed back the small one to advance upon the other. "You didn't waste any time coming here. You couldn't even give these people time to grieve for their loss! Dirt!" She sneered, her teeth baring as she hissed again at the animal, and then whipped it into the alley wall. She remembered that Stereo had old fox friends back when the littermates still had been doing their courier work, and wondered if they were connected. No one else should have been able to make it to Clowder City as fast as Video had. "Do you know Stereo!?"

She shoved the younger one back when it went to defend its friend, and then slammed her paw against the larger fox's chin. She could tell already they did by their surprise at her accusation, which made her press her claws down deeper.

"Y-Yes!" It yelped in cat's tongue, which was no surprise to Video as it was an older animal. It whimpered at Video's force.

"Tell me where he is!" She snarled and whipped its head back into the wall until she was sure she dazed it.

She lifted up her claws, ready to strike for the throat. The fox quickly shook its head and looked up at her pleadingly, lifting up its paws and tucking its tail in submission. "Please don't kill me!"

"Then tell me!" Video yowled.

"He's at the Capital! He said he'd go there and...uh...and said he was done with doing all of...this!" The small fox yelped from behind Video, surprising her with the sudden speech in cat. She released the older fox, and looked at the two once the larger one went to its friend.

"Done with what?"

"Hurting the wrong people," The older fox said. "The Jester was deceitful to him, but he said we could still come here and raid what was abandoned."

Video frowned. She seriously doubted Stereo would turn sides so quickly, especially with the dangerous risks he was already taking by being side by side with the Jester, but she still nodded. "So you say. Well, I'm telling you to get out. You're not welcome anywhere in these parts, be it abandoned or not. I don't want to see you again!" She ended the last words with a shout, and both foxes bolted away to the city wall opening.

Video pressed her paw against her head, trying to keep her vision from blurring, even to keep from succumbing to the dizziness, not to mention the feeling of being sick. It was like a wash of confusion; too much to process with the concussion. The foxes probably said such things to soften her. Stereo wouldn't be realizing his mistakes and changing allegiance so soon. For all she knew, he could be going to the Capital City to meet with the monitor who was the information leak the Jester used. In all possibilities, it could be Console, knowing he was at Capital City, too. Video, however, didn't want to think that of her eldest brother.

She prowled out of the city through the northern gates, and looked behind her for one last glance to the penthouse. She was surprised to see that the Studio Star stood at her balcony. Video's eyes widened. Video could read no expression of the leader from the distance being twenty-seven stories apart, but she knew the lithe noble probably had technology which would give her the ability to see Video. She gave a nod of thanks and sympathy for all that the Studio Star did, and all that had happened. She could only hope that one nod would be able to express everything for now, but at least she had that.

Video raced up the same trail she had with Pictures and Radio when they had lost the signal of the crystal heart. She knew she was going to have to face the same valley she killed Radio in if she kept to the same path. She wasn't ready to see it again. She wasn't ready to have to remember it all in detail, nor face what possibly might lie there now after seeing the capability of magic affecting the grounds and the living after death. Everything was unsafe to approach twice. She had to find a different path to the Capital City. Far too many times she would take an easy path for Radio, choosing any ground, any *surface*, that was easier on the noble's paws, but now she could cut directly across and head straight for the Capital.

Without another moment of hesitation Video did. She had to believe the foxes about Stereo's destination. Even if they had told her a lie, she knew she could break in and use the monitors there to locate him. Signal was never strict on where she could go in his office and while at the time as a kitten, Video was convinced his blindness was the reason why she could watch what he did right beside him without him shooing her out. Her scent and noise would have easily given her away. The giant tom really had allowed her to watch him work and it was likely why he did all the most interesting machinations and murmur to himself out loud on the days she would supposedly "sneak" in, too. Video wasn't that kitten anymore, though.

How could that have been the same father who provided the recordings which confirmed her "acts of treason"? Video almost tripped over an individual because of the self-absorption of her thoughts—startled once her paw came in contact with fur. She jumped back to see a mink couple.

"Ma'am! Please!" The woman gasped, her eyes round.

"What?" Video took a step back, knowing she likely couldn't fight and win if there was a third.

"You speak to us?" The mink woman seemed surprised, but then quickly continued, "It's our child! Strange magic happened, verified one.

She was suddenly pulled into the earth, enclosed within a tree. We don't know why, but we can't get her out no matter how hard we try, always just a whisker short for opening it enough for her to squeeze through. We need you to help us."

Video blinked in realization she wasn't as lost in her thoughts as she believed, and these minks actually ran into her to ask for help. She nodded. "Of course, please bring me to your daughter." If this was a trap, her life would be at risk, but everything she did seemed like that right now. All she could do was rely on was the truth and put her faith in others. She questioned if they should put her faith in her and sighed. If two parents couldn't break free their child with their strength, she was worried she might fail them, too.

The two brought her to a twisted and warped tree, the bark looking like it was almost woven together unnaturally. She looked nervously at the couple, realizing it could be the Jester and Stereo shapeshifting. Perhaps she was about to be shoved into the tree or slaughtered on the spot. The idea they were just a whisker short for a child to squeeze out started to sound much more foolish to believe.

Then she heard the squeak of a kit, and immediately bound up to the tree. "I'm going to help you! We're here to help!" She called out and began ripping at the bark. She saw the claw and bite marks of the minks in their own attempts to free the crying kit and followed their lead before she saw the pattern of the cracks and the strange faint lavender thread that traced up the tree. It glowed, like magic, but it was certainly nothing like the Jester's.

Video saw a small opening, and dug her claws into it. She startled when her claws, instead of splintering and breaking apart against the magic, like most sorcery caused when she faced it, strengthened and grew out. Video realized that was what the lavender thread was also doing to the tree. The longer she kept her paws on the lavender essence, the more she felt her claws heal and her pads recover. Video didn't have much knowledge of magic, but knew one color was reserved for one individual and that was purple for the Queen.

She swallowed nervously, not wanting to mess with divine intervention, but the kit let out another squeal and Video knew she had to. Once her claws were at their full growth, she took in a breath and went at it again. She ripped back the crack of the tree, pulling and clawing at it before she could get a strong grip on a large piece, and then broke it open. She tugged and tore until the parents joined her and the three ripped down the outer layer of the tree's trunk with furious and desperate speed.

Finally, the three each had a strong enough grip to pull it back. They reeled back at the same time, digging their claws and fangs into the bark with all of their strength and pulled just enough space for the kit to leap out.

All three let go immediately once she landed on the ground, nearly being swung back into the tree themselves by how quickly it pulled back to recover. Video had to catch her breath before turning to look at the other two, and then watched as the mink kit weaved around her parents with glee and love.

"Lynn, Lynn, dear, you must be more careful!" they chastised in unison.

The mink cried, nodded, and embraced her parents. They continued sobbing with fear and relief.

Video looked down at the family and then back at the broken tree. She traced her scraped paw pads along the healing bark where the lavender glowed, and her pads again healed upon contact with the tree. With the barrier or not, the Queen's magic was still here, and she was still working in mysterious ways. Video pulled back when the lavender aura disappeared and looked back at the minks, smiling shyly when the parents thanked her.

"What is your title, verified one?" the father asked.

Video blinked, hesitant since she was still technically a rogue. She felt she owed them an answer, though. "It's Video of the Rich Top Mountains. What are your names?"

"I'm Larry, and this is my partner, Lanie." He chattered, looking towards his lighter colored companion.

Video couldn't help but chuckle at the theme of their names, now knowing why they named their daughter Lynn. "Those are lovely names, sir. I am happy to help." She looked to the other two, now. "You must be careful, there are more unusual events like this ahead, and we all have to keep on guard."

When all three nodded, Video let her shoulders relax. This was why she did what she did and was loyal to Media. She was here to help the subjects and find what no one else could behind the screen of a monitor. No drone could find out why this tree had the magic it did, nor could it have helped the family in peril. This is why she was a courier and why she wouldn't give up until she was proven innocent and could continue with her work.

"I am no rogue nor tyrant." She murmured to herself, and then dipped her head to the mink parents. "Take care you three."

"We will. Thank you, loyal one. We will always remember you." Lanie murmured, nuzzling her daughter with affection, letting out small chatters in her own tongue to the little one.

Video bowed her head again, nodding to the father, and then raced back up the hill toward the Capital City, filled with new energy in her excitement and healing from the Queen.

Her mind raced back to the idea her father taught her about magic being warm and welcoming, making it deceitful to the point that it had to be avoided at all costs. Video believed him and understood what he meant when she felt the promising, warm feeling of Calotype's Forest, knowing what evil lay inside. However, the lavender aura was something else entirely. Either the Queen's magic was entirely pure and really was something good for her subjects, or Satisfaction was the most manipulative, untrustworthy mage of all. Video looked at her smooth, strengthened paws. She didn't know what to believe.

Video stopped for rest once the sun was setting again. She knew that two days without rest would leave her scatterbrained against a fight with her brother. No matter where he lay in his morals, they would never reach an understanding when it came to seeing each other. Video was certain they would always battle, and what he had done was unforgivable. She came across some dark woodland that offered protection from outside eyes. She looked around, making sure no one would see her enter, and then ran inside.

She hunted first to see if any of the prey animals had found good burrowing areas she could use, but also feasted. The animals were always so plump during the summer season, and offered just enough for Video's fill without waste. She found the perfect place to rest and curled up in the shelter of the forest's growth.

One thing she recalled: she didn't have to deal with Pictures when she slept during the day. She slept until the moon was rising in the sky, and set out for the Capital City again. The path was much easier after her paws' recovery with the tree's magic threads. Video wondered if her association with the Queen's magic was enough to put her to death, too. She was lucky there were no monitor drones around at the time. Not that monitors would understand what was going on, anyway.

Just before dawn, she reached the city gates of the Capital City and snuck inside. She followed the alleys and areas carefully where there weren't cameras. She knew she'd come across Stereo in due time for that very reason, as he would be doing the same. She snuck into buildings through windows and servant doors, knowing the monitors wouldn't bother with cameras for the lower ranked folk unless they thought one was stealing. She moved through the buildings until she came across a familiar one. Her eyes widened with surprise. It was a building Audio took Stereo and her to so they could celebrate receiving their verification. Video wondered just how sentimental Stereo might be at the moment.

She looked around and shadowed the building for a while to try and get comfortable with the layout of the rooms without being caught by any of the staff. It was for juvenile folk that were just verified, where the distinguished and retired verified would give a rundown on old ways and stories of the present and past, show new feed that wasn't classified, and outdated logs which had been removed from the current archives. Video made sure to avoid the monitor's wing and decided to travel down the courier's wing. That was where Audio had brought her and Stereo. It seemed so long ago.

Almost as if on cue, she saw the dark form of her brother. Her eyes narrowed. Their minds thought more alike than she thought, or he really was that predictable. Now she could face him though, with no monkey to stop her from giving it her all. She ran to the nearest hall and struck the emergency alarm, letting sirens screech throughout the entire building as she raced toward the direction she saw Stereo go.

She followed the tom through the rooms and halls, everyone else panicking too much to notice them now. The floors were slippery and not made for fast movement, but Video pressed her paws down hard, and kept her claws in to keep from any skidding. Her brother however, who had much less experience indoors, was moving much more clumsily. She caught up to him as he entered an anteroom and whipped him down into the wooden flooring.

"Stereo!" She hissed, and knocked her paw down on his muzzle when he tried to get up.

The tom kicked her with his back legs and batted at her, but she leapt for his throat, digging in and tossing him back onto the floor. She held her grip on him to pull him up and knock him back down, growling through his fur in anger. She was going to make him pay. He clawed down her face and yowled when she dug her fangs in deeper. With all her might, she pulled him back, lifted up on her back legs and whipped him into the wall.

Stereo dropped, dazed, but scrambled to get up. Video tried to jump on him before he could regain his footing, but he attacked her straight from the ground, making the two roll and twist in battle. They were an entangled ball of claws and teeth that ripped at each other's pelts in a frenzy, each desperate for a hit that would immobilize the other.

Video screeched when the tom sliced his claws down her sides. She felt the blood begin to matt up the fur. She grabbed at his scruff, pushing with all her weight to swing him down and hold him there. "I'm going to kill you, Stereo!" She hissed through his pelt, and began tugging and clawing at him viciously.

Stereo whipped up one of his back paws and stuck it across her face, sending her reeling back as he rose up.

"You're the only one I need dead, Video. After that I don't care what happens, Father might as well be dead in his monitor room."

Video looked at him with surprise, figuring he was against all of Media. Why just her? "It's easy for you to say, but you'll never be satisfied—never pleased with what you have done." She quickly dodged his pounce for her, looking at him with narrowed eyes.

Stereo snarled at her words. He crouched down and leapt for her with all his might. The only thing that kept him from hitting Video head on was the fact that his claws skidded on the tile, slightly throwing him off balance.

They circled each other, both their long, puffy, bristled tails lashing with anger. Stereo went to bat at Video's face, but Video leaned back and slapped him across his face with her paws, knocking him down and making him hiss at her in anger.

"You're the only reason why I've done what I've done! You and Signal, you both ruined my life!"

"Why me? Signal put Unit down, not I." The confusion started churning in Video's stomach. How could he blame her for something that happened when she was off on a mission? "Because I wasn't there?" Video knew that Stereo had a vendetta against the family after he lost his companion, but she hadn't realized it was just herself and Signal. They had never discussed it, really. She and Stereo usually had done everything together, but Video had been called on a special assignment so Stereo stayed home with their parents and Unit. After Unit's death, Stereo had gone rogue and had only ever attacked Video since.

"You were the one that took Unit from me; the one who ripped out his throat when Signal was going to take him to the Council to give testimony!"

"...What?" Video backed away, and much more narrowly dodged the next attack. She leapt for Stereo and knocked him down, taking advantage of his emotional response.

"Stereo, what are you talking about?" Video had heard the news of Unit's death on her monitor collar. She hadn't been even within a day's run distance to their house.

Stereo snarled and kicked Video away, getting to his paws and biting at her shoulder when she failed to dodge his next attack. She hissed and knocked him down, bristling and arching her spine, her tail lashing. "Speak to me, you dumb cat!"

"You killed him! You killed him in cold blood and you did it with a smile!"

Video's eyes hooded at the tom, and Stereo blinked too, realizing how stupid he sounded.

"Smile?" Video narrowed her eyes. "Why not you take into consideration what shapeshifting grinning maniac you've been working with and figure out who really killed him."

"I-I...it was you, Video." Stereo stammered, and Video knocked her paw across his face and whipped him down onto the ground.

"Idiot." Video put up with half her career having to battle the tom spontaneously, many times barely escaping with her life, and it was because he had such little faith in her that he believed she would *smile* killing his companion. That he believed she'd smile about *anything* was stupid enough, but now she realized the tom was just delusional.

"Why don't you focus on your efforts to kill the real creature that took away your rogue mate, likely because he went against the monster because of his love for you, and stop looking at the surface of things for once in your life?"

It was resolved so quickly. If Video could have even talked to him during the shard mission with Radio and Pictures, he already could have been a valuable asset. She had run into him once before that, so she supposed she only had three other opportunities before now to have cleared things up, but she felt just as foolish for not having clarified all of this before. She couldn't believe it was all just the Jester playing games, or worse, another mage that could shapeshift, but if the supposed "Video" that killed Unit was smiling, she suspected it was the Jester.

Video lifted her paw to keep Stereo from speaking and turned for the door, when she ran directly into a puffy tan lynx point.

Video swallowed nervously, recognizing Glitch. Both of them froze upon seeing each other. The feline was assigned to work in the building after the poor thing had malfunctioned half of the monitor department with a single chip she made during her technological schooling. She was probably sent in by the facility caretakers to find out if the alarm had been an error.

Glitch's eyes widened. The cat knew both her and Stereo since they first were verified as followers of Media, and even came up to the cottage when Stereo went rogue to offer her support. Video blinked at the lynx point, then back at Stereo, wondering what the tom's actions would be when she saw him stand and approach the smaller cat, and yowled when Stereo pounced on Glitch.

"Stereo, no!" Video anticipated seeing her brother rip out the tan feline's throat, but Stereo knocked the cat's head up and whipped it back down until she was unconscious, and Video was left to stare at her brother in shock.

"Believe it or not, I'm not as quick to murder someone as you are, Video. It's not like my assumption you killed Unit was really out of the question." Stereo glared at Video and started on his way out of the room.

Video followed, keeping her ears flattened and her head down. Even if she hadn't taken away the tom's loving companion, she had killed the Radio Star. She could tell by the way Radio spoke of Stereo and from what Audio said, they already knew each other well.

The tom might actually be the only one who could bring Radio comfort at a time like this.

He also could have just spared Glitch to make it seem like he was innocent. She could focus on that when they were out of danger, though. The two siblings escaped through a window of the building and ran in sync out of the Monitor's District. Just as they left, Video saw the monitors arriving around the building to check the surveillance cameras. They quickly ran out of the Capital City.

"Look," Video huffed. She caught her breath once they were down the incline just out of sight from the city. "We need to split up, I have to get to the blasted primate mage, but Radio just found out that her family fell by the hand of the Jester and she needs your help. I need you to get to her and to re-verify her as a noble in the Meridian Stretch, so she can clear my name and yours, too." She knew that Signal and Jukebox would tear him apart if he tried anything else. "You were smart by wearing that mask. There's still hope for you if you can convince her you were fooled by the monkey, as well."

"No," Stereo shook his head, speaking firmly as he turned to face his sister. "You're the one who is actively being hunted. The hunting patrol after me went dormant by last winter. I'll handle the primate, you get to her. You don't even know who he is, Video! You lost your memories ages ago."

Video stopped, and looked at him, but he continued on as though he hadn't said anything.

That was something way too important, and way too severe, to pretend like there was nothing more to his words. "No," She snapped as she stomped her paw, "No! You can't tell me that and not elaborate! I'm tired of being treated like I've been a part of something I don't know about! You thought I killed a cat when I didn't, and now you're saying I've lost memories. When did you become so mindless, you dumb tom?"

"Surely the attacks from those mages would have jostled your brain enough for you to remember how you got that scar on your foot in the first place, Video." Stereo scoffed, and carried on.

Video narrowed her eyes, suspicious her brother would bring up her kittenhood wound, and she hissed. "No, I don't! And if you don't want your ears ripped out of your skull right now, you're going to tell me!" She leapt at her brother, swinging him down into the earth and pinning him down on his back.

Stereo scoffed, but then squeaked when Video shoved her paw into his neck, and pushed her paw back. "That stupid weird colored monkey! They were here when we were kits, and now they've come back! They're the reason the barrier had to be rebuilt!"

Video's eyes rounded with horror at the very idea. "What? Wait-What *other* monkey? There are two of them!?"

"Not that you have to worry about," the Jester growled from behind her, and whipped down its cube. Video narrowly dodged it. She whirled around to look at the mage but didn't have a chance to say another word before the cube moved to strike her again.

"Stereo, I brought this stupid cat all the way to the Labyrinth for you to kill and you betray me after spending a minute with her?"

Video jumped away just in time. Once the cube landed squarely into the earth, she leapt at the monkey. "Because you decided it was a good idea to smile when you faked being me!"

The two rolled down the incline as Video made contact, but the Jester flung Video down and slapped her across her face. "You should have just left things be and stay closed up in at Audio's little shack, Video. Now you've meddled in things best kept buried!"

"No! I'm trying to find out answers!" Her voice quivered. "I deserve to know!" She kicked the monkey off of her and into Stereo, who began clawing the primate like prey.

The two dueled while Video caught her breath, but even after; she was in amazement how quickly the tables turned between the two. She thought for sure she had lost her brother to the pull of magic and revenge, but instead he faced the Jester head on after learning the truth.

Stereo shouted out in pain when the Jester drove its fangs into his neck and clawed him across the face with its nails, making Video snap back into reality. She crouched down and went to attack, but before she leapt, the Jester threw Stereo into Video.

The two toppled back, but Video weaved around her twin and went for the Jester's throat. The monkey snorted and deflected her immediately. Video realized it could predict her attacks by her thoughts. She would have to attack not knowing her own next move. Stereo struggled to his paws and went for the Jester again, leaving Video with an enough of an opening when the Jester retaliated to attack again. The two circled the monkey and struck him in sync, one after the other, until finally Video was facing the monster's front again and struck head on. Stereo pulled the mage's arms back with his claws, leaving Video an opening for the face and neck. Her claws struck against the metal collar to no avail, so she looked to the mage's eyes.

They rounded immediately as Video's thoughts went to what Film said about the former mage Phantascope going for the eyes, but didn't close them fast enough for Video's attack. She went to blind the monster, striking her claw tips deep across its eyes, raking against its face before its tail swung into her stomach and sent her back.

Video reeled back when she saw the Jester leap for her. She barely dodged its assault and had to evade each swipe and swing in a scramble of fear. The Jester's eyes went black when it reopened them, black magic mixed with blood dripping from its face where she had clawed it. Fear struck through Video. There was nothing like the depth of the darkness in its eyes—the only thing that was visible within them was a slit of bright cyan showing the creature's pupil.

She remembered the Shadow Advisor had similar eyes from Audio's stories and wondered if it was somehow passed onto the primate or if the spell was possible for every mage. Nothing was like the horror of seeing magic mixed with blood though. The monkey turned its black gaze on her for its next attack. Video was barely able to dodge as she felt the very essence of her energy drain from her paws. She felt weak just by staring at the creature and its nails sharpening into shadows brought no additional comfort.

She whipped back when it struck again and yowled out in pain when it gripped her paw and drove its nails into the back of her front leg. She took her free claw and struck the eyes with no fear. This caused the mage to release her and pull away. She flicked the blood off her paws and hissed at the monkey, only startling when its eyes burst with white and cyan mist.

The mage's eyes and claw marks healed immediately upon the mist evaporating, leaving Video clueless as to what she was going to do next.

She was thankful that Stereo could answer. Before the Jester could finish its next summon for a spell, the tom shoved his paws down into the primate's back and knocked it down. He drove his fangs into the mage's chin just above the neck and began driving his jaw down to slowly move the outfit down to get to the throat, but the mage tolerated none of it. It opened its eyes again, which glowed bright cyan as it began to return the attack. Video grabbed the monkey's tail in time before it hit Stereo, but the Jester whipped back and kicked Stereo solid in the stomach, sending the tomcat spiraling into his sister.

The two both landed roughly. Video got up and looked at the Jester, who stared at her with a conflicted expression before it disappeared into shadows.

Video's paws shook as all the realizations sank in from the battle. That was the most severe attack yet, without the cube, anyway. She never had seen magic so dark. Even in the castle when the mage's form flickered with shadows, it was nothing like the battle she and her brother just endured. She let out a breath of exhaustion, and then looked at Stereo. "What do you know that I don't? Why did it attack us like that?" she asked weakly.

Stereo shook his head and started walking again. Video frowned, and followed him silently at first, but thoughts reeled in her mind.

She thought of how Pictures said the Jester chose her and Studio for the mission, and Pictures was obviously chosen, too. The only one that was not meant to go on the journey was Radio. That was because she hadn't been in any of the information or files, which meant the primate's inside source hadn't known about her. That alone put Film out of the equation of being the leak, unless he purposely wanted Radio dead instead of the Frequency Star—as there were rumors the other noble and the gold-lined tomcat had previously dated.

Video realized it still might actually be a possibility with further thought. She wasn't sure why Stereo wasn't a part of it when they were twins. Perhaps it meant who was born last of the litter, but Video had to wonder if that had meant Stereo could have joined the group on the mission if he hadn't been a rogue. Had he just always been the Jester's backup plan after the chosen three for the journey failed?

He could still be working for the mage, for all she knew. Her tail lashed as she yelled out, "I have no reason to trust you! I have absolutely no reason to believe that wasn't staged, that you're pulling a fib on me and taking me into a trap! You're gullible, foolish, and just stupid enough to play into his games and still believe I killed your companion!"

Stereo stopped and whipped around, his face and neck still bleeding from the Jester's bite and scratches. "I had no reason to get beat up by that blasted monkey, Video! If we were planning something, don't you think he would have come up with something that didn't end up with him and me getting hurt? Regenerate or not, that mage doesn't like pain. He left because you struck a nerve." He lashed his tail and came up to his sister. "We're going home. I'm going to make things right and we're going to stop that monster." His icy gaze warmed with sadness, a stare Video hadn't seen in the tomcat for seasons. "I know the truth now, and I'm sorry, Video."

Video stared at him in shock.

Video didn't know who she could trust, but Stereo looked like he meant it.

She gave her brother a nod and started back on the path behind him. It seemed like he was genuine. Even if they had fought for their whole grown life, there was still that first half where Stereo had been the most honest feline she knew. Maybe he could be honest about the memories, too. She could start with a question, "What was I like, before I...forgot?"

Stereo blinked, and looked at her over his shoulder. "You were happy, mischievous, and evil."

"I was not!" Video's tail lashed, anger rushing back into her voice.

"Who remembers what now?" Stereo's gaze sharpened, and Video stiffened. She wanted to believe that she hadn't lost memories and that Stereo was mistaken here too, but everyone seemed to know an extra step in everything but her.

Stereo scoffed and continued, "At first we didn't believe what happened, but there was nothing you could recall about the Labyrinth or the monkey. After you forgot, you changed. All the mischief and curiosity died from your eyes. It felt like I never saw you again." He shook his head and continued, "Even our missions were hard for me because I knew you weren't the person you once were. You just put yourself into your studies, and never set foot in the Labyrinth again—besides when Signal took us in there to deactivate the traps."

Video blinked. "Had I hit my head in the Labyrinth?" Was she playing too rough? Maybe she just wanted to be careful after hurting herself, and then simply forgot the reason for doing so after all these seasons.

"Perhaps; I wouldn't put it past you, but you wanted to go back immediately after the paw bite. That's why he made you forget."

"Who?"

"The monkey mage. Your *friend*." Stereo said it with enough spite that Video knew there was memories behind it, memories that she couldn't recollect.

Friend? "Then he...it hurt me as a kit?" She whispered.

Stereo shook his head. "No, Video, he was the one who saved us when the other monkey attacked us in the jungle. When you said you weren't going to give up on finding your primate friend again and started to go with him, he made you forget. He told Audio it was to protect you."

Audio and the Jester had spoken with each other? After thinking about how the Jester was so ready to attack them after mentioning the *other* monkey and that Stereo found it responsible for the barrier being taken away, Video didn't ask any more questions. It all sounded like a bunch of charades, but she was even more hurt to hear that Stereo was sure Audio knew about this, too. That couldn't be true.

The two walked toward the Rich Top Mountains until it was nearly dawn. They found a valley dip with standing boulders they could hide under. Video chose the smaller boulder, while Stereo rested under the larger one. Video found herself staring at the tom, having been hunted by him for the entire spring and half the summer. With a strange misunderstanding rectified within minutes, she was now travelling with him.

Maybe he was still working for the Jester and this was all one big game. All of his genuineness could have been a lie with training from the mage. She wondered if Radio would ever forgive her for what she did, or ever be the bubbly cat who Video first met at the start of their journey. Video thought of herself and how—according to Stereo's claims—she apparently was mischievous and playful at one time in her life. The difference was that Video's memories evidently made her forget how to be happy, while Radio's memories were what took her happiness away.

Was mischief and playfulness really happiness anyway? The thought of such a personality more discomforted Video than anything, but she wondered if that was her, or if it was because she forgot how great it apparently was. Radio didn't give a thought to the repercussions of life. Even Pictures with as dark, cynical, and monstrous as he was, found a way to be carefree when with Radio. It was something Video couldn't even comprehend with the urgency of the mission she faced then and now.

Stereo spoke as though it was good, but she herself had seldom seen the tom happy since the loss of Unit. Was it the same for him in that sense, that Unit had been his happiness, like the Jester was for her at one time? Video wanted to retch just thinking about seeing the mage as a friend and carried on with disgust beside her brother. She thought of the battle she and Stereo just faced with said Jester. Whatever apparent friendship the two had with each other had died with her memories of it.

The idea of it continued to settle in as the day grew longer, though. She curled up and wrapped her tail around herself bitterly. Tears welled in her eyes thinking about how she was a traitor—even to herself without knowing it—and as bad as her mother for befriending a murderous traitor of Social Media.

She closed her eyes and cried silently, hoping she never had kits to have to fear for their safety. It couldn't happen as long as they were able to be pulled away into the webs and nooses of magic. She couldn't face what Signal had to every day. The tom was stuck with having a lifelong, loving companion and two kittens who had affiliated with the enemy. Video was a monster. She would have to dedicate every last breath to make it up to her father for having ever been fond of a mage.

She hoped she hadn't known as a kit that the monkey had magic, but how else would something only found in the tropics live in Media? Video could almost forgive herself if she hadn't realized it then. Was she possibly just *stupid* as a child?

Video startled awake when she saw movement in the corner of her eye. Afraid the Jester would come up from behind her and answer, she let out a sigh of irritation and embarrassment when she saw it was just Stereo standing up. She looked around in case she still wasn't wrong, and then quickly followed her littermate. She barely remembered sleeping, but the sun had already finished rising. It was best they headed out.

Stereo and Video traveled during the entire day, only stopping for a minimal time during the hottest hours of the summer day and reached the cottage in the evening. Video looked at her brother, and asked quietly, "...Stereo, what of Signal? I don't think...the Jester was both of us when Unit died." Signal had killed the tom willingly.

"I don't care," the tom spat. "It's like talking to a rock."

Video nodded slowly and carried on with him. Everyone knew Signal always chose loyalty to the land over blood, but Video also understood Signal's actions. "Unit was...an infiltrator for the mages, Stereo. Even if I had been there...I still would have..."

"I know..." He whispered. The hurt and pain in his voice made Video wonder if Stereo hadn't known about Unit's traitorous intent until it was already too late. Both she and Signal had assumed Stereo had been aware of it the entire time. She frowned and carried on, wondering if

Stereo had chosen to work for the Jester in attempts to justify his former companion's actions for himself. It was too late now though. Video kept her eyes glued to her mother's gardens.

They approached their childhood home to see Jukebox, Audio, and Radio peeking at them through the window.

Audio raced out and embraced Stereo while standing on her back legs, holding the enormous tabby tom with her paws and nuzzling him, but Video took a step back when the lithe small feline approached her next. She looked at Jukebox and Radio instead, who walked out together.

Video gave a nod to Jukebox and her older sister turned to look at Stereo. Radio tucked behind the dark tabby and glared up at Stereo.

"I'm sorry," Stereo whispered. "I'm sorry for everything."

Jukebox nuzzled her younger brother, but Radio frowned and wailed, "You hurt the only family I h-have left." Her voice cracked.

Stereo tipped his head, and murmured his apologies. Video looked at the two and then at Audio. "I'm going back to the Labyrinth to settle this once and for all. Get this all taken care of and don't sweep it under the rug." She growled at her mother and then whipped around to head downhill. It angered her that the feline didn't even flinch or ask why.

Jukebox hurried past Stereo and Radio and came up to Video. "Video, you can't. You're so close to clearing your name and you just brought back Stereo. We at least need answers before you leave. You can't take this upon yourself to go after that mage! Not when you know what it can do..." Worry shimmered in her teal colored eyes.

Video shook her head and kept walking. "I have to. I can't wait any longer. I let the monster get away last time, but it's not happening again. Not after what it did."

"You need to wait for Film and Console, Video!" Jukebox snapped.

Video whipped back when her older sister reached for her with a swipe of her paw and hurried down the hill. "I'll be back!"

"Be safe, Video." Her mother called out.

Video didn't respond, immediately reminded her mother was aware of much more knowledge concerning this dilemma than she ever presented, and continued on her journey back down to the Labyrinth with every hair on her pelt bristled.

- Chapter 7-
Timing

Video strode down the mountain without rest once more. She would only stop to drink and catch something if it came across her path, but she needed to avoid even that. She was too close to finding answers and fixing this, and perhaps possibly even putting an end to the Jester. She was tempted to just start insulting the monkey in her thoughts to lure it to her, but it seemed like it was more likely to end up sulking and hiding from her instead at this point. There was something beyond its shallow mischief and chaos going on here. This murderer was something even more than what it presented itself as.

She travelled back and forth. She moved from the cottage to the Labyrinth; to the Capital City to the Labyrinth. Video used to travel all across Central Media, but now with this Jester about and her being a borderline rogue of Social Media, she could only travel to the strange, enchanted forest; a forest where she apparently frequented quite often as a kit. Video's claws dug into the earth in anger at the thought. She knew Audio sometimes inferred that she had taken Video and Stereo down to the Labyrinth, but Video had always assumed she was mistaking the two of them for her older litter. The three bigger kits were known secretly within the family to have often socialized with the mage Phantascope, brought to the mage by Audio, before Signal put an end to it.

Video swallowed nervously at the thought, knowing that if Signal had effortlessly mangled and broken the calico mage, he likely expected her to do the same to this monkey. She certainly would for the "other" monkey, seeing as how it had somehow led to her losing half her personality. Video's tail gave a lash at that. She wondered for how long her mother and siblings saw her as only half the person she used to be, or even if it was true. At least she made her father proud—the one cat she always wanted to be like—but who says that was the case before she lost her memories? Apparently she had wanted to be like the monkey.

Well, that in itself just made Video glad she lost her memories.

The long-furred tabby approached the dark forest slowly. She wondered what the Jester might have in mind for her now that this had been brought to the surface. She further pondered how it might try to reenact the events. Maybe it would try to give her back her memories now that she was informed of their existence.

That would be a possible way to infect her with false ideas. The idea was over the top, though; he might as well just possess her like he did any other innocent creature. Video scowled and prowled into the brush.

The jungle didn't move when she entered it. If anything it was more still than usual. Video nervously stalked into the dark terrain, looking for any signs of movement or any path that might be awaiting her, but everything just seemed quiet, still, and lifeless.

Video blinked for her eyes to adjust. The more she did, the more the shadows faded from her sight. It was as though the jungle was losing its enchantment. Even the temperature seemed more regular than the sweltering heat Video had experienced whenever she came near the forest. This made her more afraid than walking through it when it was drenched in magic.

She frowned and moved forward, almost forgetting why she was there. She wondered if the Jester was looking for sympathy of some sort, now that the story was they apparently knew each other in the events prior to her mission. That was too bad, because perhaps at one time before it made her kill her companions and had smashed a cube into her skull, that might have been a possibility.

Maybe she could still play the part.

"Monkey?" She called out as relaxed as she could, but then scowled at her own soft voice and carried on with a scoff.

This just solidified the Jester was better off dead if it was this mentally unhealthy. What mage wasn't, though? Radio took a tom as her mate in less than four days!

She screeched when a branch suddenly swung down and nearly struck her spine and then gasped as the monkey swung down from some vines and kicked her across the clearing.

"Well, well, well, if it isn't fancy meeting the cat who finally decided to show up."

"That's not the way it…" Video growled as she got to her paws and glared at the primate. From the kick to the moment she hit the ground, the forest began moving; the shadows were back and the magic energy was overpowering. She looked into the Jester's cold, dark eyes, glaring into the cyan light that flickered in its pupils as it planned its next move.

"Here to end this, Video? That was quite nice of you to offer yourself to me." Video startled as the tree next to her burst into splinters down its side as though it was struck by lightning. She jumped when she felt the Jester's nail press against her throat. "Seeing as that's how easy it is to end you," the monkey sneered.

Video lifted up her chin slowly, indeed not knowing the Jester was really that powerful, and how easily it was about to be her neck that "splintered" if she said the wrong thing. "So be it…"

The Jester sighed, the monkey's eyes softening almost immediately. The mage leaned back. "You really made this difficult. I was pretty excited to play these games—burn Clowder City, murder the Council one by one—but you just keep making me have go back and retrace my steps. You completely ruin my day and make me feel…bad. It's been two weeks now, and I'm still just playing about and doing nothing, you know."

"Are the lives you affect that miniscule to you?" Video thought of the bloodline of nobles the mage killed, the innocent individuals who died as a part of mere *jokes*. Then there was the harm caused to the ones the monkey treated like partners in crime. She blinked when thinking of Pictures and Stereo, possibly Phantascope as well and frowned at the primate. "Who's beyond your mistreatment?"

The monkey shrugged. "I have yet to find someone who is."

Video opened her mouth to speak, but the Jester clapped its hands together and the world fell dark around her.

Video woke up somewhere that was moving. She startled when she realized she was still in the Unending Labyrinth. She felt the unstable vines under her and looked around to see where she was. It looked like she was in the high canopy, with the growth actively moving around her. She couldn't tell if the Jester was even there or not by all the movement. Then she saw the monkey form out of the shadows and walk across the vines with the cube floating beside it. It wasn't wearing the jester outfit for once, making Video tilt her head at it.

"I'm not playing for an audience right now, Video, nor am I dressing for show. I'm just in my abode, dear."

"Then why am I here?"

"Because you're dead." The monkey smiled, letting the cold chill run down Video's spine. She screamed as the branches fell from under her, dropping her into the darkness of the Labyrinth. The drop took the air right from her. She felt as though she was about to go unconscious once more, but was immediately whipped up and swung around a giant tree, and found herself held in the arm of the mage.

Exactly when she took in a breath and looked at the grinning monkey, she was dropped into another pile of vines. She was taken around the jungle as the vines slowly fell apart from the branches and swung her across the canopy. She squealed when the monkey came down and grabbed the vine that supported her while swinging on one of its own, not sure what was coming next. The mage flung her back as it spun on its own swing, and then jumped from the one it stood on to tackle her off of hers.

"No!" She yelled, falling in the air with the laughing primate.

She wasn't going to die as a hero in battle, she was going to die in a shameful dance with a mage using her as no more than a plaything, doing nothing but showing how meaningless and small her life had been and how foolish she was to assume she could possibly fight against the monster.

Without warning, she fell against a woven branch that broke her fall. The vines and moss that made it akin to a launching pad completely stopped her and held her in a stable position. The monkey landed down beside her. She felt the strain of the branches once it did so. She tried to catch her breath and looked up at the monkey as it began to speak.

"You're indeed dead now. You have no purpose outside this Labyrinth unless I tell you otherwise, and you'll never find your way out unless I deem it possible. You're stuck here Video, either until you die or until I see fit. There's nothing you can do to change that, unless you convince me to allow it."

She inhaled first, and then whispered. "How can I convince you?"

The monkey almost seemed offended, leaning back, completely shocked. "Well then, straight to it, Video." The primate grinned. "Well, let me work something out. Work for me. Help me clear up all the things you've held me back from. By our Stars, put me ahead! I'll have no reason to have to kill you for wasting days of my wonderful, unlimited time."

Video had slowly been rising to her paws, but when the Jester was finished, her claws dug into the moss. "No," she choked out.

"Excuse me?" The primate's eyes rounded.

She shook her head and blinked until her eyes refocused and she found herself in the drawing room.

"No! Not again!" She yowled, backing away as tears blurred her vision. She pulled away when she was stopped, looking up into the Jester's brown eyes, the dark blue rims around the mage's pupils glittering.

"It doesn't have to ever happen again if you just stop and listen to me."

Video hissed at the monkey and pulled her face away from the monster's gaze. "No! Never! I'm not making any deals with the likes of you, beast!"

The Jester stared at Video before releasing her, backing away. "Then have at him!"

Video dodged the first attack from Pictures, not sure what to do at this point. She knew this was a nightmare, none of it was supposed to be real, but the Jester *was* real. It was here with her in her dream—a vision at this point—and that wasn't right. She kicked Pictures back with one hind leg and leapt for the Jester, pinning the monkey down.

The dark mage looked up at her with apathy and wrapped its tail around her paws, lifting her away slowly. "This isn't any normal vision, Video. You're going to be stuck here forever if you don't listen to me." It drew closer to her, its teeth baring. "Magic is no fun thing to play around with."

Video's eyes rounded, as she quickly pulled her paws back and clawed the inside of the mage's tail as she freed herself. "No! I'll wake up!" She always did once *he* was gone. Pictures leapt for her and clawed at her side, ripping at her pelt like an insentient beast. She whipped him off of her and pinned him down, at this point just as viciously clawing at his flesh until she saw the black bones of his scorched skeleton.

"Not this time, my dear. I'm here," the Jester said over their battle, watching with darkened eyes as the two cats fought viciously with each other. "And unless you listen to what I have to say, he's just never going to die. You'll be stuck in this dream forever." The monkey scoffed and tripped Video, causing her to stumble and get slashed by the decaying tomcat.

Video composed herself enough to back away from them both. She dodged a leap when Pictures came at her again and then found herself with nothing else to grab onto for retaliation. She looked around for Pictures franticly, not understanding why he was gone now, but then yelled when she was grabbed and thrown down by the Jester.

She looked up as the mage laughed, offering, "What do you say?"

Video tried to free herself, but then screamed when the Jester's face split apart to show Pictures', who leapt for her and sunk his fangs into her neck.

If you die, you're dead for good! The primate's voice rang in her head.

"No!" Video yowled. Her sight went black.

Video's eyes shot open. She wondered if the mage's lack of respect for life was just because it couldn't age and had seen, met, and interacted with so many individuals. The surrounding subjects of Media ultimately lost their purpose as the monkey continued to grow in strength, but yet somehow it still took offense at her not referring to it as a *person* when it saw no value in anyone it came across. She rose up and snarled at the primate, coming up to its form with her claws out. "I came here to kill you!"

"Yes, yes, tell me something new. I'm bored of hearing it, Video. You shouldn't have come here at all, so now you have to pay the price." Video swallowed, but the mage carried on, looking away as she drew even closer. "I don't want to kill you and you don't want to die, so we have to figure out something." The monkey smiled and looked back at her after she stopped; her muzzle was a whisker away from its face.

"No," she growled low against the monkey's face, hoping the fear didn't show in her eyes.

The primate slowly leaned away from her and narrowed its eyes. "Video, you don't get an option and I really don't want to have to demonstrate why, my dear." The mage's eyes softened and it gave her a hopeful smile. It only made her more upset.

She started to respond defiantly, but instead had to catch her bearings. The force of the primate's hit completely dazed her, but what scared her even more was that she didn't have any kind of warning in order to be able to respond. She whipped up to her paws and attacked the spider monkey, but it weaved around her and threw her down again. She yowled when the mage's tail smashed down against her spine, shooting pain all the way down her legs and tail. She only dodged its next attack by a whisker. She whimpered in fear. It was moving too quickly for her. By the time she was ready to attack, she had to dodge the mage's attack instead.

"We have a few seasons to make up for, Video. I won't hide the fact you lost your memories as a kit. It was an unfortunate circumstance, but now that we're being all open with each other, that can change!" The monkey brightened as it caught Video by the tail and proceeded to swing her into a tree.

Video could barely gasp out from the pain; her throat was so constricted from her building fear. She ducked under the mage and grabbed its tail, but the primate lifted her up with it and threw her down again with sudden strength. She kicked it when it went to grab her again and got to her paws. She was finally ready to strike back. She swung her paws at the mage with full force, claws out, going for its face again, but even in its dazed state it still deflected the hits and threw her back.

She didn't know how she could face the creature when it could read her thoughts about it. Any strike afterwards, the Jester was ahead of her. Any hit she succeeded in, it retaliated with twice the force. Video began to tire out, but with the mage's energy cycling out through the artifact. The primate only grew stronger. The mage's hits began to hurt more and more to the point Video wasn't sure if she could get back up. When she finally did, the Jester put her back down.

Attacking was no longer an option. She could barely stay alive.

When she looked up, the cube hovered over her head and the Jester stared down at her with glowing cyan eyes.

"Do you remember this? I don't think you want to go through this again, because it'll happen, and then it'll happen again. I'll make sure it won't kill you. Every time it will knock you out, you'll be with Pictures. You'll wake up, and get hit again. It'll be real fun. I'm sure you'd love dealing with that every second of your waking life."

Video's paws trembled, but she wasn't going to back down! Even if she didn't have the strength to get to her paws and had to struggle to breathe, she could do this. Her immediate flinch when the cube dropped a whisker was all the Jester needed to burst into laughter. At that, sudden tears came from her eyes as reality sunk in.

She had lost.

The monkey approached her slowly, and then lifted up its hand to strike her again.

Alarm shot through every aching nerve in her body. *No more!* Her thoughts pleaded.

The Jester lowered its hand.

She had to agree, even if only for now. She had to figure out terms though, something to keep her plans from being conspicuous. "You said allow the possibility that I won't be here forever. Will I ever be free?"

"Yeah, maybe." The monkey smiled as it brought its cube back to its side.

"I'll work to get my freedom if that's what you request..." *Monster, barely an animal.*

"You also just answered what else you have to correct."

Video's eye twitched, realizing it caught her thoughts. "...If that's all, *sir.*" Video narrowed her eyes into slits.

The monkey clapped, his eyes bright with excitement. "Ooh! Yay!" The mage twirled, then straightened up and looked around. "This is going to be so much fun! Just think of the trouble we're going to get into once you're all healed up! Wait, watch!" The mage bounded up to the branches and vines. Video stared until the primate stopped and looked up at her expectantly.

She frowned, the distress beginning to set in from what she agreed to, even more so to see the primate wanted her to follow. She was barely able to lift her tail after the monkey beat her into submission. She started to shake her head, but then screeched when he blasted her with magic.

Immediate strength flooded through her limbs. The pain subsided; even her headache cleared. Her eyes rounded with complete surprise and horror as she looked down to see her injuries were almost completely gone. The mage left enough so she still felt the pain of each hit, but not enough to keep her down. Yet her facial pain, the deep scratches Radio had given her, was no longer burning. She brushed them with her tail to verify her assessment and they were indeed gone. Her ear, her face, the side of her head, it was all smooth with fur. She had just been subjected to the mage's healing ability.

Next came the realization the mage made mention of unlimited time. She could only hope that it was a simple healing spell and that this really wasn't forever.

The primate impatiently clapped for her to stand, then gestured her to follow. She blinked, then got up and reluctantly followed him down the canopy and to the low branches of the jungle. She wasn't sure what she had actually agreed to, or how she would help with all this trouble, but knew if there was a possibility of her not spending an ageless life wandering around an ever moving jungle, an eternity entrapped with Pictures in the drawing room, or getting hit by the cube as her companions were out there suffering, she was going to see where it led. She would need to if she wanted to return to her family. She had to make it through this.

What Video didn't expect was the tedious, forever-long tour and friendliness from the Jester.

The two travelled for days together in the jungle. The Jester pointed out everything Video needed to know if he was ever to assign her with a task. There were certain things he would stop explaining, as though waiting for her to finish his sentence and tell him something about the jungle, but she never could. She never knew what he wanted her to say either. She wondered if it had been something they talked about when she was a kitten, or if he thought Audio taught her more of the jungle than she really had. Audio knew the jungle in and out and knew every plant that was inside it, but that was something she said Video could learn if Video decided to pursue herbology. Maybe the monkey just didn't trust the power of his own spell and figured she would have remembered something by now.

Sorry, you were successful at obliterating anything I once had. It hurt to be around the mage knowing it, even more so for having given into his demand. She didn't even know herself anymore, if she was so willing to give up her dedication in fear of death. Her chest became tight. She had to fight to breathe with how constricted her throat was, and she was tired all the time. All she could think about was what a failure she was and how she completely ceased to object to anything the Jester had asked since. Where were her loyalties after her family did everything they could to help her? What would they and Film think of her now? Film had even reminded her that the mage problem wasn't her responsibility or mission. Video had the chance of clearing her name and presenting the Radio Star to the council alive, but instead she threw it all away.

With the primate staring at her with concern, Video snapped back into the topic at hand. Video planned to eventually learn medicine, but certainly not from a psychotic monkey mage.

"Is this what you did to Phantascope too? Did you trap the cat here to be Audio's guide until Signal took matters out of your hands?"

The monkey blinked taken aback by the sudden accusation and continued on the path, not finishing his lecture on the plant life he had been showing Video. Video frowned, but didn't apologize. It was a question she wanted to know too badly to take back.

"The story of the Shadow Advisor is a bit more complex than being a guide for lost mothers and mischievous kittens, darling Video," he said quietly.

Video shrugged, and lifted up her chin, letting her brow give the slightest arch. Depending on how long the mage could tolerate her guilt and loathing, "We have an eternity."

"Hmm…" The monkey smiled, and looked back over at Video. "Fair enough, which means you have an eternity you can wait."

Video growled, her ears flattening against her head. She prowled behind the primate with a lashing tail.

They had spent days together and yet the monkey made no move to give her tasks, leave the jungle, or really do anything besides talking about the terrain and explain absolutely everything earthly possible about it to Video. She wondered if that was the deadline to when he'd publicize her disloyalty to Media, when she knew every inch and branch and plant the blasted jungle had to offer.

Video didn't even know if it was day or night because of the thick canopy, or how many days had actually transpired. She could barely see the sky when they were in the heart of the jungle, if at all. Besides that, whenever the communication between the two was too much for Video and she broke down because of betraying her family and throwing away everything they fought for, the Jester would get annoyed enough by her distress that she would get a sleeping spell and not wake up until she calmed down. They might be here for months before she was allowed anything besides the tour at their current pace, but Video would make the best out of it until she could escape.

Radio watched the events of Media boredly from Audio's personal monitor, flipping the channels to the different parts of Central Media one at a time. She even saw Receiver and Transmitter walking around happily once, and Faith walking a little troop of baby weasels and stoats around her village on an autumn tour. At least they were alive and well, all without holes in their necks.

Unlike her.

She sighed and turned off the monitor, pressing her head against the wood surface of the counter that held the small screen. Signal had walls of monitors in every shape and size in his office; however, he did nothing but leave Audio with a single monitor in her tiny little space she called her office, a monitor in the kitchen he could watch when eating, and one in the living room.

Jukebox, her kitten and Stereo did nothing but lounge in the living room all summer. The little kitten had come up to stay with his mother while his father worked in the unit in charge of repairing Clowder City, and the boy quickly became a member of the household. The three always were together, watching the region-wide reports and listening for updates from Console and Film, or looking another sighting of Video. Radio even sometimes caved and joined them, but their daily routine didn't change when the season was over. She looked out one of the windows to gaze at the amber-colored trees outside. It seemed like everyone was waiting for a message to come back from either Video or the Jester.

The mage and his new companion were sometimes seen outside the Unending Labyrinth and Calotype's Forest, but it never seemed to go well. It was like the Jester was attempting to bring Video out in the open—wearing a mask like her brother had so that the others didn't recognize her—but it never ended well for him. He usually seemed to give up and lead her back after she would start panicking. Radio didn't understand why he wouldn't just mind control her like the other animals, but knew from what he inferred in the jungle was that it took a weak participant to have full mind control, and Radio knew Video wasn't that, no matter how distressed she was.

Everyone's worries were on Video, Film, and Console. Radio was lucky if she was checked on twice a day besides the mealtimes. Audio had given her lectures that they weren't her servants and were family, but Radio still didn't see why it would be so hard to peek a head in on her once in a while, especially after knowing the kittens were due in a day or so.

Radio rubbed her paw against her head and rose up to walk around the halls of the monitor part of the cottage, grumbling as her belly fur brushed against the ground. Maybe she could talk to Signal again and try and pick up from their bad start of first meeting each other. It's the least she could do, considering how close she was with his son. She looked toward the living room to see the two puffballs and the kitten watching their reports, Jukebox raking the top of Stereo's head with her claws when the reminder of the Clowder City attack came on the screen.

Radio's pelt twitched with discomfort. She had to keep her eyes from watering again as she went out of sight of the living room. It had been months. The city had recovered, yet it still hurt to know Stereo was capable of such destruction. His own nephew was there when that happened and was sitting beside him now. Had he known that?

She walked slowly, sighing as she looked down the walls. The hallways were long, merging between the tree itself that made the main part of the home, and the structures the family built attached to it. She still wondered how much of this was made with the help of the Council's resources and how much Signal had done himself. Audio probably told her, but she always forgot. One thing Radio did notice was that she felt a welcoming feeling when going through the house, a feeling that drew her back to it no matter how many times during her bad days she wanted to stray. What surprised her was the warmth put a color in her mind. She often thought of red when wandering the halls, and even more so while she approached the Monitor's room.

She peeked in through the slightly open doorway and pushed her paw forward to open the door the rest of the way. Radio winced as it creaked to let the blind tomcat know someone had entered. She looked inside the room and saw the giant earth-colored tabby was busy moving the controls of his devices. She realized just how unclever it was that she would approach the tom in the one room he could see in, being cursed by a mage to see nothing but his surveillance monitors and the aura of magic. He always had his door closed this summer, though. So far there had been no luck changing during the fall until now.

She was known—throughout the whole household anyway—for having bartered with the primate for magic. Since that hadn't been discussed until after she threw her collar at the gigantic tom, Radio was sure his opinion of her only sunk since. After also knowing what the tom was capable of doing to mages, she didn't ever want to approach him for that reason either, seeing as how the scratch across Video's face made by Radio was quite similar to the marks across Signal's eyes. Not that he would know that, of course. Radio wasn't sure if he ever checked on Video after the mission for the crystal fragments.

Radio swallowed and closed the door again, making her way toward the living room. There would have to be a day for her to approach the tom and it wasn't today.

It was then she heard the door open. She saw Signal leave the room. She blinked with surprise as he walked in the opposite direction as her, going toward the kitchen instead of coming at her with questions. Radio glanced at the inviting open door, the light of the monitors shining out from the otherwise dark room.

Radio's tail waved. After one more cautious glance in the direction Signal had gone, she raced into his office straight for the knobs that controlled the monitors. She had to stand on her back paws to be able to reach them, stretching out her front paws past her expectant belly to stay balanced, but she didn't let that hold her back. She began flicking and pressing the toggles that would bring her to the Unending Labyrinth, pressing the manual control to take over for the active drone closest to the area, and began flying it into the mysterious forest.

She moved and fussed with it carefully, hoping not to knock it into a tree and have to explain that to Signal. Radio began guiding it to the core of the forest, hoping to come across the Jester or Video to be able to have some update on the two. There would only be so much time before one could make the next move if either was still alive and she had to find out who it would be. She was even more shocked when she actually came across the two of them, travelling together step by step through the forest. Video was listening intently as the Jester spilled out details about the Labyrinth and how it worked. Anger built up in Radio's chest, pumping right up against her healing wound, which just made the fury rush to her head.

That *hypocrite!*

Video blinked when she thought she heard a small noise from the distance and looked around, but didn't see anything out of the ordinary.

"Is there something wrong?"

"No, I don't think so." Video answered monotonously, and looked back to the Jester. Even if something was, it was probably best Video left that for *someone else* to find out. The two of them slowly made their way back to the high canopy.

"Why don't we ever leave the forest, mage? Outside of the Labyrinth, even? I know it's only been a few days–"

"A few days?" The primate stopped and asked.

"Yes…?" Why was there a question there?

"You really don't…" He frowned when he started his question, and then shook his head. "Well, aren't you up for a disappointment." The spider monkey chuckled, and then continued forward.

Video blinked, and looked at the primate with offense. She didn't like that phrase, not after the monkey told Radio the same thing when she thought Pictures was still alive. She wanted to ask, but looked around instead. Nothing in the jungle had changed, and the monkey always carried on from topic to topic consistently, so she wasn't sure what it could mean. It could mean anything. Video was startled by her own thoughts, realizing she was in denial. She was afraid to think about it, if she was honest with herself.

Video travelled in silence until she saw something shining from below. She looked to the monkey, waiting for him to explain and elaborate on the sight, but instead, he just kept moving. She looked around for his cube as it wasn't beside him either, but the light from below was too bright even for the cyan artifact.

"Um, *sir?*" She chirped.

The monkey shook his head. "That can be explained another day."

Video sighed, frustrated at addressing him for no reason, and continued following him back to the high canopy. Her tail gave a single lash before she caught up with him. The vines were wobbly, but the travel wasn't ever beyond what she could manage. She just didn't have the grip that he did, without clawing the vines apart.

They settled in the usual spot, the hammocks hanging all around the core of the jungle, high enough that is was impossible to see from below, but still well hidden enough that the drones couldn't locate it from above, either.

Video stretched out her paws, trying to focus on them to clear her thoughts, and then curled up in her hammock. She tried to close her eyes and think of darkness, but the waves of magic kept her awake. She opened her eyes and looked through the vines of her bed, watching as the Jester wove a new bed to sleep in. Video once had assumed perhaps at one time there were more spider monkeys that lived in the jungle and that was why there were so many hammocks and nests, but instead it seemed the monkey made himself a new bed every time he slept.

"Why are you alone, sir?" she asked, her soft voice filling the silence of the night. *Besides possibly killing everyone who was once there for you.*

The monkey finished growing himself a moss pillow, and stared at Video. "I'm never alone." He answered and his cube floated up beside him. "I could say the same to you, Video," he scoffed, "It's not like you get visitors."

Video ignored him. "Besides the cube, besides me, besides all your partners in crime." Video poked her head up from her hammock and looked at him with her ear flicking. She knew spider monkeys travelled in troops—often in very large families—but this other monkey being mentioned as a whisper didn't seem like that. Other than that, this primate was completely alone. *"Did* you kill them all?"

He sighed, and rested his arms on the edge of his hammock, looking back at her. "I wish it had been my choice to decide, but no, actually. I didn't."

Video blinked and gave a small knead of her paws, waiting for him to elaborate.

The Jester arched his brow at her, and then swung his tail back and forth. "I have no reason to tell you anything, Video. You're a kit. You don't understand."

"Besides the fact that you want to share it. You want your story heard, Jester." She lifted up her chin. "Behind all the fake sulking, moping, and playfulness, there is a temper and frustration behind your action. No one knows your side of things, or why you do it."

Irritation flashed in the primate's eyes, proving Video's point, but it quickly dulled as he responded smoothly, "Maybe speculating is best. Everyone can think of me as they please and I can laugh about it."

Video blinked and replied quietly, "Only for so long, Jester."

The primate snapped his fangs and his eyes narrowed. Video dipped her head and folded her paws beneath her to seem less confrontational.

The mage frowned, guilt washing away the anger, but then scoffed and looked away. "How do these stories go? Do I start from the beginning?"

Video tried not to give an immediate response. With some thought given into his words, this primate was regenerative and seemingly ageless, that meaning there might be a lot of history he had to offer. "Yes, if you wish, sir."

"Yes, it is a *long* story. See, before, the barrier was free for mages to move through. I figured out how to close it to other magic a couple winters ago—thank the Queen." The primate shook his head before furthering, "When it was open, there was a population of spider monkeys who frequented Media, descendants of the western land's co-leader, Sanity, if what their elders told them was to be believed." Video wanted to ask about the co-leadership, wondering about the other rulers of the lands outside of Media, but the mage continued without elaborating on it. "The two lands Sanity and Queen Satisfaction reigned over are connected by a bridge without the barrier, so the tale doesn't seem farfetched. Just as Sanity had provided with her own people, the monkeys protected the remaining mages of Media from the new rulers. They offered shelter to any lost individual trying to find their path. Sometimes they were too allowing."

Video already was upset at the mood of the story changing, but listened silently as the primate explained, "One lost mage they helped was different from the rest, you see. He had the Capital and nobles specifically looking for him, having been a part of a bad incident concerning the safety of the followers of your new rulers. The monkeys offered him shelter, food, and friendship, not knowing the dangers that awaited them by doing so. They went as far as trusting the cat with their young, leaving the cat to watch over the growing troop while they searched for more stray mages to assist. One was a rather disobedient young monkey." The mage chuckled, his eyes filled with thought and melancholy.

Video didn't have to wonder who the child was before the Jester carried on, "The mage and the monkey somehow still bonded even with the small one's temper. Between the cat's lack of knowledge of proper magic and the monkey beginning to learn his, the two were at the same level. They often practiced together while the rest of the troop was away. After hearing of a further power though, the mage left, realizing he still wasn't mastering his magic. He decided he needed to seek out an artifact to boost his current power. He abandoned the boy with promises to return with the Queen's work. When he became a target at his next destination, the nobles followed the trail and found the monkey troop."

Video wasn't sure how to respond when the Jester moved his hands to his face, shaking his head again. "They slaughtered everyone they found, killing the fathers, mothers, children and elders. The boy survived the attack, slowly bleeding out as the so-called 'nobles' moved on the trail to find the strange tri-colored mage. The cat came back, having his cube to show the boy, but he was too late. Everyone else was dead, and the boy was soon to be, too."

The monkey looked away from Video, his brow furrowing. "The cat promised the boy that he would avenge his family, and would make things right by taking down the new leaders and their honored nobles, but he didn't!" The primate barked with fury. "He instead busied himself for years with his own priorities, only thinking back to the young child he trained with once it was too late, and there was nothing that could save him." The mage's fingers curled until his fist clenched, and he looked to Video. "Other means had to be taken into consideration."

"Phantascope was a dormant mage until the last few weeks of the cat's life, when he..?"

"He," the Jester's eyes rounded when he answered, but he nodded in verification.

Video remembered that Audio also referred to Phantascope as an individual, but she had loathed the idea until now. "...went haywire with his magic and began striking patrols and aggravating Signal. It was to the point Signal decided to burn the Labyrinth to flush him out." Video wasn't going to mention her father saying the mage was weak to fire, but somehow she could tell the Jester could see her thoughts about it anyway. "Signal had to end the mage himself once it attacked his kits. It was you, until the Labyrinth was burned, wasn't it? You drove the mage to insanity until he thought the only action left was to strike down Signal and his family for burning down his home."

The Jester scowled. "One might tell the story that way." The spider monkey stared over at Video again, the anger replaced with a malicious grin. "We all do strange things with the right motivation."

Video didn't really like how the mage acted under stress, because it did nothing but bring pain to others. "It's a sad story."

"It's one to learn from, though, Video."

Video wasn't sure if she could agree on the same points the monkey, but she still gave a nod. "What was the Shadow Advisor's name...before the Council verified him?"

The monkey blinked in surprise, and looked at her. "Why do you want to know?"

Video frowned, but admitted, "My mother said that he hated the title, and always requested her to call him no more than her advisor. He never told her his name, though."

"He never lasted anywhere long enough to keep one." The Jester snorted.

"Everyone has a name. I'll bet even you do, sir." Video blinked slowly. Media always encouraged to not use anyone's birth name once they were verified. Video always thought it was something that originated from the technology culture, but perhaps it was something which had been adopted from the mages, too. Names seemed to be an important thing to both worlds.

"Yes, perhaps." He scowled.

Video blinked. "Will you tell me Phantascope's name?"

The Jester winced and glared just as much as Video ever imagined the Shadow Advisor would have when Audio used the title. He shook his head and said, "His name was Curiosity."

Video never heard the word as a name before, but it sent a strike of timidness and uncertainty through her bones. She shivered, then blinked and relaxed herself. "Are mages often named after...attributes?"

The monkey looked surprised. "Yes, actually; we're named by our mentors, titled by what we cause in others or define ourselves as."

Video couldn't help it, "So Wisdom was wise?"

The Jester burst out laughing, surprising Video enough to make her fur rise on end. He shook his head. "I'll bet he liked to think so."

Video shook her head, letting out a breath in the closest way to a laugh she could muster. "What a strange aspect. I don't think the Council really has a reason why they pick the names they do for us. I don't think they know some of the purposes for the technology they verify us with."

"I never thought so, either." The Jester smiled, looking surprised at Video.

Video realized she had actually just spoken ill of her leaders and curled up in her hammock. It was hard to keep herself from shaking. She found herself thinking about Phantascope being friends with the young child this mage once was and thought back to how she was once a kitten the monkey became friends with, apparently, until he was driven to take that away from her for her own protection. What was the entire story? Video didn't know, but wondered if perhaps at the end of all of this she might understand, and possibly indeed learn something from it.

She just had to figure out what it was.

- CHAPTER 8 -
HYMN

Video was surprised to wake to the sun in her eyes, and rubbed her paws in front of her face to hide it until she realized it had been days since she had seen the sun. The revelation startled her. She quickly rose, nearly falling out of her bed from the suddenness. She was still here. She blinked, and looked up from her hammock to the open canopy and looked over to see the Jester sprawled out, sunning his dark pelt.

She wondered how easily his exposed skin burned under the sun and her brow shot up with surprise at her thoughts. She left the monkey to rest while she climbed down the canopy to get herself some water, happy to take advantage of the peace. Maybe she could find a snack, too, but she doubted she could make it that far before the Jester decided to screech from the trees to scare off everything just for a laugh.

Thoughts of the story from the night before were still fresh in her head, as well as the meaning of the names of the mages, but she wasn't sure what she was to do with the information yet. She'd just have to handle it as it came to her. The less she thought of it the better to not disturb the mage, anyway. She had to just focus on finding a water source and starting the day.

Video had to wonder about the possibility of her family coming to get her instead, or Film and Cinema wanting to get a statement from her before clearing her name. Did it even matter at this point, though? Video gave it all up when she thought she could take on the Jester and now she was under his beck and call as he pleased. She looked up into the trees, but the monkey hadn't stirred at all, so she carried on further away.

She wondered if it heard less thoughts, or maybe quieter thoughts, if they were further away. She supposed with the mage's barrier able to stretch across all of Media and his own ability to teleport where he wanted at any given time it was unlikely, but she could still try to give him some space. Hopefully just so she could think freely without being bothered. She couldn't imagine being able to hear every thought about herself, or to herself. She was lucky she wasn't well known in the land, but the Jester had been broadcast to all of Central Media and possibly beyond. She had to give thought to how much attention he tried to bring to himself and how much evil he did to become known. Did he like it?

Being ageless might draw someone into wanting something different, but Video never imagined the Jester could be doing all this just to desperately make a change in his life in order to keep his mind off other things. It made sense from what the mage said about losing people over and over again that he possibly had a lot of past to bury. She couldn't imagine destroying a third of a city and making a king vanish was the way anyone but he would go about it, though. *You could be doing good things, you know.*

Video startled when the Jester called from his hammock, "It's easier for people to think negatively than positively!"

The marbled tabby cat looked up again to see if the mage had moved, but he still laid there, only his head leaning over the hammock to glare at her. She thought of how little she trusted people after the betrayals she faced, how even she had betrayed her family to end up travelling with him now. Her trial was corrupted, the people she killed had been manipulated, and her brother had been fooled to believe it was her. It all came down to the Jester with everything that had gone wrong in her life, down to losing her memories as a kit. She had to disagree, anything bad which had happened was because of the one bad thing she couldn't shake off her back.

She had everything she had ever wanted until that point: her father's respect, her mother's love, her siblings to help as well as to count on. It had been a good life, even if it was short lived. Video hadn't even made it to her second autumn yet.

Had the Jester just always created his own problems? She clamped her jaw shut as well as, hopefully, her thoughts. She decided to keep going. It was better not to think about it while they had to deal with each other. She might make it if she just contained her constant frustration with things.

Video found a stream and followed it, hoping for a small pool she could drink from without having to stretch too far down. The water always was refreshing and was the only cold thing the Labyrinth had to offer. There was nowhere else in Media that had an enchanted heat and tropical climate. Video almost felt safe to admit she admired it, if she hadn't been raised to believe that magic was so awful. Audio always had a different perspective, and had defended it. Video always had resented that until now. From what she saw these past few days, it started to sink in that magic itself wasn't evil—it was the holder.

She had first thought Radio, Pictures, and the Jester were all unjustified in their actions and that this was a consistent trait of mages, but the only consistent thing about it was the Jester's manipulations. Radio had been such a sheltered feline there had been not a single unverified subject in Media who knew her name save her personal servants. Radio had felt compelled to trust the people she knew she was to travel with during what Video knew was her first mission. Pictures—from what Video heard him saying to Radio as well as in his reports—had been through countless homes and families growing up. Video wouldn't put it past the Jester to have meddled with his childhood like he had with Video's. Maybe he had his reasons and confusions orchestrated by the monkey too. If his eye was a spell in which the Jester could watch and see his every move, that was confirmation more than anything.

Video shuddered, and then realized she had reached a shallow enough dip to be able to reach the water. She relaxed her shoulders and her mind, deciding to just enjoy taking a long drink.

The water chilled her bones and gave her goosebumps. She lapped it up with relief, her tail swaying back in forth as she drank. No water tasted better than it did in the Labyrinth and Video wasn't afraid to admit it. She raised her head up and licked her jaws, then started walking down the stream again. She still heard no prey in the jungle, but if she had time to get far enough, there might be some in the richer parts of the area, especially if she could get to the woodlands of Calotype's Forest.

As she followed the current though, she realized that she wasn't going to the outer forest. The vines instead were coming closer together, and she was going deeper into the Unending Labyrinth. She had thought she had learned everything there was to the jungle, and that where she slept was the heart of it, but she realized where she was headed was toward that glow she had seen earlier. The aura she felt when she was first touring with the Jester.

She started forward, curiosity getting the best of her, but then heard the Jester clear his throat. Video looked to the trees, watching as the monkey mage slowly made his way toward her.

Video gave a wave of her tail as she looked up at the primate. "What's back there?" She asked.

"Nothing of your concern or interest..." He growled, dropping down.

The fluffy tabby had to admit she was proud she didn't flinch. Instead, she puffed out her chest. She wanted to object to his assumption. This was the second time she had come across the strange area, but she would give it one more time before she demanded to know. She nodded and leapt over the stream, now heading out toward the forest. She saw the stream split into a fork and looked to the mage for an opinion on which way to take in case she should jump across again, but he only shrugged as he followed her.

Her tail flicked, and she followed the path to the right. Once the Jester pulled his cube out from the canopy and began flipping it around to look at various images, Video asked, "What are we doing today?"

"I'm figuring that out right now." He mumbled in a reply.

Video scoffed and padded on, her tail starting to lash when the Jester continued, "You're starting to get too nosy, going in places you don't need to be, feeling bold enough to leave my side. I need to put you to work somehow."

Video looked at him apprehensively. "I could just...stay at your side if that's easier. I just meant to get a drink."

"No, no, I want to find something for you to do."

Regret of ever dreading the tour flooded through Video. The Jester hadn't asked anything more than for her to follow along, go to sleep, or eat, but a favor? Something to do? What was he planning? She knew he alone probably could answer her thoughts, but he remained silent.

"Ooh! I have something!" The monkey ran past her and hurried alongside the stream with his tail waving.

"What is it?" Fear built up in Video's chest at the excitement he expressed.

"We're going to catch that sister of yours and that pretty little monitor."

Video stopped in her tracks. "What?"

The monkey slowed his pace gradually, and then stopped as well to look back at her. "They entered the forest this morning. I'm going to take them out."

"Who's the monitor?" Pretty and small, did Settings come to help?

The Jester looked at her with a furrowed brow. "That gold flecked one with the curled ears and really long tail."

That tom was taller than her father! She was even more upset to see that the Jester wasn't afraid of that, though. The idea of the mage taking down a cheetah rushed into her head. "N-No, we can't do that." Video hurried up to the Jester. "It's already bad enough I threw away everything they did for me. You can't hurt them; they've worked so hard, they're trying to do good." She quickly stepped in front of the monkey and looked up at him. "Please, please, give them a chance. Just let them wander for a bit before they get lost and they can just go. I'm sure they won't bother us again."

"Video, you know anyone who enters doesn't return. I'm responsible for that." Video's eyes rounded with horror. The Jester stretched out his limbs and posed, gloating, "Yes, the one and only, it was me all along." He straightened out his posture and kept walking. "And if they come in here, and leave, saying they need reinforcements, we're just going to repeat that little story I shared with you last night. They'll come with their fire, destroy my work, flush you out, and I'll have to kill them all to get you back. We don't want that, right?"

"No!" Video wailed.

"Then you'll accept me popping off these two, so that way not *everyone* dies, right?"

Video's eyes watered. "Can I just speak with them, first? I can tell them that I...live here now, and that I don't need my named cleared and they can just live happily with Radio." *And her kittens.* Video swallowed as her thoughts threatened to give the information away. "No one has to die, and they'll understand and just leave. I'll say I never saw you here and that it's safe for me."

The Jester scoffed and looked at her skeptically. "Lie to your own family? Why Video, that sounds so unlike you–"

"Just let me!" Video snarled, making the monkey lean back with wide eyes.

He stared at her for a good couple of seconds, then chuckled and relaxed. "Okay, if you're sure. I'll let you do it your way." He rose up his hand and waved it at her playfully.

"Good. Thank you," Video whispered. She was amazed the Jester actually was giving her family a chance, giving her a chance. She nodded quickly and then carried on with her chin raised.

The Jester chuckled from behind her and followed before Video stopped and looked back at him, realizing, "I don't know where they are."

"I wondered when you'd ask." The monkey smiled. "You actually figured it out sooner than I thought."

Video scowled, but the Jester clapped his hands together and cyan lights lit up in a trail. "Follow the lights, and you'll find your darling family and brute of a tom."

"I thought he was 'pretty and small'."

"In some ways he's both." The Jester blinked one eye at her in the vaguest of winks.

Video gawked at the monkey in horror, clamped her jaw shut, and took after the lights.

The lights led her along the stream for a while, but then took her into the forest closer to the border. The Jester likely took them around in circles, already with changing the area. They probably didn't make it far. She wondered about the Jester looking through his cube and doubted he had actually discovered the two right then. He said himself they had entered in the morning. She looked at the noon sun and decided to pick up the pace.

Within moments the darkness of the canopy took away the sun and she was left roaming within the shadows, the only light being the magic in front of her. She chased after them rapidly, her claws retracting from the pressure of her paws hitting the ground. She needed to get to them quickly, before the Jester changed his mind. She followed the lights all the way to the border until they stopped.

They stopped right at a large wall of brush and Video speculated as to whether or not the Jester led her this way just for a dramatic entrance. She could smell her sister's fragrance of daisies from here and knew she was on the other side. Within a few more steps she heard them speak.

Excitement to see a family member after so many days in the jungle overtook Video. She leapt through the brush and skidded to a halt in front of the two, coming up to Jukebox immediately and brushing her cheek along her sister's. "Jukebox!"

"Oh, by the Stars, Video, you're still okay! We've been catching glimpses of you for an entire season! So much has happened!" Jukebox's brow arched at Video's silence and round-eyed look, and then determined, "Come on, we're going home." She grabbed Video by the scruff and started pulling her toward the mountain.

Video squealed, not being used to the strength of her older sister. She dug her paws in but Jukebox still had a steady grip on her and kept pulling. Film stared in shock before Video started to panic. She shoved her paw against her sister's muzzle and pulled away. "No! I can't, I'm sorry." She shook her head and stepped back.

"Video, you have everyone worried sick, Radio said she found you with the Jester and decided you needed to be corrected in your behavior. We've been watching and waiting and walking and worrying..." Jukebox's tail lashed when Video arched her brow, continuing, "We can't lose you like we did Stereo, Video. We got him back and I'm not about ready to give you up, either." Her eyes softened, "He and Radio are parents now and my kit is half grown!"

She approached Video again, but the slightly smaller feline stepped further away, shaking her head. "What...? It's only been a week, Jukebox."

Jukebox blinked, and then shook her head. "No...Video, it's been more than that. Radio had her kittens...there's three of them. She went into labor after seeing you with the Jester. We headed out then. Film finally got a breakthrough with the Council so he could come. He is here to get you and present you to the Council with Radio. They're going to give you both your titles back and clear your names. We have to go."

Video looked at her sister in alarm over the revelation, but she had to stay true to her word to the Jester if she wanted them to live. She wanted to rejoice and run off with them, but now the kittens really were at stake. "I can't, Jukebox! I live here now." She tried to think of what she told the Jester she would say and the words rushed from her mouth. "You don't need to worry about clearing my name anymore. Just get Radio protected and pour your resources into her and getting Stereo vindicated instead of me. He had been manipulated by the Jester just like Radio had and...I'm starting to think Pictures was, too. He empathized with a bleeding heart...like he told us from the start. It was all a mistake on my part. I shouldn't have done what I did."

Both Film and Jukebox stared at Video in absolute confusion and suspicion.

"Are you really Video? That won't work twice, you know. Stereo told me the whole thing." Jukebox raised up her claws menacingly.

"Yes! It's really me and I'm telling on you if you hit me!" Video squeaked.

"Oh, yeah, it's her." Jukebox lowered her paw and shook her head at Film before turning back to Video. "We've seen you with the Jester, Video. I'm not leaving you alone with that creep any longer."

Anger sparked in Video's eyes, which made her pelt bristle from her ear tufts to her tail-tip. "It was looking for me when the recording showed it to you! I taught it a lesson and chased it off. This is my home now. I'm not letting anything, or anyone, take it away from me."

Video's breath quickened when she said it and Film's eyes narrowed. "Wait, she's lying, she only does that when she lies."

Jukebox scoffed, lifting up her chin. "She'd do it all the time as a kitten."

"I never lied when I was a kit!" Video hissed.

"Not that you *remember*," Jukebox drawled as her tail lashed.

Video jerked away, taken aback by the realization that she really wouldn't. It hit her like a blast of magic straight to the chest and she couldn't even choke out a response. That's why it was autumn now. Because it happened *again*. She lost another season of her life to this mage. Jukebox saw the reaction and began to respond, but Video's face went expressionless and her eyes hooded as she did anything and everything she could to compose herself and keep her emotions down.

"Video, wait!" Jukebox yelled, alertness flooding into her sea-colored gaze.

She jumped back when Jukebox reached for her and ran out from the clearing, only looking back when she heard the Jester drop down on the two. "Hello!"

"No!" Video yowled, whipping around.

The monkey was pulling up the roots from under the two, knocking them up in the air. Video rushed back to them, but the vines held her down. Jukebox flipped into the air and dropped onto the monkey, biting his face and pulling him down with sudden strength and fierceness. The monkey screeched and ripped Jukebox off of him, but was yanked by the tail by Film and swung into the closest tree.

Video skidded to a halt when she saw the cube flash past her shoulder. She couldn't take another hit from it and one glare from the Jester made her freeze in place. She swallowed and her eyes watered as the Jester flung a blast of cyan magic at the tomcat and grabbed her sister. He barked at her and tumbled down with her when she grabbed his throat and yanked him down again. The two battled in a frenzy as Film fought against the vines that pulled at his legs and held him back, wrapping around his neck and tugging him away from the battle.

The Jester jumped free of Jukebox and swung his cube into her skull, knocking her out cold.

Video screamed as her sister dropped to the ground, limp, and ran back to them, the anger and fear for the two overpowering any fear she had for the Jester and his magic. The Jester scooped up Jukebox, tossed her into the brush, and then leapt for Video and threw her down.

The air was knocked out of her as she landed on her back and the Jester slammed his hand down on her throat, cutting her gasp of air short.

She tried to struggle rapidly, shoving her back legs into the Jester in a panic, but his eyes stayed cold and menacing, narrowing into slits as she continued to struggle.

"I'll make them suffer longer if you don't stop," he growled low.

Video stiffened, and pulled back as the tears came back into her eyes. She shook her head as she closed her eyes and curled her paws back to herself.

The Jester let her go, making her open her eyes to see him glaring at her before turning back to Film.

The giant smoky tabby tugged against the vines under the gaze of the Jester, his eyes rounding as he stared at Video. "Go for his throat! Don't stop until he's behea–" Film's words were cut short as vines wrapped around his head. He clamped his jaw shut to snap the vines caught in his mouth and yowled. He stared at Video fiercely, but Video remained frozen and on the ground as the Jester laughed and spun the cube menacingly. She looked over at Film pleadingly, hoping he remembered his words acknowledging she couldn't take another hit to her head.

Did it really matter, though? Video wasn't going to remember the rest of her life, anyway. She looked up at the primate, remembering how Stereo started at his chin then worked his way down to the throat to push the primate's metal choker back. While the Jester looked up, it was a clear shot. She could save them all.

But what if she failed?

"Run, Video. It's hopeless," the Jester whispered as he stepped off of her. He stomped on her tail, shooting pain up her spine and making her yowl in alarm. She scrambled to her paws. The Jester hit her across the face, knocking her in the other direction. "Run, or I won't stop here!"

Video turned her head and looked Film in the eyes. She saw the final gaze in his golden spheres, a look of both dismay and disappointment as her eyes once again pleaded for his understanding. She turned away for the brush. She couldn't do it, she couldn't see more, and she couldn't risk the Jester hurting anyone more. If he took his anger to the Rich Top Mountains, Video couldn't live with herself. She had to protect her parents, Radio, and the kits if she was to ever make it out of the jungle alive, losing half her memories or not.

She leapt through the thick growth and kept going, hearing the tom's screams and shouts as she bolted into the trees and headed into the canopy far away from them.

Video crawled the rest of the way once she found a tree with a hollow. Tears streamed down her face when she was left alone with her pathetic self, knowing she had abandoned her own flesh and blood and the tomcat who had risked everything for her. Her body wracked out a sob. She curled up into the hollow. Video wrapped her tail around her face and ears, shutting out any noise her mind was still imagining and cried. She had never cried so hard before, not even when she first started travelling with the Jester. Her paws were unsteady and shaking as her whole body quivered with emotion. She shook with each sob and it wasn't letting up.

Seeing the harm she had allowed and didn't try to stop would haunt her for the rest of her life. How could she have done this to them? How could she have chosen the possibility of the rest of her family being hurt before she chose the people being harmed in front of her? Jukebox had been right when doubting who she was. At this point, Video didn't know who she was if her loyalty had really worn this thin. She'd never be able to hold herself with pride again. She wasn't going to make it out of here alive either, if she bent so easily.

Video stayed curled up in the tree for a long time. She never fell asleep, the sound of Film's screams still fresh in her ears, as well as the painful sound of the cube striking her sister's skull. She pleaded to whatever magic might listen that Jukebox was still alive, had woken up, and simply fled out of the Labyrinth. She hoped with all her heart her sister was okay and wished she had anything to be able to verify that she was.

She startled when her vision darkened through the fur of her tail. The marbled tabby looked up to see the Jester staring at her at the entrance of the hollow.

Her hopes for her sister were gone. Video saw the gold flecked tips of Film's fur stuck to the Jester's outfit. What had the monster done with Jukebox if even Film hadn't stood a chance? She hoped the magician had forgotten about the dark tabby mother, but from the stare she was receiving, she knew it wasn't the case. The beast didn't have a single scratch. The thought repeated in her mind. How could she abandon them like that? The tears came down her face. She had let them all down. "How could you? What do you have against them...?"

The monkey blinked, then brought a hand up in a shrug. "Film and I go way back. Jukebox was just something that was long overdue."

Video looked at the primate in horror, tears still falling down her face. She wished she knew why. She wanted to ask, but her throat was too tight to say anything, and the Jester didn't answer her thoughts. He stared back at her coldly, but when his brow started to furrow as though he was about to speak, he closed his eyes and walked away instead.

"You lied to me. You said I could tell them to leave," she whispered, coming out from the hollow to follow after him.

"Uh, you did, sweetie," he mimicked Audio with a laugh, making Video's eyes water again. "You said everything you asked me to allow you to say, but then you ran off having one of your breakdowns again. I took that as a free chance to do what I wanted since they obviously weren't in your favor anymore."

Video shook her head. "I would have stopped...I would have realized I had to go back."

"And what if you didn't? What would they have done? They knew you were lying about me being here, Video. They would have brought the whole force of Media into my home." The Jester's hand trembled as it clenched into a fist. "I don't need to deal with that again! Never again." The monkey's voice lowered to a growl before starting for the deeper jungle.

"Why have I been here so long? She said it's been a season, Jester!"

"Because you don't handle things well, Video!" The Jester whipped his head around and growled. "I've had to deal with your incessant wailing, pleading, and begging just to get you out of your hammock all summer! We were both tired of it! I found what worked with you, decided to keep what worked, and throw away all the failed attempts!"

"That took you months? Constant touring around the jungle was the only thing that made me able to tolerate you? What else have you tried? How can you think this is acceptable?" Video whimpered, her paws unsteady as she trailed behind the mage.

The monkey took a few more steps toward her, and then slowed down to a stop. He stared into the darkness of the jungle for a moment, then looked back at her to answer, "Everything will come to light after you're dead, Video. I'd like to say otherwise. I could tell you more, but you can't handle it, because I've tried."

Video looked away from the severity of the Jester's gaze and swallowed. He only further proved her fear and fleeing had been for nothing. If she had at least died there, she would have died doing all she could. She stopped again and let the Jester walk on, unable to follow him after accepting the realization. There was no point for anything anymore if this was how it was going to end.

For the rest of the day Video was left alone. She and the Jester had been sleeping in the day to avoid the nightmares from Pictures, but after what had happened, Video didn't sleep at all when the sun was up. Nothing failing to eliminate itself from her head this time. She mourned for most of the day, so frustrated she clawed apart as many vines and branches she had the strength to destroy.

She raked the jungle to pieces until every last bit of energy was gone from her. She could barely lift up her ears by the time she was done, but she didn't find much point in trying, either. It was nighttime now. Video was worn to bits and the impending nightmare hadn't even come yet. She collapsed against the ground and shook her head, trying to keep herself awake, but it was to no avail. She wouldn't make it to morning and the Jester was sure to open the canopy just enough for her to tell the moon was at its highest peak. She closed her eyes and gave into the darkness, giving in to what terrors awaited her.

She blinked open her eyes to see the drawing room, and barely dodged Pictures when he attacked her. The silver tomcat's tail lashed as he looked at Video, as though sensing she had no energy in her to fight. He leapt for her and she swung him down with a heavy paw, but with one sweep of a twist, he pulled himself free and struck again.

Video flinched as he struck her across the nose like he had in the actual castle. The burning sensation was just as intense and it filled Video with alarm. She looked back at the solid tabby and dodged his next swipe, sending one of her own into his shoulder to knock him down, but she knew she'd only be able to do it so many times before she collapsed.

Pictures rose back up as Video staggered and glared at her with his glowing amber eyes. The two grabbed each other at the same time and clawed each other ceaselessly, but this time Pictures wasn't falling apart like he had in the other dreams. Video could actually feel his fur as she grabbed him, and his eyes had more genuineness, too. They stared into her sienna ones with a burning, frightening fire of anger.

"I'll make you pay!" He hissed.

Video gripped him at the neck and threw him down, pinning him at the throat and staring into his eyes again; there was no sign of blue, not a bit in the room. This wasn't a vision cast by anyone except Pictures and Video was going to take advantage of that. She needed a moment to herself—a moment of lucid thoughts without worry, without being watched. Even if she had a murderous tom in the room with her, "I've killed you all week, no, all *summer,* and it's not going to be different this time either, Pictures," she murmured quietly.

Pictures looked at her with offense, and then knocked her in the face with his back leg. Video reeled back as the tom's back sprouted out the orange threads she saw in the castle and extended above his head. He glared at Video ferociously and leapt at her with full force. "You messed everything up! She was the only one who didn't have to die!"

That was new. Video's eyes rounded before she focused back on the battle. The two twisted and clawed at each other in a frenzy, both furiously whipping their paws and fangs at each other. Video took out all the anger she had built up over her time in the Unending Labyrinth on the tom, but he was also ready for the battle. Tonight, she felt like she was really battling with Pictures and not some image or memory of him. She needed this and Pictures seemed not to mind getting some successful hits on her, too.

They fought vehemently. Video could barely pull away long enough for a breath, let alone to ask, "You really did love her, didn't you?" She took advantage of his hesitation and whipped him into the stone of the fireplace, missing the furnace by less than a paw-length. She shoved him closer to it and demanded, "Tell me if this is real or just in my mind, and answer me!"

The silver tabby looked at her with pain and dismay that Video could have never imagined alone, and the true feeling in his eyes convinced her he had truly loved Radio. Video regretted she had to kill him to wake up, but at least she knew. She felt some of her old fire return to her mind and paws, and continued with full force.

Video slammed Pictures against the ground repeatedly and clawed at his throat like pulling apart old insulation from a building. Pictures writhed and twisted in pain. Video lifted up her chin, trying to stay calm even with the revelation. "For what it's worth, Radio's alive." His eyes opened and rounded with shock, so Video continued softly, "She thinks of you every day and wishes she still dreamt of you." She watched the silver tabby's eyes fill with sadness, making Video shake her head, unsure what to think. "She loves you with all of her broken, black, tiny little heart and I say that with full honesty."

Video watched his eyes water despite the heat of his form. Amber tears formed in the edges of his eyes. Video was amazed the tom had really felt anything for the noble at all. She only wished his love had overpowered his greed for the heart of glass. His voice sounded clear in her mind that moment. *Thank you for that, Video...In return, I have words for you to heed. Fear the one who stands at your paws, more dangerous than you know, and understand that I couldn't be saved by him, but only because of the fire. Use your aura to face him, Video.*

Fire...Her eyes rounded at the thought. Saw the pleading in Pictures' eyes as he begged for death. She thought for a moment about telling him of the possibility of kittens, but didn't want to give him further incentive to fight, or to come back like the Jester wanted. Instead she dug her fangs into his neck, just like she should have with the Jester, and then snapped it like a twig.

She picked up the corpse and went to throw it in the fire, but it burst into light instead, and the drawing room turned into darkness. Video scrambled for a grip in the disappearing area, but her paws caught nothing, and she fell down into the black surroundings.

Video closed her eyes and opened them to see the Jester with the cube, glowing orange as he took the light from her form just as he had from Radio when Pictures guided her down from the noble's fall through the canopy. Her eyes rounded with surprise and sudden fear when she thought of Pictures' words, but knew she couldn't give them any thought now.

"Am...am I done with...the nightmares?" She asked as the cube faded back to cyan.

"Yes. It seems like you resolved any issues you had to with him. It was easy to grab him this time." The monkey arched his brow.

Video nodded, deciding to stay silent.

The mage scoffed, eyeing her suspiciously. "Just a couple more away, you know. Soon he'll be whole again."

Video ignored the words as she tried to keep her thoughts clear, so he lifted up his chin. After another moment, he walked away, his tail lashing and the cube glowing brightly beside him. Video swallowed and sat back down, trying to think of anything but what she had learned from the dream. Her paws perspired from her nervousness. She exhaled slowly, but then got up and followed after the primate, knowing it was headed toward the canopy where the hammocks were.

Video followed without a thought on her mind. She only registered enough to be able to follow behind. It was easy enough to do after the dream; she felt like she hadn't slept a wink, and it was already dawn. This was the time they usually slept, though.

Video watched the mage settle into a new hammock it wove with the cube. She looked away and let her thoughts clear again. She needed to wait. She didn't know for what, or for when, but her dream didn't happen without a reason. She was going to figure it out. She felt the fire burning, strong in her heart, melting any of the ice that had frozen over it these past two missions.

Once the sun finished rising, she heard the snore of the primate. Video looked over at the sleeping mage. Her eyes flooded with alertness. She needed to think of anything except a direct thought, something to get her out of here and to get her newfound knowledge to her parents, even if she was sure she wouldn't get far enough without being stopped.

Then her eyes fell on the key. She looked at the cube when it flickered amber, and her heart started pounding. She could never...magic was evil...but was it? Video swallowed, knowing the power was only dangerous by what the holder did with it. She was certain using the cube to send a small message wouldn't corrupt her, not after the determination Pictures gave her. She rose as slowly as she earthly could and climbed out of her hammock as silently as possible.

She held her breath, pulled herself onto the branches that held her bed and looked across. The cube was in the hammock two trees away from her, but she would be able to use the thick branches, climbing across without any drastic leaps. She could get there, if she was careful.

Video let out her breath and then started for the first tree. She was able to reach it easily enough, but it swayed in the slightest with her weight. She kept from swallowing in case her throat made a noise as she reached as far as she could to grab a thicker part of the limb. Video pressed her weight down and quickly put her other paw as far as she could ahead and slid onto the next branch with minimal movement. She pulled herself onto the branch all the way and released her breath silently. She shook her head because of her slow progress, but then climbed onto each branch just as carefully toward the next three.

She froze when the monkey's pelt twitched, but decided to focus on the cube when she realized she didn't wake *others* when she moved silently. She couldn't think of a single person directly, she just had to think about the cube and what she was going to do next.

The cube went from amber to a soft orange as she drew closer, beckoning her with its warmth. It wanted to help, it wanted to be free. Video could tell. She reached for the branch connecting her to the second tree. She was so close to the artifact, but couldn't quite reach it. She had to jump.

Video took in a breath and leapt, no hesitation. She pulled up her hind legs so her front paws landed first, then slowly let the rest of herself fall onto the branch.

No movement came from below, so Video peered down and looked deep into the cube until it turned into a rich sienna. It beckoned her, but how was she to grab it? It looked so effortless when done *by others*. Video stared at it for a while and then the rest of Pictures' words came to her about using her aura. What was her aura? Her beliefs, her wants? Did

Video just have to want the cube to come to her? She kept her breath still and figured it was worth a shot. She had never heard words used to conduct its magic, so it had to be from the mind...or perhaps the heart.

Video felt her chest and head pound from her apprehension and worry. Maybe she couldn't do this...but she already had doubted herself enough as it was. She focused her gaze with intensity on the object, and with her will and command, she had the crystal artifact lift up and come to her. Warmth flooded through her fur instantly. It felt like she had just wrapped up in a blanket laid out in the sun. The entire world seemed richer. All the darkness faded from the Labyrinth when her eyes focused, making her almost scream and stumble before she caught herself. She quickly moved away from the hammock and made her way down the tree with the object at her side. Video had it, she had the Queen's artifact. She took off for the deeper part of the forest where she couldn't be heard.

She felt the strength and energy rush through her as she ran with the cube beside her. She willed herself to be silent and it was so. All she could feel for the moment was shock. It was only now she understood how truly alluring magic was and why so often in the reports the mages sought more. Video raced through the forest with the Queen's artifact at her side and felt like she could take on the world.

Then she felt it. The glow that came from the forest the Jester...no, the glow she wasn't allowed to see. Video swallowed nervously, but didn't think anything more of the matter. She couldn't deal with her own...inquisitiveness right now, not when she needed to get a hold of Audio and Signal.

Video turned back to the cube and swung it with her paw, trying with all her might not to yowl when her pads came in contact with the surface. She felt a blast of power shoot through every pore and hair on her body. She didn't know her fur could stand on end like that. Her eyes rounded at the power and she made sure she kept her distance. Once she recovered her breath and her thoughts, she could try again. Contact with the object was not the answer. Instead, she began hovering her paw over the artifact and slowly turning it with a demand of her thoughts.

She willed it to show her parents, and saw them immediately within the surface of the artifact. Audio and Radio were watching closely on the monitors, while Signal was on a different panel of the cube, looking at his own monitors. Video pondered which one to contact, hesitant in case Audio didn't see the direness of the situation, but Audio would relay things to Signal, who would see the urgency through Audio's subtle wording no matter what. If Video contacted Signal alone, he would only notify the Council if he found it urgent and would leave Audio out of it. Audio might tell Radio, Stereo, even Console. It was best trying to contact her.

With another swing of her paw, she demanded to be within the screen, to be in contact with Audio. Immediately the cube showed them looking face to face.

"Video!?" Both Audio and Radio startled in their seats, bristling and leaning back.

Video pulled back her paw and stared at them with round eyes. "Can you hear me?"

"Yes, yes! Sweetie, are you okay–"

"There's no time for that, Audio." Video said curtly, feeling the magic light up her eyes with her fierce tone. The two jumped again in shock, and Video made herself relax before continuing, "I'm contacting you through the Queen's artifact and I need you to listen. You need to call for help within the Capital immediately. Film and Jukebox were taken down by the Jester and I did nothing to help them. We're in an urgent situation and neither of them can help us now. I don't know if they're alive, Audio, which is why you must act fast." She looked to Radio and swallowed. "Pictures still haunted my dreams until last night. He is happy you're alive, but he also told me how we can stop the monster. He connected all the pieces for us." When she knew she had Radio's full attention, she turned back to Audio. "I need you to contact Signal and tell him everything. Audio, the Jester *is* Phantascope. We already discussed how he was defeated. The only way to end him is–"

"Putting down annoyances once and for all." The Jester whipped the cube down from Video's paws and backhanded her, his nails racking across her cheek and slicing an open cut.

Video landed roughly, but got to her paws before he could strike again. She looked in the corner of her eye at the cube to see Audio nod and run off, and then looked back at the magician and growled.

"Your attempts are futile, Video. You see, I can't die anymore…and there's nothing you can do that will stop me." His eyes hardened.

What a thought. She knew she had to think of something else before the mage got too irritated with her, but at least she felt better about herself after successfully reaching Audio. "But I did." She *had* been trying to do all she could. "The only thing that has ever held me back was the monster with power out of my control." She said out loud. It didn't matter anyway whether it was said or thought, he'd hear her anyway.

"Way to exempt yourself out of any guilt, Video. I'm proud of you." The monkey sneered as he drew closer.

She looked up and stared at him. "Do you disagree with me?"

"You'd be surprised how much of this you brought on yourself. You can't pile everything onto others." The primate's eyes glittered with anger.

"I disagree, because my only problem is the one in front of me. I think if I defeat you, I won't have any more heartache or pain. I have a supporting, loving family–"

"That keeps secrets from you," the mage growled.

Video's tail lashed. "–that kept me from the dangers around me to protect me! I was apparently a foolish child who thought a destructive, pessimistic monster with more power than it could reasonably control would make a good friend, as did my mother. The only good thing it ever did was make me forget it."

The Jester flinched with hurt at her words, but she kept going, "You'd think it could have stayed that way, but it came back into my life, more destructive than ever. It took away my king and threw my family into chaos and worry about me when I had to accept the mission to pick up the mess it made. It had me kill someone who only wanted to be my friend, framed me with the help of its ally to be one of the most hated subjects in all of Media by killing two of the sweetest people I ever met and saying I did it, and then put me up against the same apparent ally, who I had to kill after travelling with him for nearly a solid week, eating, sleeping, and tackling this horrific mission together!"

Video's paws shook, but she kept going, her heart pounding with her anger and fear. She shouted, "You destroyed everything I've ever had, you beast! You took my form to kill my brother's closest partner and blame it on me, likely after the said companion was already working for you! Did you kill him once he also saw through you and saw how destructive you were? He was going to give up being a spy, wasn't he!? You kill all that is good, Jester!"

"Stop calling me that!" The monkey snarled, bristled head to tail tip.

"No! I won't, no matter who you are!" Video wailed. "You're a joke! A real laugh to anyone as sick as you. I can't believe you think bringing pain to others is something entertaining, something fun! You are nothing more than a jest and you should be dead! You should have been dead before I was born! You hate yourself so much—as much as we do— that you can't even walk around in your true form, that disgusting creature you really are. Ashamed of your abandonment, trying to justify it by making others do the same, but we don't!"

"It's not that simple!" The mage shouted back, his eyes rounded with emotion.

Video carried on anyway, not letting the gradual steps of his approach scare her. "Jukebox and Film risked *everything* for me and I'm not about to believe they're dead yet either, mage! You're worse than anything you make us out to be because you took the form of the one child who waited for you while you fetched a stupid cube to feel better about yourself, and then defamed his name like it was nothing! You took his form and destroyed who he really was, all because you didn't want to look at yourself any more than we do now! We would all be happy if you weren't here, *Curiosity!*"

The entire area turned pitch black and Video flattened herself to the ground. The Jester looked at her with round, cyan irides, glittering tears streaming down his cheeks. His irides and sclera faded to black, only showing the slits of bright blue pupils and the magic tears that fell down his face. "I just wanted you to be my friend again…I thought if everyone hated you and you lost everything else, you'd come back to me."

Video swallowed, and she whispered, "N-No...you could have just helped people...you could have shown everyone magic was something good like Queen Satisfaction did..."

She whimpered when the mage snarled and looked away when he took a step closer.

His eyes hardened. "You might have showed me that if you would have given me a chance, but instead you decide to insult me. You invalidate all of my efforts to better myself and treat me like this...monster. I'm tired of being called a monster when I'm trying, Video! If you want to see a monster, *I'll show you!*"

- CHAPTER 9 -
EFFORT

The primate snarled as black magic washed over its form, distorting its voice as it pulled apart and twisted into a strange hybrid of a shadow animal sprouting magic, flowing wings like Pictures, but distorted, dark, and chaotic. Video had never seen anything like it. Her bones chilled to the very tips of her claws, but she refused to plead for mercy. There was sudden concern about realizing the black shadows had an immediate effect on her energy, though. She felt her paws wobble as the form became darker and her eyesight began to wear away. She looked over and noticed that as the mage's shadows expanded more, the cube's orange hue began to wear away to cyan. With that in mind, Video pulled it away, ignoring the pain, and stepped back, cutting off a bit of the monster's source of power.

There had been an immediate reaction and change to the expanding form, which made Video realize how reliant the magician had become on the artifact. She swallowed and moved it even closer to her after another step towards the stream.

The form washed into the unclothed primate once more, nearly immediately after she stepped back. His eyes were still cyan, but they were rounded with alarm. Video's tail tip quivered apprehensively when he took a step closer. She took another step back as he seemed to make attempts to calm down and speak again.

Video shook her head. It was too late for words at this point. She commanded the cube to her side and bolted away.

"No!" the mage shouted and chased after her.

Phantascope is Curiosity, the Jester is Curiosity. It made no difference at the moment; it was a mage trying to kill her. Video tried to rapidly think of any memories of her father teaching her about the calico mage, but realized with the monkey taking away her memories of himself, with how vastly he could read her thoughts about him, it was likely all her memories were gone of learning about Phantascope, the Shadow Advisor, too. Video now understood why she struggled during her younger seasons, always feeling like something was missing, as well as her frustration when Signal claimed she had learned these things about his experience with mages already, but it had just motivated her to learn more and to never forget again. She never realized it was the fault of having her memories of what she learned forcibly stripped from her mind. Yet everything made a lot more sense now because of it.

Video had to run with all her might, faster than she ever had before. She bolted past the trees and traps, snapping anything which posed as a threat with the cube. However, even with the artifact at her side, giving her all the boost she could ask, Curiosity was too quick with his magic. She screamed when he caught up to her, ducking down when he leapt for her. She whipped her head back up and ran in the other direction, looking for anything that she could use to buy time before Audio figured out how to save her or to get her out of the Labyrinth.

She didn't know if she was going to make it. Even with how quickly Audio might be able to find a solution, the mage had been taking down its opponents since before Video's grandparents were born, if not even before then. Signal was Phantascope's defeat and Video didn't know how that happened, but the monster, even then, hadn't truly died. Video was very well aware of this as she had to dodge another attack. She needed to figure out something to stall for time that was unlike anything the mage had faced before.

Video looked to her side and realized what that might be. Since the days of Wisdom, Phantascope was the only one ever sighted with the cube until the Jester came along, and with the times merged together it had been ages since the magician faced an opponent with the same strength. With how many times she had successfully injured him before without the use of magic, even if only temporarily, Video was ready to see what she could do with Satisfaction's power at her side.

That and the fact he hadn't succeeded in killing her before.

She whipped around and willed a blast out from the cube to strike the mage. She screamed when the blast hit her instead.

"Be more specific, you stupid cat!" Curiosity leapt at Video in her moment of daze and swung her into the ground, punching her with a sudden slam of his fist against her chest.

Video reeled back with a yowl and quickly commanded a barrier to protect herself. She gasped for air and tried to make herself relax, but it was impossible. The mage slammed a blast of cyan magic at her force field. It immediately began to dissipate and was gone in seconds. Video's eyes rounded. She leapt out of it before it burst into pieces of light, scattered away by the magician's own plasma.

She bolted up the stream, willing and begging the cube to blast magic at Curiosity to hold him back. She now comprehended the importance of names to the mages; quite possibly to the verified of Media. Did the mage have to know Video's birth name to be able to cast magic against her? She defined herself as Video, so she imagined it wasn't the case, but she knew to be more skeptical about sharing her title with anyone she didn't trust. It was something to worry about when she didn't have a homicidal mass murderer on her tail.

Phantascope had destroyed entire villages, murdered town leaders, citizens, and mutilated some of the most respected subjects in all of Media. She had just unveiled the wrath of the being he had tried to become in order to *better* himself. What would lie in wait if she didn't kill him now? She whipped to the side when she heard a blast coming from behind and then turned on her paw, spinning around to face the mage. She reeled upwards and brought up the earth around her with her stretch, the magic flowing up from the toes of her back paws to the claw tips of her front, then flung the stones and earth at the primate.

He leapt over the first wave, but then Video yanked down and swung her tail up, flinging a giant boulder right into him.

Once it struck the monkey down into the ground, Video turned back around and raced up the incline. She had to think of something quickly before it was too late. She had to get away immediately. Her mind went to watching Pictures teleport in the castle, but she was afraid she'd teleport below ground and crush herself if the cube was that specific about things. Nowhere else was safe that Curiosity wouldn't destroy if she thought of it, so all she could do was ask the cube to strengthen her lungs and limbs to be able to keep the pace she needed to fend this monster off.

If she was going to survive this, she needed to hide and not let her thoughts give her away. She looked to the artifact hovering beside her, still glowing its deep orange while under her control, and took off into the deep forest where she hadn't been taken yet. She needed to get to that other glowing area. Nobody would sense the cube where there was already a bank of magic.

"Signal!" Audio snapped.

Signal blinked once but didn't look away from his monitors. If anything, he turned his ears further away from the two after they barged into his office to explain the situation.

Radio came up beside the taller feline, bristling. Audio knew the feline was upset after finding out that Video and Curiosity were travelling together, but after the small noble heard about Video's distress signal and found out Audio was going to demand Signal save her, she had jumped on board. "Listen to her! Your daughters and the most important monitor in all of Media–"

"Uh, Radio…" Audio swallowed.

Radio didn't listen. "–Are in danger right now, and you're going to be worrying about what you're authorized to do as a Monitor consultant? You are the sorriest sack of fur I've ever met, and I'm disgraced my family has used you as a resource and married you!" Radio didn't let up even as Audio gasped, instead stomping her paw on Signal's tail to hold him in place, which only worked because the tail was already flat on the ground and he was sitting, but she didn't care. "I demand you to fix this. I authorize you as the Radio Star. I hold rank over you, single rowed or not! Go take care of it, Signal of the Rich Top Mountains!"

Both Audio and Radio's fur raised in the slightest as Signal turned his blind gaze toward them slowly, the silver lining almost glowing with his intensity.

"You're no longer verified as the Radio Star without your collar, *untitled.*" He growled, low, making Radio's lip quiver. "It's the only thing that gives you power. Right now you're just a weak little offspring living off of your ancestors' fame to no avail. I have no answers for either of you." He shook his head and looked back at his monitors, his ears flattened against his head as he pulled his tail out from under Radio's paw.

The tom hadn't heeded either of their words. The two felines watched in shock and dismay as the giant tomcat shut the door, using it to push them from his office.

Radio burst into tears immediately and ran away to the living room. Audio took in a breath and sighed, and then followed after the noble. She would give Signal two minutes before she spoke to him again, but for now she could focus on Radio.

She approached the living room and saw the noble in the corner. The small seal-mitted feline was clutching her mangled collar. Her tears fell onto the sapphire gems, dripping down to the silver panels which had once kept the choker together. Audio wished Stereo wasn't hunting right now. The little noble could use all the support she needed. "I'm sorry, Radio...he may just be stressed."

"Rubbish...that cat only cares about what the Council says. He doesn't give a flying feather about Video. She ripped out my throat and I'm more worried about her than he is! Jukebox has only been there for me since I've met her! Now both she and Film, the only c-cat in all of Media who knew me, might b-be d-dead." Radio's voice cracked into a sob and she whimpered, burying her face in her collar.

Audio frowned, and stepped closer. "We can't give up yet. If we move quickly, there's still a chance!" She pleaded, wanting to believe her words as much as she wanted Radio to believe. "We need to think of something else."

Radio lifted up her head and nodded. She swallowed and asked, "W-what about S-Studio?" Her sobs interrupted her speech like hiccups. "Can we get a c-command from her to tell h-him?"

Audio's tail bolted upright with hope. "It's worth a shot!"

Radio quickly got up and the two rushed to the monitor. Audio put in the command to activate the remaining bot in the utilities, and brought it up to send it over to Clowder City.

The mission was crucial, but Audio could make it go no faster than what it was set to go, and the two had to watch it creep across the sky. Both the other drones were further away than the one Audio was controlling. At the point they were hoping to switch and override Signal's command, it would have taken longer for the other two, even heading toward the Capital, to turn around and overcome the utility bot. Radio and Audio's tails both flicked with impatience, but there was nothing more they could do while regular correspondence was cut out from the penthouse in Clowder City.

With the time it took, the two could do nothing but converse. The first thing noticed was how the resolution was distinguishably different from the other drones' recordings. "...Jukebox was telling me how the other two drones were named, what's this one?" Radio asked.

Audio blinked, and then responded, "Machete."

"Machete?" Radio chuckled weakly. "So, Gun, Chainsaw, and then Machete? Who came up with these names?"

"Video did, when she was a kitten." Audio shook her head in disbelief, pondering, "I don't know where she got such names. She was such a playful, silly girl."

Radio squinted one eye at her in doubt and then turned back to the screen.

Once the drone flew past the start of the remains of the glistening black city, Radio and Audio's ears perked up. They quickly focused on driving it to the penthouse. Radio's fur began to rise with excitement when she saw her auntie's silhouette in one of the windows. The penthouse balcony wasn't closed to surveillance, so they had the bot fly right into the building.

Radio let out a squeal with excitement at seeing the familiar room, but her heart stopped when they entered the room where they had discovered the last shard was undetectable. She remembered her travelling companions' anger. Her vision blurred with sudden tears, but she quickly wiped them and told Audio, "It's just down that hall. She should be at the end towards the left."

Audio nodded and began controlling the device again. The device automatically stopped at the Monitor's station, where Screen was, but Radio shook her head when she saw the silver tom. "Don't talk to him...both Video and I thought something was off about him..." From what Jukebox had said, it seemed like the mostly-blind cat enjoyed being the temporary mayor more than Radio would hope to admit and more than what Studio probably could bring herself to, either.

The drone hovered past and went to the room at the end of the hall. Radio took in a breath when she saw her beautiful auntie. With the extra time on her paws, it seemed the regal brown tabby had curled her fur and made it shine. Radio wished the rest of Media was in the same condition. "Auntie Studio!" Radio stamped her paw on the audio box and purred into the mic.

"Ra-Radio...?" Studio looked over at the drone, and her eyes rounded. She bounded off the windowsill and hurried over, fresh tears in her eyes. "You *are* alive!"

"We need your help! Video's in trouble and we can't get Signal to help us! Write the nastiest letter you can think of and make him see he has to get off his rump!" Radio wailed.

"Radio!" Both Audio and Studio chastised, but then both smiled at recognizing each other's voices.

Radio shook her head but furthered, "I mean it! We found out that the Jester was that old mage Phantascope, the Shadow Advisor you banished!"

"I will, but we need all the power we can get for this mage...I already sent a message of that to Video. I never even thought to give it to you Audio, I am so sorry. I'll write something to Signal now." Radio and Audio's eyes both rounded, and Studio started writing as she quickly explained, "After the funerals I attended, I went to seek out Phantascope to see if he would help us by using his prior name, but instead I only came across the Jester. I don't know how else to explain it..."

"We know," Audio whispered, "It seems many of his current actions are based off of his anger from the past."

Studio shook her head and slid her message into the drone. The paper faxed to Audio, who ripped it from the machine and ran off. "Stay with Studio and find out as much as you can! I'm going to Signal!" She called to Radio as she raced down the hall.

Radio blinked and turned back to the camera. "Do you know anything else about the mage we might be able to use?"

Studio shook her head. "No, I only ever knew him as a teacher and friend until this. The best way I always found to defeat him was by embarrassing him...but Radio, this whole ordeal is on a different level than anything I imagined...I have nothing."

Radio frowned, but nodded. She saw the charge was running low on the surveillance and noticed her auntie's discomfort, so decided to cut it short. "Alright, thanks, Auntie. We'll be in touch if anything more happens. Video's older brother, Console, is working with Film to get everyone back into Social Media on good terms. We're going to get you out of there!"

"Thank you, Radio! Be strong!" Studio purred.

Radio smiled, giving a small giggle, and turned off the correspondence.

Studio watched as the monitor bot flickered its lights and hovered away, and then allowed her shoulders to slump. The whole mission would have been easier if she and Curiosity had never known each other. She felt awful lying to Radio about not knowing her niece was alive, but how would she be able to explain that she could hear the little noble thinking about her? How could she tell them the reason Curiosity could predict their every move and know every thought directed toward him was because of Studio asking him to learn it when she was a kit?

Video held her breath and closed her eyes as she pressed herself against the cold stone. She couldn't believe what she had found on the other side of the trees. The cube had almost pulled itself away from her side when she had seen the pool. The body of water was unlike anything she had ever seen! The moment the cube had touched the already glowing pool, the entire thing lit up into a bright orange ray, comparable to a bonfire. Video had to make sure her spot hadn't been given away by the amount of brightness coming from the pool, and had quickly run over to the other side of the stones surrounding the water. There was a narrow passage within the stones that led her under the waterfall that fell into the pool, and was just deep enough to hide the cube's light from outside eyes.

She looked down at the artifact, her eyes narrowing as the dramatic brightness contrasted with the darkness of the hole and her closed eyes. It took every effort not to grab onto the cube and clutch it to her with such little space, but already from just the small instances her paw had touched it or swiped along its surface, Video knew she wouldn't willingly ever do that again. She wondered if that was what it would have felt like if the panels from the barrier had touched her, and hoped no one had to have felt that when the plasma broke apart. The entire situation was terrifying, but Video knew she couldn't give it any more thought. She couldn't risk anything which might give herself away.

Video lay there and had to hold back from sighing. She curled her paws into the fluff of her chest and closed her eyes again, not giving the cube any commands or thought until she saw it dim through her lids. She opened her eyes again to glance at the object, admiring the crystal detail within it. It looked so different when it wasn't glowing. There were threads that weaved and twisted within it just like in the old barrier. Video's eyes watered. She barely stopped herself from holding onto the cube when she thought of what was gone. She took in a breath and held it, closing her eyes again when she knew she had to control her emotions. She couldn't think of what happened if she didn't want to get caught.

She had to think about something else. Her thoughts flashed to Pictures, and how he was free from her dreams now. She thought of how he helped her and how he gave her the courage to contact Audio and Radio...but knew she couldn't give him too much of her mind, either. She had to be careful. What about her days with Faith? No, they had been affected and ruined by the guardians' corruption. The Ruined City? Meeting Receiver and her raccoon friend was nice. She hoped Transmitter recovered well with the plantain poultice treatment. If only that blasted wolf...but the wolf wasn't in power of its mind.

This was terrifying. Video had to find something that wasn't involved...that had no relation to why her memories were lost. Even herbs weren't something to think about because of the interest shown in the Unending Labyrinth. Video swallowed nervously when the very corners of the cube began to show cyan, watching as the faint light started expanding toward the core before she willed it away and the cube turned orange again. She willed it further away from the passage opening, and hoped with all her might the magic wasn't seen from the outside, or sensed, for that matter.

Video flinched when she heard a footstep outside the passage. Pebbles fell down the loose stone, and she heard several more steps along the stones surrounding the pool. She hoped that the noise of the falls drowned out the sound of her gentle breath, but worried how it seemed the magic enhanced everything, and if it was going to protect her. She held her breath now, hoping she could for long enough until the...until it was safe.

Her heart beat hard against her chest. She couldn't bring herself to continue using the cube, and watched it fade back into its clear crystal. She watched as the cyan light slowly moved toward the other side of the cube before it began fading away. She listened until the footsteps were no longer audible, and let out the breath she was holding. She begged to the Queen to allow that just thinking of the footsteps was vague enough. She closed her eyes again. She needed to figure out something, anything to ensure her safety until she could escape. She wrapped her tail around herself and looked into the cube, begging it to show her parents.

Audio was running to Signal's office, a piece of paper in her collar. Video tilted her head, and then scrolled the angle of the cube to show Signal, who was taking notes. Video blinked with confusion and went to check on Radio, surprised at how easy it was to find these people with the cube. It was also unnerving, with...how...how *others* might be able to use the ability. Video's ears flicked. It felt like holding back a sneeze while trying to control her thoughts. She needed to be more careful. She looked to see Radio messing around with the third drone of Signal's. Stereo just came in, though, and she started rambling and yelling at him. Video closed the image. The thing that made her the most upset was seeing the trees outside were orange and the grass was fading. It really was autumn.

Video shook her head and then asked the cube to show her Jukebox and Film, wishing with all her heart that they weren't gone.

She was surprised to see Jukebox walking in the Labyrinth. Her eyes rounded and she flinched when her whiskers touched the cube in her eagerness, lighting them orange before she pulled away. She looked and listened, but there were no sounds from the outside that suggested she was heard from her quiet peep. She let her shoulders relax in relief and looked back to the cube. Her sister looked to be in good health, determined, even. Video was relieved. She went to change the cube to Film, but the moment she saw the vines and blood she cut out the image.

Video was completely shocked. Had she really just seen the limp form of Film? Were the drops of blood all of it, or was she only whiskers away from seeing a fatal wound? She held her paws against her muzzle and flattened her ears. She couldn't cry, she couldn't yell, but the anger was rising in her chest. She had to control her emotion and thoughts if she was going to survive this, but what had happened? She was afraid to look back and see if he was alive, but knew she'd regret not knowing if she didn't. Her paw hovered along the cube and recast the image.

She slowly moved the angle to see the rest of the tom, and her heart skipped a beat when she saw he was breathing. He looked injured, but recoverable. He was tied at every limb and around his neck and muzzle was held in place in midair with a fortress of bramble berries surrounding him. It would keep him from being seen from the outside. The area beyond the bramble's canes was covered with brush and growth, but Video knew exactly where in the Labyrinth that was now.

Something had to be done. Video startled when she realized that the cave was turning black around her. She stared in shock for a moment before she realized it was the enchanted shadows. She quickly started for the exit. She was afraid of what the darkness might do when the cube's light already had such an extreme effect. She felt weaker when she first faced it with the Jes...the form from earlier. She ran out of the hole with the cube at her side.

She panicked. The rest of the Labyrinth was black and she just almost gave herself away. She ran blindly, only from memory to where the pool was, hoping the magic would come back to it and it could overcome the darkness. She startled when she felt its water, even more so from the loudness of the splash her paw made. She blinked, hoping the ebbing magic might give her enough light to see around the Labyrinth, but her sight of the jungle never came back and her energy began to drain quickly. She put the cube into the water to light it up again and looked around.

She startled when she turned her head to stare right into his glittering cyan eyes.

"There you are."

Audio shoved open the door to her partner's office and slammed the note down on the desk where he was writing. "There you go! A command from Studio herself to go get my little girl. Go! Straight to Video! Now!" she snapped, her spine arching and neck fur bristling with her increasing anger.

Signal took one glance at it, ran his paw along the holes that enabled him to read it, scowled, and turned away. "She has no authority over us. She is under house arrest and under questioning from the Council for her association with the enemy."

"Signal! She *is* the Council! I could tell you the very day she was appointed!"

Signal whipped around, startling Audio. "Audio! I am not going to rescue the stupid child who put herself in the situation! She willingly went to that mage and now she is paying the price! Everyone who went into that Labyrinth knew the risk and affiliation with magic there. They entered under their own discretion, including you!" He snarled, his tail lashing and fur rising.

Audio leaned back, shocked, and shook her head. "You would have come...You would have rescued us if anything had happened to me and the kittens, right?"

"No," the answer startled Audio, as her supervisor and partner explained, "That monster attacked the kittens on *my* territory. You had no authorization to be entering that forest and were under advisement not to, but decided to listen to who you defined as your trustworthy *mentor* instead over me, dallying and playing! I was revolted, humiliated, and ashamed!" the tom hissed.

Audio looked at him with shock and confusion.

Signal's blind gaze narrowed into slits. "Taking our kittens to the beast, spending your days with it. I was blinded before I knew what our last litter looked like, but it wasn't beyond the timing that I would have been suspicious if the creature hadn't had the tri-color pattern." The Shadow Advisor's brightly colored face was the last thing the tomcat had seen before he was blinded.

Audio gasped, her eyes welling with tears, but the tears were barely caused by sadness; she was seething with frustration and anger. "You think I..." Her voice cracked, but she started again, "Signal! He was a childhood friend, an advisor!" She swallowed at her poor choice of wording, knowing Signal had also known the calico tom as the Shadow Advisor. The mage had told her many times to call him Advisor and she had yet to break the habit. "You're going to bring this up when our kittens might be dying out there!? He...*it*, was a mentor and my first teacher of herbology; like a father who actually asked questions of me and showed interest in my knowledge and growth instead of treating me like a commodity the way my..." Audio swallowed, knowing Signal respected her father. She couldn't bring herself to say anything negative about Logistics. "My mentor was never, ever anything beyond that, not since my kittenhood crush. You're the love of my life, Signal." Her voice grew quiet with sadness, as she furthered, "You have been since...within moments of my being assigned here as your assistant."

She took a deep breath, her expression one of questioning until it changed to one of determination. Audio's tears had dried, but her tail continued to lash, and her neck fur rose high. "You think I pined for that creature and regretted what you did to it after the mage tried to kill our kits? I was only ever sad that someone I had once cared for so deeply was not who I thought he was and could think the action he...*it* should take was to hurt those I love," her eyes grew soft then, "Those I would give my life for in order that they could live. My regret was standing there in shock and bewilderment as I only began to comprehend the betrayal and hatred toward such innocent beings as our kittens were."

Signal looked surprised, but didn't give her any words in return. Audio's paws shook and she looked up into her partner's blind gaze. "Because I couldn't comprehend it...I was useless to them. It would have cost them their lives if not for you, Signal. In that hesitation, I failed both you and them. I have to always live with that shame."

When Signal still didn't respond and instead turned around, Audio continued with a raised chin, but she herself didn't know if she was doing it defensively or defiantly. "You saved them and you destroyed the Shadow Advisor, Phantascope—the Jester. They are all the same. It was the right thing to do and I am ever grateful to and proud of you for that. However, I couldn't bear the desecration of my former mentor's body and the way you left it there where the children could see it. That's the reason I took the body to the pool in the Labyrinth." Her voice shook, but she carried on with her posture held high. "I was closing a chapter in the story of my kittenhood. It was only herbology I learned from it. However, I knew it was a mage, so I felt it had to be returned to its world, as it wasn't a part of ours." Her voice grew strong again. "The Rich Top Mountain could once again be ours as a family. When Video and Stereo were born I was sure we were once again a unit...but I guess it's only been you and the commodities, the kits, I provided." *Just the way my father saw me.*

Signal whipped around, his tail lashing. She jumped back when he rose up the claws of one of his paws, but her eyes softened when she realized she may have actually hurt him with those words. She didn't know what else to say, except whisper his name, "Signal..." She took a small step toward him as he raised his paw and again whispered to him, this time saying, "It's the truth, dear one, there has only ever been you...and our kittens, my love. I cherish all of you with my entire heart." She wanted to go to him, comfort him from the hurt her words had inflicted, knowing he wouldn't harm her, but knew this was not the time; she had to stay strong and show she meant everything she said.

He flicked his paw upwards and growled, then stomped it on the ground, and took off for the outside. Audio raced after him, leaving the house, but stopped once she realized he was heading down the incline for the Labyrinth. She went back inside and ran to her monitor.

Video yowled as Curiosity slammed her into the pool. She whipped around in the water, trying to find where the bottom was so she could find her way to the top, and tensed when she felt the rocky ground. She quickly swam up to the surface and jumped out from the pool, then bolted away with the cube. The cube's heat and energy warmed her fur and dried her off, so she focused the magic on clearing the shadows and strengthening herself again as she raced through the trees. She heard the primate and knew he wasn't far behind her. She ran as fast as she could. She bolted into the trees and decided to run for the canopy, but the mage met her at the top of the branch, and leapt for her.

Video screeched in surprise. The primate whipped the cube out from her paws and smashed her into the trunk of the tree, pinning her down and biting into her neck. She kicked him off and twisted up to her paws, but by the time she got straightened out, he shot for her again. Video reared up, growling as he drove his fangs into her chest, but was able to stretch her neck down and bite him in the back of the neck. She slammed him down onto the branch. Their combined weight made the branch swing the limb back and forth, but just then he yelled and bit her front paw, pulling her down with him. She took her other paw and raked her claws against his face. She pulled back at the same moment and yanked free, then grabbed him by the throat and swung him around, slamming him into the tree now, too.

Curiosity shoved his fist into her muzzle and then slammed her back. Video expected him to let up, but he then pinned her down against the tree branch and snarled, "I could have been someone! I tried to be everything I could, but I can't be something I'm not, Video. You're right."

The primate brought up the fully cyan cube and spun it threateningly. Video leaned back in fear, thinking of her head injury, but was startled even more when the primate burst into the shadow creature and snarled at her with all his might. Video yowled out, but even when she tried to fight and writhe out of his grip, he held her tight. She gasped and clawed at the shadows, but they just came apart and reformed. She threw her head back and yelled as she felt the darkness take her energy. It was too much for her to be able to break free.

Video glanced at the cube and asked to see her parents one more time. It showed Audio and Radio watching on the monitor in the living room. Video peered closer, making the image zoom in. She saw a shape running in the recording, but it was too dark and blocky to make out at first before she realized the two were watching Signal. She quickly requested the cube show her where Signal was. It swung outside and down the incline, where her father was running down to the forest. Her tail flickered with excitement before she tucked it back to herself. She hoped he was coming for Jukebox and Film and could make time to help her escape on the way, but the dread that Jukebox would tell him about her betrayal sunk in her stomach. They might say it's best to leave her to rot after what the Jester probably put them through, if they were even alive by the time Signal arrived.

She shut her eyes and jerked back when the mage flicked his hand. She expected the cube to hit her after that instant, but when she opened her eyes again and looked, the mage tossed it back with his shadow tail and raised up his arm. He punched Video right above her eye, missing the socket only by a few whiskers.

Blood dripped down into her eyes. Video cried out when her sight became clouded and he threw her back. She wiped the blood out just in time to see him leap at her, but wasn't fast enough to deflect it, and both were knocked out of the tree.

Video spun in the air and landed on her feet, but so did Curiosity. The two leapt at each other and raked their claws and nails against each other's pelts. Video clawed and ripped at the shadows until she came across the mage's black hair, and drove her fangs into his ribs.

Curiosity yowled and slammed his tail into her face. He grabbed her and threw her across the clearing. Video landed roughly that time, her fur becoming matted with mud and leaves. She gasped and struggled to her paws, the blood dripping back down into her eye. She swallowed the bit that fell in the back of her throat and hissed. No matter how scared she was, she was not about to back down again. She was lucky she could see at all after knowing her father and Screen's fate. She looked behind her, and saw there was a long drop to the ground below, with a tree stump struck by either lightning, or more likely, magic. The spikes of the tree split looked fatal, and Video swallowed nervously before turning her head back to the mage.

"Try all you want to stop the users of Media, but we will forever be loyal to our leaders as their followers!" She called out, and then spat out the blood that fell down from her head.

The shadow creature's tail lashed and he stared at her boredly. The shadows dissipated and revealed the monkey once more as he stepped closer. "Loyal to the death, I've always commended you fools for it. I'm not looking to defeat you, Video. Not enslave, conquer, overtake, no. I just want every single one of you *dead!*" The last sentence ended with such bitterness that it chilled Video, but she just rose up her chin and glared, not letting her shakiness make her wobble with all her strength.

The two glared at each other with pure loathing at that moment. Curiosity looked down at the blood soaked dirt, his face now hidden by the shadows. Video watched as Curiosity pushed the cube aside and stood up on his back legs, overcome with anger and frustration. Video was now unsure of the situation. She watched as he took one step towards her and clenched his right fist. She scrambled back, not ready for another hit. He slowly raised his head so his dark eyes could be seen. The blue eyes flashed to freeze her in place. She tried to jump back but her paws wouldn't move. What was going on!?

Suddenly, he jumped forward, his clenched right fist thrown forward towards Video. She saw it go for her already bleeding injury and panicked, realizing the monkey's intent to kill her with this swing. She demanded the cube to overpower his strength and free her, jerking her head backwards at the same time in attempt to dodge or at least lessen the blow, but the primate was too fast. Curiosity's fist slammed into her head and further, into her eye. He punched with so much momentum the blow shattered the skull's protection around her socket. She heard the snapping of the bone fragments and felt immediate, immense agony. What made it worse was the movement landed uncomfortably from her struggle, causing pain to him, as well. The two screamed in horror as Curiosity's hand snapped and splintered from the strike and Video's skull cracked right above the eye that hadn't been bled on yet, blinding her.

Video was left screaming and crying at the pain while Curiosity backed away, waving out his hand and regenerating the bones and flesh. After that moment, all Video saw was red and black. All she could hear was her heart pounding the blood in her head as it leaked out like water. She gasped repeatedly, shaking and quivering from the sensations. She panicked and wailed when she heard the primate come closer. She attempted to back away, but fell down, going into shock from the pain and blood loss.

Curiosity approached her that moment, but both of them heard the sound of propellers at the same time. Curiosity watched as the black and red device immediately flew to Video. The mage caught it in his tail and turned the camera to look at Video, snarling, "Take one last look at your daughter," before he snapped it into pieces with his tail and threw it back into the brush. Video listened to his breath as he opened his fangs to bite into her, but then she heard a sudden movement—a crack of a twig in the brush. She kept alert, hearing Curiosity stepping away after the snap. She had no idea why, until his words rang in her ears.

"Signal," the primate growled.

Video forced her working eye open and gasped, seeing her father through her blurred vision. Her body trembled, but her eyes watered even more with gratitude. She might live today, she could live. She tried to stop the bleeding to her face, grabbing any large absorbent leaves, and was relieved to see a clump of moss growing along the closest tree.

The spider monkey lashed his tail when the giant feline took a step closer. "Get out. I don't need to deal with the likes of you. Leave your traitorous children to me and go about with what little of your life you have left." Curiosity sneered.

"I'm not leaving without what's left of her, Jester."

Video slightly resented that, even through all her pain.

"And you will die again if you try and stop me." The dark tabby's tail lashed, and he started walking over to his daughter.

The primate stepped in front of Video. "I don't think so, Signal. Who are you to act like this, anyway? Where's your little slip of permission? You can't do anything without the sweet words of your precious Council, and we all know they haven't processed anything to you for weeks." The monkey snorted and grinned.

Curiosity flinched when the long-furred tomcat turned his head to face him with fierceness, the blind gaze surprisingly piercing and direct. "This is personal business, Phantascope." He started advancing toward the primate instead.

"Wha...hey, now," the mage stammered. Video could hear the fear building up in the primate's voice. She blinked her one open eye for the instant she needed before everything went red and black again, starting to see the mage Signal was talking about when she was nearly complete with her verification training. Whatever Signal had done to manage to kill a regenerating mage, it mustn't have been nice to see the mage so timid now.

The tomcat spoke bold and low, "You once killed a protector of the subjects of Media who went by the name of Calotype, a red mage with the power of the exemplars of Satisfaction herself, in hopes of ending her bloodline for good. You did not succeed. Calotype had a grown litter before you destroyed her forest and claimed it as your own. Those kits lived to have more. I am proud to avenge my great-grandmother by ending you for good and I will continue to have her bloodline live on!" Signal's irides flourished into red light until the red mist burst from the sides like flames.

Video and Curiosity both startled in fear and surprise. Flames shot up from the ground and began burning the trees and brush rapidly, sending the jungle ablaze within seconds. Curiosity snarled, backing away. "You're Calotype's..." His voice shook, and then he shouted, "I didn't need more reason to *hate you*, monster!"

Signal sent a fire blast at the mage and jumped for him once he went to dodge it. The two rolled around against the burning earth, snarling and hissing at each other as they bit and clawed at each other, leaving Video in shock. She grabbed more of the moss and some mullein that grew around the tree, pressing it against her face wounds and trying to slow her both bleeding and breathing. She wouldn't be able to make it much longer if the two fought too long, or if the fire got too bad, but she could try to hold out as best she could.

She watched as Signal grabbed Curiosity by the head with his front claws and drove his fangs into his skull, startling Video. She had to regulate her breathing again after that. She closed her eyes, unable to watch what was unfolding. All she could hear was their screaming and shouting, blood spilling, branches cracking, magic being cast, and burning fire. She could barely contain herself. She didn't understand either of their words and she could barely keep herself conscious. When she opened her eye all she saw was red again, which was starting to scare her, as she had to keep her eye clear to see the world around her.

The fires were growing at a rapid rate. Signal was using that to his advantage against Curiosity. He kept throwing the mage into the flames, facing multiple forms of the beast as he shapeshifted in desperation to escape. Video had never seen a battle like it. The magic, the anger, the risks, the reality of her father being a mage and fighting his old foe right before her. There was only so much time now, though. Video had to drag herself away from the blazing heat with her free paw as her other one held the plants together against her head. She already had to replace the absorbent moss and mullein as they had become too soaked with her blood.

She had never been in so much pain, nor felt such sensations. This was an experience of a lifetime if she could live through it, one she hoped to make it through with her father if he could defeat the monster for a second time—and from what she saw, and that was a possibility.

The primate leapt for the giant cat. Signal quickly whipped out of the way and spun around, propelling himself onto the monkey and digging his fangs into the back of his neck. Curiosity yowled as the feline drove his jaws as close together as possible, breaking fragments of the monkey's back and ripping the flesh apart by shaking and pulling. He slammed the monkey down into the hot ground, letting the burning plants ignite the monkey as he ripped him apart with his teeth and claws. Video stared in horror as her father continuously clawed at the screaming beast, which barely resembled a monkey at this point. The dark fur was slowly wearing away into only flesh and white, and the shadows were overtaking to protect the rest of his form in desperation.

Video never thought she would see the Jester defeated in such a fashion; in such barbaric action. She screamed and startled at the sight of the mage as Signal pulled him back up from the earth, and startled even more when it still *moved.* "By the *Stars!*" she choked out before she began coughing up her blood.

Signal began to throw the mage, but it gripped him and whipped him down. The tom was as surprised as she was, even more so as the black shadows sliced across her father's pelt. Video yowled out, but Signal didn't give up. He rammed his claws into the exposed flesh of the creature, causing them to battle out once more.

Video realized the two were drawing close to the pit, however. She began dragging herself closer, hoping Signal would notice her and realize how close he was to the fall, but neither of them seemed to notice, only Curiosity, if anyone.

She realized her mistake. The mage grabbed Signal and shoved him toward the drop, beginning to regenerate from the claw wounds the instant it was free from the tom. Video was surprised to see what regenerated was white, long fur, and was wondering if she was seeing what Curiosity looked like as the Shadow Advisor.

She figured she had guessed correctly when that only seemed to anger Signal. Curiosity whipped upwards, third cat, third shadow, third mangled, broken, burned monkey, and choked out, "You'll never kill me. I'll always come back."

"And I'll be there that time, too." Signal snarled.

The reply shocked both Curiosity and Video. Signal had sensed the drop, and he launched himself at Curiosity, grabbing him at the throat and chest as he sent both over the ledge.

Video yowled in horror and pulled herself to the edge of the drop, watching as her father and the mage fell toward the split tree below. Her eye widened with horror, realizing she was about to witness her father be impaled with Curiosity at the bottom, but the tom whipped Curiosity down and propelled himself off of him, letting the mage's mangled body pierce the jagged edges and slice through his form as he landed a whisker length away from the trunk of the magic-struck tree.

Video watched the body slowly come apart upon contact with the spikes, and shivered as the shadows dissipated into a strange mix of the monkey and cat he once was. He was dead, his eyes were dull, and he was nothing more. Video couldn't believe it. He was gone. Signal rose up on his back paws, sending burning fire at the tree to completely destroy the mage once and for all, but the tree deflected it, sending the flames back at the tomcat.

If Video actually trusted her sight during that instant, she would have said that the tree was glowing lavender. It had the same hue as tree did with the mink family, and the way the outline of Radio's body had, but Video's sight started to fade immediately upon noticing it.

Her heart pounded. Her breathing became rapid and the last thing she remembered was looking into the furious red gaze of her father below before she blacked out.

She gasped awake when she realized Signal had grabbed her by the nape of her neck and lifted her up. He started running through the forest with her scruff in his jaws. She curled up as much as she could instinctively. She winced as her tail and back of her legs hit against the ground, but at least it took the pain away from her head. She realized the mullein and moss was now tied carefully around her wound with vines. Signal had treated her wound before he had picked her up.

Her fur was singed, but she was not burned. The tomcat took her through the forest at an incredible speed. Video realized the flames were dissipating with each step of the tom and that he was putting out the fire. She felt the magic flowing through him as he moved faster and stronger than she ever knew him to. Alarm flooded into her once she realized they weren't alone in the Labyrinth, though. "Signal! Jukebox and Film! We can't leave them!"

"I'll come back for them. For now, I'm getting you out." He answered, muffled against her fur.

Video blinked and stayed quiet then. She barely remained conscious for the rest of their time in Calotype's forest. Once they were out and Signal put her down, she felt herself give way. She gave one more look to her father and let the darkness of her sight surround her.

- EPILOGUE -

Radio sat at the windowsill of her bedroom in Audio's home. She had decided to stay there after she and Video's names were cleared. Audio cared for her, Stereo was there for the kits and there was peace. Video and Signal were almost always together after the events in the jungle, for as much as Signal allowed, anyway. The two seemed to have learned something about each other during the rescue in the Unending Labyrinth. Signal even visited Video often in Audio's infirmary.

Video and Film had come back severely wounded, but even with the resentment Film and Jukebox built up toward Video after she abandoned them—according to Jukebox, anyway—Film still made sure that Video came with him for treatment and surgery. His team had to wait to work on her skull until the inflammation was down around her eye, but then they got to work immediately. Radio had never seen wounds like the ones the two came back with. Jukebox had gotten off lucky with just a few scratches and bruises from the jungle traps.

Radio rubbed her raw neck, feeling the healing wound. She knew their pain and hoped each one was able to recover without magic. Radio had an advantage with her agreement with the Jester. With the ongoing regeneration from her magic, her scar had been healing faster. It was nearly completely healed now that they were approaching the beginning of winter. The fur hadn't grown back yet, but that left two pink hearts on her chest and cheek. Radio pressed her paw against it gingerly. Video was lucky it ended up looking cute. She would never forget the agony of that moment though, no matter how much she tried to bright-side it.

Radio startled when her kittens started poking her and kneading her side for her to roll over. She furrowed her brow at their demanding mewls, but she complied, laying down on her side and stretching out. She let her eyes close for a moment, then opened them to look at the corner of her room, where her sapphire and silver necklace lay. Her collar had been repaired by the noble forgers, who made the royalty and nobility collars and the crown in the depths of the castle. The collar's cracks were still visible, remolded together with lacquer and powdered metal and stone, much like what Studio used for her city. The lacquer was mixed with gold for the silver, and amethyst for the sapphire gems, used to display her strength and resilience. Despite the compliment, Radio said she was not ready to take on the responsibility of the three fallen nobles. She didn't say it out loud, but Radio just wanted a bit longer with her new family.

She knew Resolution had loved her, but Radio's mother never could speak up for her, quite literally, but also never made ways around communicating what her daughters needed. Frequency always managed to voice her wants, but Radio had always just kept to herself when it came to her family since they didn't like her going out. She still didn't know why she wasn't in the logs or why there weren't any records of her, but now she didn't have anyone to ask. Radio had only been able to count on her servants for emotional support and after learning how her father strayed. Radio understood Resolution had enough of her own problems than to have to deal with Radio's miniscule needs. Radio still had hoped she would have been able to ask her why they hid her from Social Media, though. The one person who would have found the answers, her devoted head servant, Stella, was gone. She missed Hana and Leil so much, too, but they were in the Capital still recovering.

Radio figured her parents had been ashamed of her for some reason, but this family wasn't like that. Audio, the light brown feline, was a healer, and her life revolved around her family. Radio felt loved. Jukebox had treated her like a sister, Stereo was there for both her and the kittens, excited to call them his own, but also so shy with them, afraid he'd squash them that Radio couldn't help but laugh when they were together. Video had been through as much pain as Radio had by the time she got out of the Labyrinth with Signal and Radio would tolerate her at this point. She had to, with how Video gave her entire family to her. Radio couldn't have said she would have done the same, especially since she knew she was already jealous of Video getting along so well with Studio.

One day, maybe, she would live with her aunt once everything was put behind them, once Clowder City was restructured and things were happy again, but Radio would just keep it to calls for now. At least until the kittens were old enough to travel. Radio didn't want to risk anything, nor really explain to Studio that Stereo was their father after she had chased the tom out of her city just this summer for his attack on Video. At least Studio was out of her house arrest and finally mayor again. That was almost unbelievable, but the only determination Studio deserved. Film, Console, and Settings worked tirelessly to clear everyone's names and now their verification ceremony was just around the corner.

So much had changed.

Radio squealed when one of the kittens bit into her and got up, popping them all off. She looked down at them, already planning their titles when they were verified. She wasn't sure if she wanted them to become nobility. She might do it in the future, but for now she didn't want to repeat the fate for her kits which she had to go through. Being locked up in their home, only being called out for special appearances, not getting the time to know anyone outside of their family circle and servants. It wasn't a good life, but as a noble, she could choose the kittens' verified names. She already had.

Circuit, for the puffy dark brown tabby with mitts and a white face just like her. She loved the little flecks of black on his torso. They resembled the blotches Stereo had on his ruff, but were smaller and broken up into pieces like wave signals. Video had been upset with her after seeing the kitten look so much like the bulky tomcat, but their bloodline split generations ago. There was no connection anymore and Video would have to understand that.

Pixel, for her only daughter. The little tabby had Radio's coloring and white face, but her markings were spot on with Pictures. She had his same exact stripes and build, even his eyes, too. Radio adored her. She was just too cute to have any other name. Radio purred until she realized Pixel was the one that bit her.

Then little Image, for her middle-born who was the smallest of the three. Radio imagined his name should have been Pixel instead of her daughter for his tiny size, but his silver striped pelt and mixed paws reminded her too much of the image of Pictures and she couldn't resist. He had her fluffy black tail and her black arms, but the one front paw's white coloring stretched up in the back side of his leg just like Pictures. The thought made her purr again.

They were all perfect, and Radio knew they were going to take up all of her time as they got older. She walked away from their protesting mewls, her tail waving in the air as she hopped down from the windowsill. She needed to eat, too. Audio always had extra food now for when she, Jukebox, her kitten, Stereo, or even Video needed a snack and Radio took advantage of that fully. The healer seemed to be overwhelmed at the four mouths to feed; eight, counting Radio and Jukebox's kittens, but Stereo and Jukebox both hunted incredibly well while Video healed and Radio was happy to learn how to cook with Audio while she couldn't stray too far from her kittens.

Her excuse, anyway. She just liked talking with Audio, really. It seemed like the two could fill in their seasons of not having anyone to talk to with each other and really be themselves around one another. Radio learned about Audio's perspective of magic, and how she had been trying to advocate for mages since she was young, determined to show how good they were, and how good magic could be, but she had put her faith in the wrong one. Radio swallowed at that, because she still held the Jester's magic in her own essence. Audio always seemed to understand that, however, and encouraged Radio to use her ability for good almost any time it was mentioned. Radio felt bad for the older cat, having dedicated so much of her time and life to a mage who ended up doing what it did to her family. Radio understood that mages were individuals just like anyone else, but Curiosity in particular was hardly a person at all.

From Video's words, Radio understood that the mage had intended on her failing the request to retrieve the shards from the beginning, doomed to die by Video's paws without either knowing they were played. Radio herself had been fooled, so she couldn't hold it against Video, either. Her mind wandered to the new plasma barrier which surrounded the land and how it had become a mage's prison for Media's followers, but the Council had put her family under a prison sentence as well. It felt no different to Radio.

Image climbed down from the windowsill to pounce on her tail. Radio squeaked, but glanced over and smiled as he picked it up with his teeth and looked up at her with pride. He started to bring it to his siblings before he tripped on her long fur and fell over. Radio shook her head and pulled her tail back up and around herself, but let her thoughts wander again. She wondered if it was because of her magic that the Council confined her family. After what Audio and Video said about the battle between Signal and Curiosity, Radio wondered if her kittens would have magic, too, knowing it was in their parents' lineage. The monkey had told her it was the case when they both realized she was expecting Pictures' kits, and advised her to just be rid of them after they were born.

Radio immediately bristled at the idea, shivered even. She would be even more protective of them for that. She wrapped her tail around the trio, all having come to her from the windowsill, and nuzzled them as they purred. The Jester could say all he wanted, these were the loves of her life. Once the kittens settled down again, Radio rose back up and walked out into the hall. She was surprised to see Stereo, Audio, Signal, and Jukebox with her kitten all together, but understood why when she heard Audio's exclamation of joy. Video had successfully opened the eye that had been struck by the primate, and recovery was going well.

Radio wanted to join them in congratulations, but felt awkward doing it when Video still made her uncomfortable to be around.

She gave a smile to Audio, and then continued her way to the kitchen. There was something that was lifted from their family's shoulders, even if it took away Radio's family for it to happen. Everyone knew the truth about each other. Seasons of guilt, bitterness, and secrets had been unburied when faced with the enemy. Radio hoped it would stay that way for them, and hoped maybe one day she could fully be a part of their rejoicing with time.

Nothing could defeat the strength and bravery which shone in their hearts. After the events that had occurred, they could face anything, and that was something Radio felt comfortable promising herself.

Video, Studio, Stereo, and Radio stood side by side inside the King's throne room for their verification ceremony. The four looked up at the giant cheetah with round eyes, and their tails quivered in unison. Radio couldn't help but glance over at Video then. She had never seen the marbled tabby so nervous. It wasn't obvious to the crowd, but when she had travelled for so long with the stoic feline, the apprehension was evident.

Radio only blinked at her slowly and looked back at the rest of the courtroom. She knew Video wouldn't dare take her eyes off the ceiling above as the King gazed down at them intensely. She'd do nothing to jeopardize this moment. Very few verification ceremonies actually included the Council in person, let alone the leader of Media. The only time Radio had seen Video look away from the Council and King was when the giant tabby seemed relieved to see a hawk, bobcat, and fox sitting proudly in the corner. She'd have to ask about that story later. Right now, the focus was their titles. The Cinema Star had offered personally to give the four their verifications back and to clear their names once Film and Jukebox returned them to the Capital City.

Signal was kind to have claimed the two dark felines were too injured to deliver her and Video to the Capital City, but Radio knew there was an underlying bitterness from them directed toward Video after she had left the pair to be victims of Curiosity's wrath in the Labyrinth. Film got the brunt of the primate's fury, but he still pooled the rest of his and Settings' resources to get the two to the Council safely even despite how hurt he had been over Video's cowardice and betrayal when facing the mage. Radio was lucky she had been exempt from judgement from the family, but also resented that they had higher expectations for Video than her. She tried to catch a glimpse of Stereo in the corner of her eye, but the tomcat just seemed to be trying not to fall asleep.

She now glanced to her auntie, Studio. The tall, dark and white tabby was standing tall and proud. Radio didn't want to stare too long when she saw a flash of annoyance from the noble before looking back at her niece. Studio gave her a warm smile and then a bright grin, so Radio quickly returned it before looking to Cinema. She slid her tail up against her aunt's with excitement as their grandmother approached the four. She was an ancestor to all of the felines, only separated by generation from Radio, Stereo and Video, to Studio. Radio swore she could hear Video's heart pound from where she was, but it was probably just her own. There was something about looking at Cinema which made Radio feel tense, like her throat was tightening. Her heart pounded against her chest with force as she stood in front of them.

Cinema smiled at them as she bestowed their reverification, the elder's raspy voice making Radio smile just as big as she had at Studio. It was an old voice, but a strong one, one that spoke with power. *With arrogance.*

Radio shook the strange bitter thought out of her head subtly and tried to pretend something was in her ear. The voice didn't even seem like her own.

She quickly brought her attention out from her thoughts when Cinema began to speak. "I verify you as loyal users of Media. With this registration, you agree to our terms of service, and agree to never forfeit your handles of Stereo, Video, the Radio Star, and the Studio Star, nor your devotion to Social Media."

"I agree," the four chirped back at once.

"You agree to serve the users of Media and to swear utmost loyalty to your Council, respecting the title and command from them above all else," she stated as she lifted up her chin.

"Yes," they answered boldly.

The towering noble's eyes softened upon their words. "Then congratulations," Cinema purred, and came closer.

She touched the nose of Stereo, and then Video, but it made Radio's stomach immediately ache. An overwhelming anger was overwhelming her thoughts. Thoughts she felt she couldn't control. It was as though there were shadows clouding her vision with nothing to focus on but Cinema's eyes. Filthy, traitorous eyes that took the ones she loved away from her. Radio felt her own eyes begin to burn with the magic sensation and quickly blinked it away. It *hadn't* been her own voice. Cinema had done nothing against her personally. She realized it was Curiosity's thoughts of resentment. His feelings were spinning through her mind! All Radio could think of was what Video had said about Pictures' blue eye and how he had kept an eye on all of them when they were on their mission.

The mage could see through her eyes.

Dread enveloped Radio. When Cinema went to touch her nose she reflexively pulled away. She wanted to hurt her great-grandmother for things which happened before she was born. Things she didn't know happened until now, but memories that weren't her own started rushing through her head. Cinema looked at her with offense and Radio gave her a sheepish smile, but all she could think of was Cinema standing over the bodies of the people she loved, the family who had accepted her, the only friend she had. Radio had received the anger of the mage's memories from the moment they made the agreement back in the valley which had cost Radio her life, but this was the first time it was so vivid, enough that Radio felt it had happened to her personally. She now knew it was Cinema and two others who single-handedly killed three different parties associated with the supposed last mage of Media, and it seemed the mage regretted letting the old queen live.

How could she explain she knew that, though? Cinema gave a censuring stare at Radio and walked away from her to touch noses to Studio, making Radio's head fall. She was devastated over the fact she had denied her great-grandmother's approval for something which wasn't relevant to her, especially with the fact that Cinema had worked so hard with Film and Console to clear their names, but it just wasn't right. Radio looked at Studio, who was staring at the elder feline with a cool expression, and she realized the high-ranking noble also knew the pain Cinema had caused for the other mages. It made perfect sense since Studio had been acquainted with Phantascope before he had started hurting people again.

He had likely told the city leader while they were getting to know each other.

Radio quickly looked away before Studio could make eye contact with her. Neither of them knew the Jester was watching them through her eyes; all they saw was Radio snub one of her ancestors. The realization that she wouldn't be able to tell anyone why she did what she did without being put to death again settled into her throat, but she couldn't throw her life away now that she had kittens, she had to live for them.

The knowledge that this all could have been avoided if Radio just hadn't agreed to take his power made her chest pound. What kind of person was she to have accepted his power?

Studio apparently knew Phantascope, but she had never made deals with him, unless there was a story behind the surface of Clowder City's color disappearing. It was something Radio would have to ask later, too, if Curiosity's memories didn't answer it for her.

Cinema actively worked to destroy him before retiring for her kittens, but Radio jumped right into an agreement with the sorcerer. He had even said to Radio that the last shard of the heart artifact would have been found if she had just let it be. He made sure to let her know as she died in front of Video's blood drenched paws.

Studio purred as she and Cinema's muzzles brushed against each other. Cinema arched her brow at her granddaughter then turned to her great-grandchildren. "May you travel safe and abide by the rules well, my darling children."

Video visibly relaxed and settled down, Stereo blinked his eyes open and nodded without understanding what the Council member meant, while Studio got chipper and purred. The three all noticed Radio's demeanor when glancing at her, though, and seemed to be in sync as they weaved around each of the smaller feline's sides and began leading her out from the throne room toward the drawing room.

Radio had read the report that Pictures died in that room and immediately started pulling away. She shook her head at the three larger felines and then started walking in the other direction.

"This is a time of celebration, little Radio." Studio whispered.

Radio blinked, and looked over at the three. Her eyes watered, but she came back to them and buried her head in the fur of Studio's shoulder. Studio purred soothingly, and groomed the top of her head.

"I'm sorry…" Radio whispered.

"Radio, you know you deserve this title as much as either of us do, yes? That we love you, and have fought for this day for *all* of us?" the golden eyed feline nuzzled her little niece.

Radio realized they assumed it was just the guilt over her magic. She knew she couldn't tell them the truth, not if she didn't want Video's claws ripping into her again. She turned her dull gaze up at the giant long-furred tabby's dark sienna eyes. They shone with concern and worry for her, but Radio knew how quickly that could change if Video felt threatened. She looked at Stereo, who also gave her a comforting look, but Radio knew she couldn't trust him with the information either, not after he learned Curiosity was responsible for the death of his former companion.

"Yes, I know, Auntie," she whispered back, and then smiled at Video and Stereo. "Thank you."

"Your mother would be so proud of you," Studio murmured.

Radio saw her aunt's eyes watering, and immediately began crying, too. She brushed her head up against Studio's chest and nuzzled her. "She would be proud of you, too."

Radio had often seen pictures of Studio in her mother's office. She knew the sisters had rarely communicated with each other after Studio made her city and Resolution took Flash as her partner. Yet the evidence of them keeping so much of the other's accomplishments in their sights proved that they had still cared for each other more than Radio thought. Neither would be able to say what they had held back for so many years because of the Jester. Now Radio had to hold the secret she still carried his magic and knew his thoughts even after the harm he caused them.

For now, they could be oblivious. The monkey was dead, anyway. It was probably just old thoughts associated with the power he gave her.

She had to keep quiet.

In depths of the Unending Labyrinth, the jungle was silent. The flames had died out, and all prey had fled from the fire. Within the center of the enchanted domain, the split tree remained still, but the shadows dissipated from the shattered center. The darkness drained into the earth and followed the stream, sliding through the ground and into the water until it made its way to the large, glowing bank of water and magic where the power it needed awaited it.

The shadows stayed dormant in the water until they slowly began to rise to the surface, slowly contaminating the light and magic that filled the pool with the tenebrous poison. The cesspool burst from the core the instant it reached the shore of the water and expanded out. Once the darkness began to solidify, a dark-tabbied and white furred feline clawed his way out from the pool. His scorched paws brushed against the holes in his throat and eye, beginning to regenerate the area with black, leathery skin.

A black and silver eye formed in the cat's empty socket. Once it focused, the remaining eye rolled around in its head until the eye focused on its surroundings, dark with the only light visible within the very depth of the pupil. He pulled the rest of his dark, scarred body out of the pool and darkened the remaining warm orange of his pelt into a dark, dark gray until no color was left. His tail and fur grew in length slowly, and then whipped up. Black, white, and silver-colored chaotic wings spread out from his back and rose above his head, a wave of cyan static running through them only for an instant before all of the color dissipated for good.

The crystal artifact followed behind him, emerging from the pool and spinning cyan until it faded into white as well. The mangled feline looked at it sternly, but then gave a nod thankfully before he started to walk out from the pool and into the deeper part of the jungle. He submerged the cube in the body of water so it wouldn't give him away. The artifact could only remain colorless for so long out in the open, but with an enchantment cast upon the lagoon, it could hide within the water and have it stay undetectable as long as Audio didn't remember, or more likely, mention, that he stored it there in his old form.

After that, he needed to find a place. Somewhere not here, that was safe. The parts of the jungle which had stored pockets of his magic were burnt to a crisp, and he knew Signal had done it on purpose. The giant beast would likely come back for him once he sensed his magic again, so he quickly desaturated it to white to help it remain undetectable. It could buy him the time he needed to find a hiding place and a conduit for his next attack.

He couldn't handle this in his own form anymore; he had to take control of another. Each step shot pain up into his legs, but he couldn't risk going into the shadows if he was too weak to materialize back into a solid form. He wouldn't be able to come back into his current state if he injured himself anymore in his condition. The regeneration wouldn't work to heal his burns. If only he had Pictures, but the tomcat's essence still wasn't complete enough to bring him back yet. He needed more time. Anger built up in his open chest where he had been struck by the jagged open trunk of the tree, making the pain even worse. It was crucial for him to get somewhere far away to a place where no one would look, but it had to be close enough for him to keep his eye on things, close enough to be able to strike back when the time was right.

And end everyone for good.

- END -

THE PROLOGUE

CHAPTER 1: KIDOLOGY

CHAPTER 2: IMITATION

CHAPTER 3: LATENCY

CHAPTER 4: LATITUDE

CHAPTER 5: ENDURANCE

CHAPTER 6: DARING

CHAPTER 7: TIMING

CHAPTER 8: HYMN

CHAPTER 9: EFFORT

The Epilogue

ABOUT THE AUTHOR

Teelia Pelletier is the nineteen-year-old author of Strong Hearts Are Mandatory: Heart of Glass and Straight to Video as well as the four upcoming books in this series. She lives with her family and many cats in rural United States, spending her free time making digital art and animation while she works as a nursing assistant at night. She is working toward a nursing degree and also pursues her interest in criminal justice and library science. This novel was a Camp NaNoWriMo entry in 2017. Look her up as Teelia to find out the statuses of the upcoming third and fourth books after Camp NaNoWriMo in April and July of 2018!

Search "LadyTeelia" on Redbubble to see the chapter headers and cover in full color, ready to be printed on all types of clothing and other products to your liking!

Thank you for reading!

CPSIA information can be obtained
at www.ICGtesting.com
Printed in the USA
LVHW03s1553150818
587067LV00016B/1707/P

9 780998 851310